THE BISON

&

The Butterfly

FRED AFFLERBACH

Llumina
PRESS

This is a work of fiction. All similarities between the characters and real persons are coincidental.

© 2016 Fred Afflerbach

ISBN: 978-1-62550-303-9

Printed in the United States of America by Llumina Press

the road was the common denominator

the missing link

noble arbitrator

great healer

the road did something no one could

Part I

The Load Out

"...you may all go to hell and I will go to Texas."

— *Davy Crockett*

One

Jeremy Taylor scratched and clawed at the glass as if gravediggers were shoveling dirt on his face, burying him alive. "Hey," he shrieked. "Hey, how do you roll down the window?"

"Take it easy, kid," the truck driver said. "It's the switch by your elbow."

Jeremy flicked the switch and pushed down on the slow-moving glass until it disappeared into the door. He draped his torso out the window almost to the front tire and beat the side of the truck with the palms of both hands. "Hey, Mom, hey, Dad. It's me, Jeremy. Pull over. Pull over."

"What are you doing, dude?" The driver said and creased his eyes at the strange teenager he had just picked up at Sid's Truck Stop.

Jeremy pulled himself back inside the truck cab. His face throbbed and burned and his eyebrows arched upward. An icy chill carved through his spine. "My, my parents," Jeremy stammered, "they're in that car beside us. The new Toyota they just bought."

"Okay, okay. Don't have a seizure," the trucker said and tapped the air brakes. "Get their attention and we'll stop at the next exit."

Jeremy pushed his head and shoulders out the window as if he was trying to crawl out of a hole six-feet deep. His thick hair shot straight up into a cone. He looked down at the empty lane next to the truck. White stripes rushed under the wheels. The diesel roared. Jeremy pulled himself back into the front seat, looked at the driver. "They're gone," he said. "Gone, just like that."

"Where'd they go?" the driver asked.

"Never mind," Jeremy said in a monotone. "It's too late now. Too late."

"Are you okay? Maybe taking this trip wasn't such a good idea," the driver said. "I can turn around. Run you back to Sid's."

"I'm not okay." Jeremy ran both hands through his wild hair. "But I'll be all right. I think." Jeremy stared out the window for

1

several more miles. The trucker, known as Flapjack, snuck a couple glances at the teenager. Something about this boy was not right. A mile later, Jeremy broke the heavy silence. "Mind if I lie down?"

"Suit yourself," Flapjack said.

Jeremy reclined in the sleeper berth and stared at the ceiling. His head was spinning like the time he got drunk on cheap vodka a friend snatched from his old man's liquor cabinet. His thoughts drifted back to Sid's Truck Stop where he had hooked up with the long-haul trucker, Flapjack.

Two

A neon stack of pancakes revolving counter clockwise on the roof of Sid's Truck Stop had been a beacon of hope to weary travelers for several decades. But the city of Philadelphia had methodically built above it with skyways, tunneled below it with subways and circled around it with bypasses. The once-busy hub had been reduced to a hangout for local drivers. On a warm June morning in 1992, Sid Quatro was pouring a coffee refill for a tow truck driver when the string of bells dangling from the front door jumped to life. A rawboned teenager who looked like he'd slept with Romulus and Remus stumbled in.

"Mister, can you get me a ride to Texas?"

"Geez, kid, this is a truck stop, not a bus station."

"I know, but I'm in a hurry and don't have much money. I figured since you and my grandpa are old friends you would help me out. I have to get to Texas. Quick. Real quick."

"Who's your grandfather?"

"We call him Grandpa Truck. You know him as Ubi Sunt."

"You're one of the twins?" Sid asked, squinting.

"That's right. I'm Jeremy."

"You used to play out back with your twin sister. What was her name?"

"Molly."

"That's right, Molly." Sid shook his head, marveling at the lost years. "You two crawled inside that stack of old truck tires like chimpanzees."

"Yes, sir," Jeremy said, a wild look in his eyes. "I need a ride to find my grandfather. He should be in Texas."

Sid pointed to a booth near the front door. Sit here, son. Jeremy slid across the red upholstery; his long legs bumped the pedestal below. This kid has sprouted like a willow tree. "When's the last time you ate, son?"

"I'm not hungry, Mr.Quatro. I just want a ride to Texas. Can you help me? Please. If you can't, I'll hitchhike. I'll sleep in truck stops."

"Hold on, young blood." Sid held up both palms. "I didn't say I wouldn't help you. But first you got to tell me why you are running away from home. Musta had one helluva argument with the folks."

Jeremy's bloodshot eyes radiated desperation. His thick, black hair sprouted in all directions—north, south, east, west.

"Okay, kid. What chew done?" Sid said in a sharp tone. "Knock somebody up?"

"No, sir."

"Knock somebody out?"

"Thought about it."

Sid rested both arms on the back of the booth. On his left forearm, the faded image of a long-nosed Freightliner. "Look, I can't help you if you won't—"

"Mom and Dad got killed in a car wreck two weeks ago," Jeremy blurted. "We couldn't find Grandpa Truck. Probably on the road. So he missed the funeral and everything." Jeremy's chest heaved. "Then my other grandfather, the one who lives here, he got angry. He said Grandpa Truck is an irresponsible, itinerant something-or-other and fired off a letter to the address in Texas. So that's where I'm headed. I'm going to beat that letter to Texas, even if I have to crawl."

Sid leaned forward. "How old are you, Jeremy." His coffee and cigarette breath made Jeremy's eyes burn even more.

"Eighteen."

"Give me a break, son. If you're going to bum rides all the way to Texas, you're going to have to lie better than that."

"Gonna be eighteen soon."

"When?"

"February."

"This is June, but never mind. Don't you have any other relatives? Anybody else who can help you?"

"Mom and Dad didn't have any brothers or sisters. We got no aunts, no uncles," Jeremy said, shaking his head. "So we're living with my dad's parents. That's all we have, other than—"

"Your Grandpa Truck in Texas," Sid said, nodding.

Sid leaned back and sank low into the upholstery. "It breaks my heart to hear what happened, Jeremy. And you got good reason to find your grandfather. I lost track of him years ago."

"His phone just rings and rings. No answering machine, nothing," Jeremy said. "Maybe it's been disconnected or he got a new number. All I know is he owns a little trucking company in Texas."

Sid drummed his fingers on the table, itching for another cigarette. He knew few men like the kid's Grandpa Truck, men who cut through the bullshit and laid their cards on the table. "Damnit, I'd take you there myself, but my wife's laid up with the shingles and I, well, I got no one to run this place," Sid said, a touch of melancholy in his voice.

"I thought you could find me a trucker headed west," Jeremy said. "I don't have money for a bus, and if I did he would probably call the police, FBI, or whatever."

"Who is he?"

"My other grandfather. The one I just told you about. He's some kind of corporate lawyer. We call him the Attorney General," Jeremy said. "All he talks about is winning big cases for big money. After the accident, he took over everything. Asked us how we felt about nothing."

"Sounds like a regular hard ass."

"First it was the funeral arrangements. I begged him to wait until we found Grandpa Truck. He wouldn't listen. Next he made us move in with him and my grandmother. She's not so bad. Then he tried to put us in a different school right before the end of the year. Can you believe it? But Molly and I, we started a hunger strike, like Gandhi."

"So that explains why you look like a ragamuffin."

Jeremy ignored the slight and continued. "We refused solids for six days, but somebody at school noticed how pathetic we were looking and called a state agency. So he backed down on changing schools. But then he wrote that hateful certified letter. It said he had no use for someone like Grandpa Truck and he would make sure nobody from Texas could come riding in, messing up our lives by trying to patch things up." Jeremy rubbed his eyes with the back of his fists. "Mr. Quatro, if anybody can find me a trucker headed to Texas, I figured it would be you. You've known Grandpa a long time."

The tow truck driver dropped a dollar bill on the counter. "See you tomorrow," he said and yanked open the front door. A trim man in his seventies, wearing a black suit, pushed his way past the wrecker driver.

"Anybody here who can pump gas?"

Sid climbed out of the booth and approached the stranger. "Sorry, mister, but it's self serve. Been that way for ten years."

"You expect me to pump gas wearing this?" The man held out his arms. "You know what this suit cost?"

"This ain't no country club, mister," Sid shot back, offended. "It's a truck stop in South Philly where people aren't afraid to get a little dirt under their fingernails."

"My vehicle is running on fumes. I have an appointment with a district attorney in a half hour. I can't go in there smelling like gasoline."

Sid turned and marched outside. Only one car was at the pumps. A shimmering, silver Jaguar sedan. He looked up at the man. "I guess you want the premium?"

The man nodded and held out a twenty. Sid stopped the pump at twenty bucks. Before he could return the nozzle to its holster, the car shot out of the driveway. Jackass.

Back in the truck stop, the seat where Jeremy was sitting was empty. Oh wait, the kid is all curled up, lying flat on the booth.

"What the hell are you doing, son?"

Jeremy slithered back up on the bench seat and peered out the window. "That man driving the Jaguar. Is he gone?"

"Yes, that asshole is gone. What about him?"

"He's my grandfather."

Sid's eyes peeled back. "That man is your *other* grandfather?"

Jeremy's head bobbed up and down.

"I'll see what I can do about getting you that ride to Texas."

Three

Jack Benson was looking for a load home to Houston, but all he could find was a shipment of car parts for Laredo. On his way out of town, he pulled into Sid's Truck Stop, fueled and picked up this kid that the broker said needed a ride to find his grandfather in Texas. Don't know what that's about, but Sid's Truck Stop had been a mainstay, about the only place between Baltimore and Boston that treats you right—fresh coffee, decent chow, especially pancakes, clean showers and no lot lizards banging on the door at three in the morning. Speaking of pancakes, Sid has a giant stack, rotating on the cafe roof, all lit up with syrup dripping down the edges. Either that or he got relatives from Mars.

Jack owned and drove a new, long-nose Kenworth with bunk beds situated behind the front seat. It was propelled by a purring Cat diesel engine. Jack ran through a half-dozen gears and eased the rig onto the interstate. Jeremy looked around the spacious truck cab and plush interior. Before today, Jeremy had seen the interior of only one rig—Old Ironsides, his grandfather's Peterbilt that must be one hundred years old.

About fifty miles after Jeremy climbed in the bunk, he crawled back into the passenger seat, still a little unnerved by the image of his dead parents riding down the road beside Flapjack's Kenworth.

Flapjack broke the ice. "Back at the truck stop, Sid mentioned your grandfather's some sort of truck driving legend."

"He used to be," Jeremy answered. "Lived on the road for thirty years. Now he owns two or three rigs and hauls grain across the Texas Panhandle. Says he's too old for the long hauls, but day trips across the High Plains keep him from going nuts."

"When was the last time you saw him?"

Jeremy blinked twice, three times. He couldn't remember. "Been a while."

Jack's foot fell heavy on the accelerator. The rig emitted a low growl. "Sweeter than Big Red soda water, the way this baby pulls."

"What's Big Red?"

"You never heard of Big Red?" Jack said. "You have had a deprived childhood."

"Where do you get it?"

"Back home," Jack said, leaning forward and caressing the steering wheel with long arms. "Before I leave Texas, I usually grab a case. Lasts me three, maybe four weeks."

"What's so special about Big Red?"

"It's not just special, kid, it is a *booiful* experience." Jack loved twisting the word beautiful and reshaping it into *booiful*. And he often added a wistful touch, almost like a whisper when he used *booiful* to describe something he was passionate about. "You have to sip it slowly. Let it foam up and then simmer down. Suh-weet and so red it'll stain your teeth." Jack grinned, and sure enough you could see a red tint to his smile.

Jeremy looked across the cab at the driver, about thirty, slender face with sharp nose, shoulder-length black hair falling on his unbuttoned blue denim work shirt.

"Where'd you get that name, Flapjack?"

"My old man gave it to me. Growing up, all I wanted to eat was flapjacks. Banana-nut. Blueberry with whipped cream. Pumpkin-flavored at Halloween," Jack said. "Anyway, five years ago when I took to the road I didn't have a CB name. It was just natural to take that handle, Flapjack."

"You sound passionate about flapjacks," Jeremy said.

"Damn straight, I am. Flapjacks—the food of the gods. Ancient Romans ate 'em. Ben Franklin loved corn flapjacks. And here's a little secret. Most drivers stay awake at night gulping coffee, but it's the carbohydrates in flapjacks that keep me going."

The Kenworth hummed along, got a little close to a Volvo with a *Bill Clinton for President* bumper sticker, then merged into the far left lane. White lines were specks on the highway.

"Are we going to get a speeding ticket?"

"Guess I better back it down," Jack said and eased off the accelerator. "Got carried away talking about flapjacks. But here's something else you should know. Back at Sid's Truck Stop, he sometimes uses melted snow in his flapjacks. Makes 'em rise up like inflating an air mattress." Flapjack shook his head left to right. "Booiful."

One hundred fifty miles down the road at the Roanoke truck stop, Jack treated his new sidekick to a full stack smothered with boysenberry syrup. But Jeremy's stomach was a tempest of nerves and acid and anxiety. He picked at the pancakes, but couldn't choke down more than a few bites. Jack helped himself to a short stack topped with blueberries and whipped cream. The pancakes vanished behind a blur of flying elbows and smacking lips. He pulled out a spiral notebook, a pancake journal that he kept.

"Not bad, but they won't make my top ten list—three stars out of a possible five," Jack said, his pen moving across the sticky page.

One day on the road and Jeremy was beginning to think he had entered a world where space and time and reality were all askew. His deceased parents appeared on the highway like ghost riders, and his first ride was with a man who drove pedal-to-the-metal and worshipped flour, milk and eggs whipped up and fried on a hot griddle.

Back on the highway, Flapjack prodded Jeremy about his outburst. Jeremy again explained that his parents had been killed in a highway crash and he was on a quest to find his estranged grandfather. But he didn't have much time, nine days to reach Texas and return, or else. Or else what? Let's don't even think about that right now.

Four

The high school band where Jeremy played saxophone had scheduled a retreat to the Poconos after the end of the spring semester. But when Jeremy found a copy of that stinging letter on the Attorney General's desk, he vowed to race across the country like the Pony Express with a message of his own. That night, Jeremy told Molly little about the ruse.

"I'm not going. I changed my mind and I'm taking a trip of my own," Jeremy said, sitting on the edge of Molly's bed as she brushed tangles from her sandy-blonde hair. "I told the band director I was looking for a summer job."

"What did you tell *him*?" Molly asked.

"Nothing. As far as he knows, I'm still going."

"Are you sure you know what you're doing? If he catches you—"

"If he catches me, well, I don't even care," Jeremy said. "I really don't care about anything anymore. I know it's wrong to say that, but that's how I feel."

Molly continued brushing her hair, looking at Jeremy in the vanity mirror. Back in elementary school, her brother had idolized Grandpa Truck, decorated his room with postcards from the road, crawled all over the cab of that old Peterbilt when Grandpa drifted into town. So she had a strong hunch what Jeremy was planning.

"If I get caught, you know nothing," Jeremy said. "I don't want to drag you into this."

"A little late for that, don't you think?" Molly said. She dropped the brush on the vanity and looked at her brother's reflection in the mirror. Jeremy sat mum on the edge of the bed. "Don't worry; I'll keep your secret." Molly turned around and faced her brother. "And get a haircut while you're out there, you've probably got woodchucks living in that mess."

Jeremy had nine days to get to Texas and back, to meet the bus full of returning band members at the school so that the Attorney General would not catch on that his grandson had duped him.

The morning the bus was scheduled to leave for the Poconos, Jeremy sniffed the armpits of several T-shirts and stuffed the ones that smelled cleanest into his backpack along with a couple pair of jeans. Next he latched tight another piece of luggage—a hard plastic case with the letter J embossed on the lid. After the Attorney General and Jeremy's grandmother, Katherine, dropped off the twins, the grandparents hung around the school parking lot and wouldn't leave. Jeremy had to climb aboard. The bus clattered off in a cloud of diesel smoke. Jeremy cupped his hands around his face and peered through the back glass. Geez, they're still watching.

Forty miles down the road, Jeremy persuaded a friend to beg the driver into making an emergency pit stop. The band director had chartered a cut-rate transportation company so the buses had no toilets. And it was overcrowded with students wedged three across most seats. No way the bus driver would miss one kid. Jeremy grabbed his backpack and the hard plastic case and disembarked with several others. Out of the bus driver's sight, he vaulted a guardrail and hoofed it down the frontage road.

Jeremy spent all day and much of that evening walking, jogging, riding the subway, catching a city bus, more walking, until he glimpsed a faint light flickering several blocks away. A neon stack of pancakes spinning like a vinyl disc on a turntable illuminated the truck stop. Deep in the back lot, he crawled into an unlocked, rusty trailer that Sid used for recycling cardboard. He curled up on a stack of flattened grocery boxes, backpack for a pillow. Then a tug on a shoelace. Another. Jeremy recoiled, pulled his knees against his chest. Clawing and scratching sounds inside the trailer walls kept Jeremy awake almost all night. When hazy sunlight slanted through a hole in the roof, he staggered into Sid's and asked help finding a ride to Texas.

Five

Jeremy nodded off but refused to climb in the bunk. Whenever the Kenworth hit a bump his head snapped back like a bobble head doll and shook him awake. He would then sit up straight and act like he hadn't fallen asleep, as if by dozing he had betrayed an unspoken obligation to stay alert and indulge Flapjack by listening to more stories. But more than that, he was afraid what he might see in his sleep. His parents had already appeared to him while he was awake, what could happen in his dreams?

Sipping his portly coffee mug, Flapjack reveled in the twilight that had descended onto the highway. Roadside pine trees cast long shadows across the asphalt. Silhouettes of eighteen-wheelers burning amber clearance lights rolled on like furtive giants. With sparse traffic on this rural route, a hush came over the highway.

Jack's rig sliced through southwestern Virginia, a narrow and remote appendage of the Old Dominion. Early evening slowly morphed into black night. Low clouds drifted in and smothered the highway. Headlight high beams bounced back into drivers' eyes. Jack yearned for Houston, the Bayou City with its mucky heat, pregnant white clouds that dropped showers on sizzling pavement almost every afternoon, margaritas and shrimp enchiladas and guacamole salad like you get nowhere else. Although visibility was poor, Jack couldn't help but let the Kenworth stretch her legs. Seventy, seventy-five, the rig was a comet racing through the blackness. The headlights were the nucleus, piercing the night, illuminating the path ahead. The smoke and exhaust that billowed from twin stacks was the tail of trailing ice and dust particles that disappeared into nothingness.

Jack reached across the truck cab, prodded Jeremy on the shoulder and pointed with his thumb to the lower bunk. Get some rest, kid. Jeremy shook his head, said I'm all right.

Ah, night driving. Jack savored the late hours when the amateurs left his workplace and headed down exit ramps for home. Now that the road is empty, you have a little wiggle room. Don't have to worry about a four-wheeler disappearing into the blind spot, a truckers' Bermuda Triangle halfway down the side of the trailer where cars can't be seen in the mirror.

Oooh, night driving. Sensual. When the highway is empty and pitch-black you see only a short distance, so other senses kick into high gear. Little noises are magnified, like the turbocharger whistling on the uphill. And with that heightened awareness, you become one with the road. You glide across the smooth stretches like there's no friction, no wind resistance. Other times, the aggregate in the asphalt feels like goosebumps on your skin. The steering wheel shakes in your hands. A little twitch runs down the back of your neck.

An all-nighter? Sure, those flapjack carbs have kicked into overdrive, but still can't go for that. Heard about one driver who bounced little white pills off the windshield and into his mouth like M&Ms. Maybe just a myth. Anyway, that catches up with you down the road. Don't need the jitters and stomach cramps that go with it. Two a.m.? Three o'clock? That's late enough. Any time after that, no matter how alert you are, it doesn't feel right. Not worth the risk when the head starts nodding. Sure, you can roll down the window, hang your head out. That works for a while. And blasting hard rock on the cassette—Led Zeppelin's *Ramble On*—can get you a little farther down the road. Another trick— smoke, smoke, smoke. Light one from the other by holding the fresh cigarette in your mouth and pressing it against the embers from the one you just finished. Now watch this. Hold the glowing cigarette butt between your middle finger and thumb, flick it out the window. Up it soars, red tip sparkling as the cool night air hits it, shooting sparks like a bottle rocket. Then it crash lands onto the middle of the highway and, with one last gasp, emits more crimson sparks.

CB radio sounds different at night, too. Voices bounce around the cab kind of hollow-like. And some drivers got a gadget they call an echo chamber hooked up to their radio. Bizarre in the day—but late at night when the caffeine and nicotine and full moon are all at their zenith, and the lanes are empty, no headlights, no taillights in either direction—that's when it's downright freakish, those voices ricocheting around the cab.

"Westbound ... bound ... bound. Got a nasty hailstorm outside Birmingham ... ham ... ham," the anonymous voice would fill the cab.

You can pick up distant, AM radio stations late at night. The play-by-play man's scratchy voice, announcing a St. Louis Cardinals game going into the twelfth inning; a self-professed UFO and alien authority expounding his theory about a government cover-up; a Bible thumper without the aid of an echo chamber exhorting us all to "*repent, repent, repent*" and mail him a check.

Sweet night driving. Love how it gets you past that closed weigh station, like pushing a herd of Longhorns across the river before bedding down for the night. Dreadful night driving. Hate how it gets you trying to fudge the logbook that next morning. Might have to explain to a state trooper how you drove eight hundred miles in one day, but recorded only eight hours behind the wheel. And that last hour before putting the pedal up feels like there's someone standing behind you, pushing down on both shoulders.

Oh you seductive, yet perilous, night driving. The pleasure of having the road to yourself. The danger of drifting into the ditch. Best to quit while it's still fun. Hit the right turn signal and start dropping gears on this steep exit ramp. Watch that rig parked on the shoulder. And when you're tired and the transmission is obstinate, the downshifts don't come smoothly like when you were fresh. Now the truck stop is jammed, sixty-foot sardines packed in rows. Let's see if we can squeeze in that narrow spot in the middle aisle. Better get out, walk around the rig. Shadows can play tricks on you. It doesn't pay to get in a rush when it's late and you're fuzzy-headed. Okay now, got 'er wedged in nice and straight. Not much room on either side, but it will do.

Late night driving. Exhilarating. Exhausting. Excruciating. Kidneys on fire. Screw it. Going to take a leak right here in the parking lot. In the blind spot. Now I gotta wake that kid passed out in the passenger seat and tell him to climb into the top bunk. Aw, hell. Look at him. Wiped out. Let him be.

Six

Jeremy sat up, blinked, and rubbed his eyes. The brilliant morning sunlight burned through the windshield and warmed the cab. *Where are we?* Last thing Jeremy remembers, Flapjack chain smoking and flipping cigarette butts onto the road. So when is he going to wake up? Hate to bother him, but it's Texas time. Maybe it's better to leave a thank you note and find another ride.

Jeremy rolled down the electric window and poked his head out, looked in the mirror. Thick and shaggy hair gone wild. Teeth feel like they're covered in slime—hadn't brushed in two days. Okay, got to keep moving. Let's find a restroom and a ride. But first, grab this pen off the driver's console and a receipt from the truck stop in Roanoke. Got a little pancake syrup on it. Oh, well.

> *Jack, thanks for the ride but I got to move on. If we meet again, down the road, maybe we can make a toast to the perfect pancake, with a swig of Big Red.*
>
> *Jeremy*

Inside the truck stop restroom, Jeremy didn't think his bladder would ever empty. Then he edged up to an open sink, elbow-to-elbow with several truck drivers sloshing water on faces and hands. When was the last time they cleaned this place? Wet hair sticking to the porcelain. Green calcium growing on faucets like stalactites. Okay, here goes. Out comes the toothbrush and toothpaste, scrubbing and spitting and don't care who's paying attention, got to get the grime out of the gums and teeth. Now, handfuls of cool water splashed across the face. Again and again. Keep splashing. Got to wake up. Got to get to Texas. Where's the paper towels? Never mind. Pull a T-shirt from the backpack, use it for a towel and wipe the face. Now let's get out of here. Grab the backpack and go. Out in the lobby—Hallelujah—a hot chocolate dispenser, jumbo cups and baby marshmallows. Might live after all.

Jeremy sipped the hot chocolate and stared at a wall map. He found a red arrow with the words *"You are here"* pointing to Farragut, a small town in eastern Tennessee. Wow, Jack must have gone through a pack of Marlboros and a stack of Led Zeppelin cassettes last night. No wonder he's sleeping in. Oh great, here comes a sheriff walking toward the coffee counter. Let's skedaddle outside. Standing between a Coke machine and a newspaper rack, Jeremy pulled from his hip pocket the small atlas Sid gave him yesterday with a note scribbled on the back.

To Ubi Sunt, my old friend from Texas, if you are reading this then you must not be dead and your grandson survived 2,000 miles of bad highways and bad food, 'cept my blue ribbon flapjacks, of course. May the two of you reconcile and find peace wherever the road may take you. My condolences for your loss. Sid Quatro, June 8, 1992.

Jeremy's eyes followed the shortest route to the Texas Panhandle. Nashville, Fort Smith, OK City. That's the route, all right.

Outside in bright morning light, more than a dozen diesel pumps chugged nonstop, dispensing fuel into one-hundred-gallon saddle tanks. Jeremy bobbed in and out of sight, ducking behind trailers so the drivers didn't know where he came from until he was standing beside them.

"No, kid, can't helpya. I'm headed to Miami."

"What the hell? How old are you, boy? You don't look a day over sixteen."

"Sorry, son, I'm headed to Rochester with this load of Florida grapefruit. But I overheard a driver at the fuel desk say he was going to the West Coast. He should be running the interstate through the Texas Panhandle. He's driving that GMC pulling out of the wash rack over there."

Jeremy looked up to see a strange beast poke its head out of a cave. The creature batted its eyelashes back and forth, swatting aside water that was streaming down the windshield. It came to a stop, standing proud and alone in the middle of the lot, headlights on bright, four-way flashers blinking, water puddling underneath it.

Behind the cab, the rig carried a camper bolted to the truck frame. Made from sheet metal, it was the size of a small shed. Windows on three sides. Air conditioner affixed to the top. All sorts of antennas sticking out of the roof and hanging onto mirror brackets. And painted on both truck doors—a porcupine standing on hind legs, smiling. Must be the driver's CB handle.

The driver swung open the door and climbed down from the rig. His dark green T-shirt rippled over thick biceps and an ample belly. Black hair sprouted from his arm pits and the back of his neck. But there wasn't much neck to speak of; his head sat directly on his shoulders. Porcupine rooted around the truck with a critical eye. Perusing the perimeter of the sixty-foot rig, paper towels in hand, he wiped dry the turn signals and tapped the lazy amber lens on the left front until it resumed blinking.

Jeremy approached this strange man driving a strange vehicle.

"Nice rig."

"How ya doing, kid?" Porcupine bellowed. "Looking for a ride?"

"Yes, sir. Going to the Texas Panhandle to see my grandfather."

The driver looked over the skinny teenager. Seen many like him. They take to the road for lots of reasons: violent parents, divorced parents, over-indulgent parents, no parents.

"Where your folks?"

Jeremy wanted to blurt the truth. You really want to know? They're in Atlantic Memorial Park, just outside Philadelphia. Don't believe me? Go see for yourself. Look in the new section in the west corner, past the big maple with the 'Y' trunk. Look for the couple who died on the same day a few weeks ago. Look for the fresh flowers and fresh mound of earth. You asked, mister, so now you know.

Rather than unload all that pain and anger on a stranger, Jeremy choked back the truth. He offered the story he had rehearsed lying in bed back home, after the funeral, when he had decided he was going to defy his lawyer grandfather and trek to Texas.

"My folks are on vacation in Florida. They left my sister and me home alone. So I'm going to visit my grandfather because I haven't seen him since I was a kid. Mom and Dad wouldn't approve, but that's family history. I think they should forgive and forget," Jeremy said, shuffling his feet, looking down.

The driver cocked his head and squinted, eyes veering off in different directions. This young man was trying to pull something—something other than sneaking one past his folks, something other than a weeklong trip to see his long-lost grandfather, followed by a quick return home, with Mom and Dad none the wiser.

The truck driver bowed his head like he was praying, then looked back up, eyes askew but full of compassion. "Sorry, but I got a full house."

Jeremy then noticed the driver was pulling a Deaton Van Lines trailer, the same company that Grandpa hauled for until he opened his own outfit.

"My grandfather drove for Deaton," Jeremy said. "For about thirty years. You might know him as Ubi Sunt, or the Southpaw."

"Are you talking about the man who drove Old Ironsides?"

Jeremy nodded, yes, yes.

"Well, hell's bells. He helped us out of a jam near Duluth," Porcupine said and raised his index finger. "Hold on." The driver shambled over to the rig's cabin, climbed three steps and disappeared inside.

A minute later, a soft voice drifted through an open window. "Just a minute. We're finishing a lesson."

Jeremy leaned against the side of the truck and closed his eyes. The sheet metal hut twitched and the side door eased back. A woman, about thirty-five, stepped onto a small landing. A rig rolled past and kicked up a gust that blew her long, black hair behind her shoulders, revealing high cheekbones, olive skin, and slender lips curved upward in a tantalizing smile. And those eyes, can't tell what color, but they twinkle like headlights on a lonesome highway. Jeremy tried not to stare; this woman was almost old enough to be his mother. When he managed to snap out of the trance, his gaze continued downward to narrow hips snuggled inside a pair of faded blue jeans.

The woman studied the teenager. Goodness, that crumpled T-shirt and wrinkled jeans are hanging from a skeleton. Looks like he hasn't eaten for two weeks. But oh my, the thick, rich, head of black hair.

"You may call me Sacajawea," she said. "When was the last time you had something to eat?" Jeremy gazed into Sacajawea's eyes, unable to answer. "Must have been a long time."

19

"Uh, pancakes," Jeremy stammered, "yesterday, somewhere in Virginia."

"Come in," Sacajawea said, "and I'll serve you pimento cheese."

Jeremy slipped his backpack free from his shoulders and hefted it in his right hand. Something was amiss. Jeremy's throat contracted. His face turned ash-white. His stomach knotted up. "Hold on. I forgot something."

Jeremy sprinted across the truck stop parking lot, zigzagging between drivers and vacationers who glared at him and shouted, "Hey, watch where you're going." Inside, he squeezed past truckers lined up at the fuel desk and walked head down toward the back. In the men's room, no hard plastic case with a capital J on it rested near the sink where he had cleaned up. Jeremy slammed open the restroom door, squeezed past a heavy woman pawing over stale donuts and made his way to the fuel desk. Both cashiers were busy counting change. Jeremy leaned over the glass counter. There it is. *Thank you, dear God.* Jeremy said excuse me, two, three times, but all he got in reply was a palm held up indicating wait your turn. Jeremy circled the counter, noticed the swinging door was not latched. He eased it back and took two steps into the area for employees only. Then he looked up at the cashier nearest him, a tall woman with hoop earrings, about forty years old.

"Thanks for hanging on to my luggage," Jeremy said, picking up the case.

Without looking back, Jeremy pushed open the truck stop door and marched across the parking lot toward Porcupine's rig. He clutched the hard plastic case against his chest, arms folded across it. A minute later he was standing before Porcupine's rig. Sacajawea was waiting on the small landing that served as a front porch. She smiled and asked, "What's in the case?"

Jeremy shrugged. "Nothing."

Sacajawea held the door open. Jeremy scaled the small ladder and entered the camper. He slid across a bench and propped his elbows on a tiny table. Two pimento cheese sandwiches, sliced diagonally, waited on a paper plate. Each half was impaled by a toothpick with a green olive riding atop it. Clattering pistons and hissing air brakes shook the table. Porcupine was apparently pulling out. Then a scraping sound emanated from a sliding door in the back of the cabin and a beaming, pinkish round face looked up at Jeremy. It was a young boy with the build of a snowman. His brown eyes veered to the side—headlights out of adjustment. And the whites were hard-boiled eggs.

The boy examined the sandwich. "You have an isosceles triangle," he said. "The two angles are congruent, forty-five degrees."

"This is our son, Newton," Sacajawea interjected. She then addressed the boy. "Newton, remember, you should look at someone when you're speaking to them."

Jeremy said hello to the rotund kid with the buzz haircut, plucked the olive from the toothpick and offered it to the boy. Newton rolled it in the palm of his hand. He said, "This is an oval," and popped it into his mouth.

"What do you say?" Sacajawea prompted.

The youngster finished chewing and swallowed. "An oval is like a rectangle with rounded corners. And it means egg in Latin."

"That's not what I was asking," Sacajawea said in a stern tone.

"Oh, thank you for the oval." The boy said, revealing a red speck lodged between his front teeth. "I mean olive."

The truck suspension creaked and groaned as Porcupine ran through several gears, engine whining and exhaust stacks vibrating. Jeremy bit a corner off the triangle-shaped sandwich. The boy continued staring, not directly at him, but staring nonetheless. People rarely visited their little home mounted on the back of the GMC diesel rig. Mom and Dad liked privacy.

"I'm seven," the boy announced. "I should be in second grade, but my parents are road schooling me."

"You mean you're living on the highway, out of this truck?"

"Yes, sir. I'm too smart for a conventional classroom, Mom says. I read on a sixth-grade level. I was tested last month." Newton swished his tongue against the inside of his upper lip. "Salt, that would be the chemical compound $NaCl$," he said. "We got a classroom and laboratory set up in the back. Mom calls it the Wickiup."

Sacajawea asked Newton if he had answered all the geometry questions in the exercise.

"Yes, Mama," Newton said, eyeing another oval perched atop another isosceles triangle.

21

"Then you need to work on your daily writing assignment," Sacajawea said, pointing toward the Wickiup. "Check the schedule."

Jeremy held out another olive. The boy took it, said thank you, and rolled it between thumb and finger, examining it for texture and color.

"Newton, you get back to work," Sacajawea scolded. "I'll be there in a minute to check your geometry."

The boy tilted his head back, opened his jaws, and tossed the olive into the air just as Porcupine mashed the accelerator. The rig surged forward. The olive began its descent. Newton thrust his neck and head forward and the little green oval landed softly on his tongue. "Almost forgot, velocity equals distance divided by speed," the boy said, smacking and chewing. "We must be moving at forty miles an hour."

Newton wobbled into the Wickiup. Jeremy stuffed more pimiento cheese into his mouth. He looked out a small window. Green tree canopies and blue sky floated past. Sacajawea raised a kettle that was plugged into a wall socket and poured boiling water into a pear-shaped, porcelain travel mug. The truck shook and Jeremy bounced in his seat. Unfazed by the rocking rig, Sacajawea slipped into the booth across from Jeremy. For some reason unbeknownst to Jeremy, Sacajawea felt the need to explain her family's lifestyle.

"Some people disagree with how we're raising Newton," she said, dipping two tea bags into her cup. "Especially how we're taking Newton out on the road."

"That's your business," Jeremy said with a quick glance toward the woman. What a gorgeous face. No makeup. No wrinkles.

"Newton came home from school one day last fall asking what spaz meant. Later it was retard. Then he said kids were calling him Pickle Boy. I blew up at the school principal and that did it. My husband was already on the road at the time, so we threw everything we own into a storage unit, added this cabin to the truck frame, and away we go." Sacajawea stared into the bottom of her cup, then looked up at Jeremy. "The way I see it, the only thing Newton is missing by not going to any kind of school, public or private, is potty jokes and bullying and waiting on the rest of the class to catch up on a lesson he's finished and completely bored with."

"What about friends?" Jeremy said.

"Did you see how he examined that olive? Your sandwich?" Sacajawea said, looking up from her tea. "He doesn't play with other kids. Just gets lost in his own world."

Jeremy's eyes drifted toward a horizontal light fixture above the door. Three naked bulbs. All different colors. Sacajawea answered Jeremy's unspoken question.

"Green is when we're in highway mode and everything looks good. Yellow means no moving around the cabin because we're riding on rough roads, sharp curves, an exit ramp, stuff like that. Red, grab each other and get on the floor with a pillow over your head because—" Sacajawea paused and glanced out the window. "I can't remember when we last had a red alert."

"Does Porcupine have a switch up in the cab to turn on the lights?" Jeremy asked.

"We both do." Sacajawea said and swirled a spoon inside her mug.

The walls rattled and the table shimmied as the rig rumbled over broken pavement. Sacajawea cradled her mug with two hands, sipped the tea, and decided it was time to probe the heart of the boy's story.

"Soo ... Jeremy."

Oh, no. Here it comes. Now begins the interrogation. She's got that look in her eyes. Instead of sparkling, they're piercing. A laser cutting through skin and bone to a vulnerable place locked deep inside.

"Tell me . . . Jeremy." Sacajawea's spoon swirled inside the travel mug. "What's really going on here?"

Jeremy squirmed in the bench seat. Looked across the table. How can you lie to a pair of eyes like that? Jeremy pushed the plate away. The pimento cheese had lost its appeal. He looked around the room. The walls were looming larger and closer, a vise squeezing and compressing. He wiggled out of the booth. Stood up.

"Are you okay?" Sacajawea asked. "I'm sorry if I upset you. Maybe you should lie down in the Wickiup. It's really quite comfortable."

Jeremy's stomach churned. His face, pallid. He inhaled, but it felt like someone had stuffed a pillow in his face. "I don't feel good. How do you give a code red?"

Sacajawea slid out of the booth and flipped a wall switch up and down three times. Jeremy gripped a handrail by the door. The truck engine lost rpms. Sacajawea clutched her tea mug as the rig pitched and shuddered to an abrupt stop. Jeremy leaned against the doorjamb with his right hand and pushed the latch with his left. Open up. Open, you stupid, damn door. A willowy arm then reached around him, flicked the latch sideways. Jeremy flung the door back, stumbled onto the porch and vaulted the low railing. He landed flat-footed on the grassy road bank, but a knee on the downhill side gave way and he tumbled and somersaulted into the bottom of the ditch. Lying on his back, he looked up. Fuzzy cotton balls swept across a blue canvas. Jeremy took a slow breath. Then, someone kneeling at his side—a face covered with whiskers blotting out the sky.

"Move, please."

"You all right, son?"

"Please get out of my face." Jeremy waved a hand.

"Okay, kid. Take it easy," Porcupine said. "Can you get up?"

Jeremy's breathing was coming easier now. "Gimme a second," he said.

A low-hanging cloud drifted into view, hovered above and dimmed the sun. Rays shot out in all directions, turning the sky into a wheel. Gray and white spokes radiated from the hub. Jeremy took a slow breath. The burning sensation in his face and the wrenching in his gut had subsided. Then, the wind pushed the cloud away and Jeremy caught the sun's glare head on.

"Take my hand, son." With his low center of gravity, Porcupine offered ballast on the incline.

"I can get up by myself," Jeremy said and climbed to his feet. Sacajawea looked down from the tiny porch, raven hair falling past her shoulders.

"Okay if I ride up front?" Jeremy asked.

Porcupine nodded. "You can ride wherever you want."

A few moments later, Porcupine mashed the accelerator until it was rubbing the floorboard. The GMC rig lugged the trailer up a grade, whining like it was about to blow a gasket.

"Shoulda done one thing different when I extended this truck frame and built our little cabin on back," Porcupine said. "Wished I had rebuilt this Detroit diesel engine, gave it some guts." Porcupine eased off the pedal for a second. With hands quick as a boxer, he maneuvered the stick shift to the next higher gear. "You know what they say about a Detroit 318?" Jeremy shook his head, no; Grandpa Truck was a Caterpillar man, swore by that engine. "To slow it down—all you got to do is hold up a picture of a hill."

Jeremy noticed the approaching blue-and-red medallion-shaped highway sign with Tennessee stenciled on it. For a moment, he had forgotten what state he was in. "Where are we?" he asked.

"Just west of Knoxville," Porcupine said and grabbed another gear. The truck took a liking to a long, downhill stretch, picked up speed, almost hit sixty-five.

"I must've slept through the last hundred miles last night," Jeremy said. "I never saw the Tennessee line."

The truck lumbered on for several miles, wind whistling through tiny cracks between windows and doorframes. Then, a hill approaching fast. Not a picture of one, but the real thing. Steep and long. Right foot on the floorboard, it was an all-out run to gain momentum. Still, the truck lost speed halfway into the climb and Porcupine dropped two gears. The rig labored along, hugging the right lane. A charter bus headed to Guitar Town, Nashville in CB lingo, swooshed by. One more downshift and the GMC crested the hill.

"Up and down," Porcupine complained. "Up and down." The truck regained speed and Porcupine wrapped his stubby fingers around the black shifter handle. Trigger fingers twitching, he waited for the rpms to reach twenty-two hundred, then pushed the knob up and away from his right knee. "They say don't ever get into a fight with a man who drives a rig with a Detroit 318."

"Why's that?"

"Constantly shifting like this, you develop a lethal right hand." Porcupine flashed his teeth and held up his fist. "With the camper on back and a full trailer, we're hauling about seventy thousand pounds, a damn heavy load for this old girl," Porcupine said and checked his gauges. "Anyway, Sacajawea takes care of the kid, I keep it between the ditches, carry on best I can. Got three days to make Shaky Town."

"Where?"

"Shaky Town, you know, Los Angeles."

"Oh sure," Jeremy replied. "Of course. How long before we're in the Texas Panhandle?"

"Tomorrow, maybe noon."

The sun beat down on the GMC's twin windshields. Porcupine pulled a pair of sunglasses out of his T-shirt pocket and slipped them on. Jeremy rested his right arm against the passenger door, wedged it against the glass. "Kinda' stuffy in here," he said.

"That's because these big-ass windshields act like a giant magnifying glass," Porcupine explained. "They can almost blind drivers headed in the opposite direction. Heard a few hands on the CB call it a fish bowl."

"It is a lot of glass. But a great view," Jeremy said, rolling with the conversation. "Okay to open the window?"

"Suit yourself."

Jeremy gripped the steel handle and cranked it round and round until the glass disappeared inside the door. He draped his arm out the window the way he saw Grandpa Truck do many years ago. The stiff breeze blew his matted hair straight up into a pyramid.

Porcupine ran the bypass around Nashville, past the suburban maze of shopping centers with chain stores crammed one against the other, the brick and steel and glass office buildings, the nondescript hotels and sprawling, homogenous subdivisions. West of town, Jeremy marveled at the Tennessee hills and meadows draped with blankets of fresh green shoots set before a backdrop of hickory, sugarberry and beech trees, all with that pale, lime green of early summer. Behind every hill lay another verdant field, pasture or paddock. With more than seven hundred miles in the rear view mirror, Jeremy started to relax. Philadelphia was a fog. Texas, a rainbow. Making good time. About eight hundred more miles to find Grandpa Truck.

But a lot could happen in eight hundred miles.

Seven

Split rims, those damn devils. Steel rings like enormous washers wedged between a big rig's tire and the wheel itself. Probably the worst engineering idea to come off an automotive draftsman's page and onto the tractor-trailer rigs that roamed North America in the twentieth century. One tire repairman lost half his face and all his vision when a split rim exploded while he was inflating a tire on the highway shoulder outside Rapid City. The poor victim had extracted a six-penny nail from the tread, sealed up everything with that goo you slap between rubber and steel, had the air compressor humming, got to about ninety pounds pressure when KAPOW! The damned iron donut busted loose. His name was Henry Jackson, just a kid six months on the job. He was leaning over the wheel holding his gauge to the valve stem when it cut loose. Like a 12-gauge shotgun blast, it sent him sprawling. The truck driver then waved down the next car, and a good Samaritan rushed Henry to the nearest emergency room. Poor Henry couldn't find another job after that, but the truck stop owner took him back. And damned if Henry didn't go right back to fixing truck flats. But by then, the truck stop owner had bought an iron cage for inflating tires. Air hose in hand, he could reach through the bars and insert the nozzle onto the valve stem, protected from flying shrapnel in case that sonofabitch rim let go. As young Henry grew into old Hank, he learned to repair tires by feel and sound and intuition and became a whiz at his job. A local newspaper reporter came out once. Took a picture and wrote a story about him. You can see it today, framed, on the wall inside the coffee shop entrance.

Jeremy felt the explosion like a firecracker detonating under his seat. It shook his body and shattered those tender nerves that had finally abated. He felt the rig tug toward the grassy median. Porcupine wrapped his fingers around the wheel at ten and two o'clock and fixed his gaze straight ahead. Narrow eyes. Veins popping out of his neck and the back of his hands and hairy forearms. T-shirt sleeves stretched tight against bulging biceps.

Jeremy pushed against the dash with both hands. Shoulda strapped on that seat belt, but too late now. The truck rocked side-to-side and careened onto the left shoulder. Porcupine couldn't let go of the wheel to hit the toggle switch that would warn the family riding in the camper that they should hunker down. But all hell had to be breaking loose back there and they didn't need a fire alarm to tell them to hit the deck.

The rig continued to pull violently toward the left, the cab listing toward that side. Then a change in road noise from a hard asphalt hum to soft dirt and grass splattering against the rig's chassis. A voice on the CB: "Ride her, baby, ride her."

Porcupine squinting, grimacing, gripping the wheel with iron claws. Something banging, flapping under the cab near the left front bumper—thump, thump, thump—and it's growing louder as the truck rights itself in the bottom of the median. Losing speed, the thwacking noise slows down and the rubber finally lets go with a thud. Porcupine finally flips the code red toggle switch. The GMC rocks along another thirty yards, limping like a runner with one shoe, and comes to a stop.

The CB explodes with chatter.

"Hot damn! That rig looked like it was going to capsize."

"Hey, driver, that split rim shot by me as I was passing eastbound, saw it roll into the brush about a couple hundred yards ahead of where you stopped."

"You need to get rid of them split rims before you get yourself or somebody else kilt."

Porcupine shut off the engine and looked at Jeremy. "You okay?" Jeremy swallowed the grapefruit that was lodged in his throat and nodded that he was fine. "Come on back to the camper with me. I got to check on the fambly."

Porcupine and Jeremy climbed down from the hobbled rig and were standing before the small landing when Sacajawea slammed back the screen door. "I knew it. I told you those split rims were dangerous. Newton's crying from a gash on his forehead. And he banged his elbow on the floor when his chair turned over."

"I'm sorry, baby. I'm sorry." Porcupine bowed his head. He couldn't look his wife straight on. "We'll get new tires and new rims," he said, looking down at the truck's front bumper, inches above the ground. "Soon as we get out of this ditch."

"The Wickiup looks like an earthquake hit it," Sacajawea said, holding up both hands. She pushed back her raven hair and using a tissue dabbed a red gash on her forehead.

Out of nowhere, a low-centered, Ford Galaxie 500 pulled out of the hammer lane onto the shoulder and traversed the slippery embankment. The rear tires looked like they could use several pounds of air pressure, and the tail pipe dragged the ground, plowing a furrow as the vehicle plummeted into the ditch. The original hood ornament had been replaced with a small, polished silver replica of the Rodin masterpiece, The Thinker. The Thinker was in his original pose—nude, right elbow propped on his thigh, hand under chin—but in this rendition the left hand was holding a book. The Thinker wasn't cogitating some universal truth. He was reading.

The car slid to a stop beside the stranded rig. The driver's door swung back, rocked on its hinges, and wedged open in the muddy ditch. A slender, white-haired man with a gray beard that fell to his waist stood one foot on the grassy median, one foot still in the car.

"Looks like you're in a real quagmire here, quite a predicament," the man said at lightning speed. "I'm no tow truck driver but maybe I can help. My name is Percival, traveling dictionary salesman for eleven years, traverse the South in winter, head north for the summer. Last year on the Fourth of July I sold seventy-six hardbacks in Wapakoneta, Ohio."

"How are all your dictionaries gonna help me get out of this ditch, mister?" Porcupine's forehead wrinkled and his eyes shot darts. "Unless you can use them books to jack up this eighteen-wheeler." *Of all the characters out on the road, why this kook the one to stop?* "Now, I'm running late. Gonna spend hundreds on new wheels and tires. Got a bruised wife and son, a teenage runaway tagging along, and all you can talk about is —"

"I'd like to see one those dictionaries," a soft voice drifted down from the truck's camper.

"It's Webster's Sixth New Collegiate Dictionary," Percival said and flicked his long beard over his shoulder like it was a scarf. He feasted his eyes on Sacajawea's almond skin, long silk hair, shimmering eyes. But oh, a blemish, a nasty gash on her forehead. Is nothing perfect?

"Did you know less than ten percent of American families own a dictionary?" Percival said, launching his sales pitch. "That's a sin against literacy in my book, pardon the pun."

Percival high-stepped through the mud and popped open the trunk. Like Moses holding up two stone tablets, he hefted a dictionary in one hand and a thesaurus in the other. "Got a special going right now. Two for twenty."

Sacajawea shook her head at the sight—a man selling books in the middle of an interstate highway—but saw an opportunity. She was still using that dog-eared dictionary she bought at a college bookstore years ago. A new dictionary would be a wonderful way to teach Newton all the treasures that come with exploring new words. "I'll take them both."

"You are a wise and beautiful woman." Percival approached the small landing like it was an altar. He placed both books into Sacajawea's outstretched hands. "That'll be twenty bucks cash, sure you wouldn't like a couple of pocket-sized paperback editions, too, or I have a few copies of "Bartlett's," wonderful quotations that inspire, encourage and uplift, never know when you —"

"Would you please get the man some money?" Porcupine said, holding both hands together like he was praying. "This is ridiculous, buying books while we're stuck in a ditch."

Sacajawea cut her eyes at her husband, handed over a twenty, and thanked the man. She said she needed to attend to her son. Holding the new books close to her breast, she disappeared into the camper.

Jeremy had been observing this interstate commerce with keen interest. What a scene. But his mission was paramount, and after examining Porcupine's predicament he determined he could not afford to wait. He had to beat the mailman to Texas.

"Here comes the tire truck," Jeremy said, looking up at a rattling red diesel flatbed rolling down the highway shoulder.

Porcupine, Percival, and Jeremy followed the driver, a young man wearing greasy coveralls, around the rig's perimeter. When it became obvious that the GMC would have to be towed to a shop to be outfitted with new wheels and tires, Percival said he would be on his way.

"If you don't need anything, I'll be shoving off. I'm scheduled to meet a group of teachers, librarians and parents tomorrow in Oklahoma City."

Relieved at the prospect of getting this weirdo out of his hair, Porcupine forced a grin, little lines at the corners of his mouth turned upward. Maybe he had overreacted. Still, this ratchet-jaw salesman was annoying.

"I appreciate you asking, but you need to get along," Porcupine said like he was talking to a child. "Thanks for the books."

Oklahoma City, Jeremy remembered from studying the road atlas that Sid gave him, was about three, maybe four hundred miles from Amarillo. That would put him three-quarters of the way to Grandpa Truck's depot, warehouse, or terminal, or whatever he called it.

"Can I hitch a ride?"

"You buy enough dictionaries, he'll take you all the way to The Promised Land," Porcupine said, forcing another smile.

"Very amusing," Percival replied. "Indeed, I would enjoy the companionship, the opportunity to imbue the love of language with an impressionable young man, share the wonderful world of antonyms, synonyms, homonyms—"

"M&M's too," Porcupine said with eyes on Percival to see if he was getting under the man's skin.

"Touché!" Percival threw his right hand into the air. "Well done, sir. Now, we must be off, through Arkansas, dreadful state for dictionary sales I might add, and into the Sooner State."

Jeremy climbed the steps and slipped inside the camper. He had just met the most extraordinary family of his life and now he had to say goodbye. Is that how it is on the road? Meet 'em, greet 'em, leave 'em. Sacajawea was sitting at the breakfast nook explaining to Newton that the truck had blown a tire and they were waiting on help.

"I—uh, I'm going to catch a ride with the dictionary salesman," Jeremy stammered. "But I want to thank you."

"I understand," Sacajawea said, lowering her eyes. She asked Newton to say goodbye to their new friend and then finish the science questions he was working on before the blowout. Newton said in what seemed like a rehearsed manner, "Nice to meet you." He disappeared into the Wickiup.

Jeremy felt a ting of sympathy for the kid with a brilliant mind but strange body. What price was Newton paying for his parents' nomadic lifestyle? Was road schooling really best?

Sacajawea smiled. Her cheekbones pushed up high on her face. The forehead gash had stabilized and looked like a small cut. Jeremy stared, again transfixed by her shimmering eyes. "You better hit the road, Jeremy. That dictionary salesman is probably tired of waiting."

Eight

"Do you know how fast you have to drive to outrun your headlights? Take a guess. Ninety miles an hour? One hundred? One hundred twenty? Ever heard of anyone doing that? I performed such a feat on the salt flats in western Utah, interstate so flat and straight you could drive with your feet up on the dash. And here's another road riddle: You know how many white stripes are in a mile? I counted up to one hundred ninety-eight, then I missed a curve, rolled into a ditch outside Walla Walla, trunk popped open and dictionaries spewed out covering a quarter mile of the median. Say, you don't talk much; I mean are you picking up what I'm putting down? That's okay, people say I talk enough for a room full of politicians and preachers but I'm just practicing the language, harvesting the beautiful bounty from the literary seeds our forefathers planted when they learned to use their tongues and mandibles for more than grinding nuts and licking their gums; you know without language we'd be savages, grunting and gesticulating. Of course for some of us out here on the protracted road that holds true, no offense to the truckers and your grandfather in particular——but alas we are in a crisis in this country until we make the effort to improve our lexicon. Anyway, about truckers, my Ford blew a tire once in the Nevada desert and I didn't have a jack but a trucker stopped and changed the flat and since then I've felt an obligation to remember travelers share the same common denominator despite what we drive and where we're from. On the road we live in this suspended state of animation and we are all vulnerable to a degree, and most of us revere the road because it allows us the freedom to be alone with our thoughts and you know sometimes that's the only way I can have an intelligent conversation, not that anyone would get much of a word in edgewise. So that's my story what's yours? Looks like you're withering away if you don't resent my blunt rhetoric. I've seen some troubled youth before and you've got the weight of a string of adverbs on your shoulders. Oh my, I hadn't noticed. When did the poor lad fall asleep? Oh well, the lad is distressed, destitute and desperate, need to let him be; let's concentrate on making the Arkansas line and the opportunity for correspondence with my sweetheart, my beloved, my jewel Josephena. Oh, how I adore that woman."

The Galaxie bounced across western Tennessee, snout in the air, tail dragging, and approached the Mississippi River at Memphis. A large break in the asphalt shook the car and woke Jeremy. He looked out the window in a daze. The broad and muddy river meandered far below the interstate. If a car fell in there, boy, it would sink like an anchor. Percival pushed the vehicle across the expansive bridge and down into Arkansas. The Galaxie chased a patchwork of pavement littered with cracks and potholes through the Mississippi Delta. Shotgun shacks and decrepit buildings on stilts disappeared in the rearview mirror. Percival spurred the Galaxie to a speed where the car finally leveled, like a boat planing out. Jeremy dozed. The car skimmed the broken road across eastern Arkansas into Little Rock where it weaved through lanes jammed with cars, buses and trucks. Percival refueled the vehicle west of town, and with a keen eye for the highway patrol, chased the horizon across western Arkansas. The scarlet sun sank low in the sky, winked and ducked behind low-flying pink and violet clouds.

A few miles after crossing the Oklahoma state line, Jeremy woke to the sound of Percival sniffling and wiping his nose with a white pocket handkerchief. Jeremy sat up, looked out the window. A rest stop, dark and empty.

"Are you okay?" Jeremy asked, miffed at the man's sudden turn in demeanor.

"I miss my Josephena," Percival said, looking at Jeremy through watery eyes. "I know I'm obnoxious and boorish, but she accepts me for what I am and I'm in heaven when we're together. She's . . . she's . . . uh . . . see what a hold she has on me, I cannot speak. And as you know, I tend to blather on."

"I hadn't noticed," Jeremy said.

The dashboard gauges illuminated Percival's face. Pink from crying. Bottom lip sagging like a trout. Embarrassed for the strange and somewhat obnoxious man, Jeremy waited for Percival to pull himself together. Percival touched up his face with the handkerchief. Jeremy asked, "So, what are you talking about?"

"This is the prearranged drop spot for the letter," Percival explained, his voice muffled by the damp cloth. He finished wiping his nose and folded the handkerchief into a neat square. "The letter must always be taped to the underside of the picnic table located at the westernmost point."

"I still don't get it."

"I'm picking up a letter from Josephena in this rest area, and yes I know what a post office box is for, but this is exotic and quixotic and that's how we do things. I shall retrieve the missive and read it late tonight. Perhaps this time she'll be ready to slow down long enough for a rendezvous; good heavens memories of that week in Ashtabula have warmed my soul for countless nights."

"Does Josephena sell dictionaries, too?"

"She's a travel writer, working on a book about offbeat Americans. Been working on it for years. We've had this long-distance relationship for . . . well, a long time."

Percival retrieved a flashlight from under the seat. "Wish me luck," he said and skittered across the rest area toward the picnic table where he expected to find his lover's correspondence. Shortly he returned with a small, damp white envelope covered with spiderwebs.

"Must've been placed here weeks ago," Percival said, brushing away daddy long-leg remains. "Oh, it must be pregnant with expectation and elucidation about our forthcoming engagement."

"Aren't you going to open it?"

"In front of you? Heavens no. A document such as this must be read in privacy." Percival held the envelope to his chest. "I'll wait until I have taken a hot shower and am snuggled in bed, reading by the dim light of a motel room bedside lamp."

35

Percival reached over the seat and opened an ice chest full of diet cola. He grabbed three cans. One for the young lad and two for himself. Percival chugged one in a long gulp. A dreadful habit, swilling this soda, seven, eight per day, but one has his vices.

The Ford continued westbound down the interstate, Percival's right hand clutching the steering wheel, left hand gripping the letter. The big V-8 engine chewed up chunks of Oklahoma as if Percival was again trying to outrun his headlights. Jeremy's head fell hard against the passenger window glass, mouth open wide. Twenty more miles and Percival at last felt he could let go the envelope. He leaned forward and slid it inside a dictionary afloat on the dashboard. A safe place for his treasure.

Under a moonless sky, the Ford Galaxie assaulted Oklahoma in a westerly fury. Insects had peppered the hood ornament all day and all night. Bug-splattered yet undaunted, book in hand, The Thinker peered into the dark night ahead.

Nine

After midnight on the west side of Oklahoma City, the Galaxie veered off the freeway and into a small community of motels, cafes, convenience stores and truck stops. Percival's eyelids felt as heavy as manhole covers. He eased the Ford under a sagging carport clinging to the front of Nick's Motel and turned the key to the off position. The hot engine block ticked. Percival's eyes clamped shut, his head snapped back, and his mouth opened wide in a yawn that contorted his face like a Halloween mask, revealing several fillings in yellowed molars. "Good heavens, that felt good."

Percival spilled out of the front seat. A naked light bulb dangling from an extension cord above flickered on and off. Percival's knees shook and buckled. He steadied himself with a hand on the warm hood. Standing before the Ford, motor still ticking and cooling from the marathon through Arkansas and eastern Oklahoma, Percival jammed his thumb into the night bell at the door until a light appeared in the office and a voice barked out an open front window.

"Hold your horses. I'm coming."

A car door slamming alerted Percival that his passenger was awake. Percival turned his shoulders and saw Jeremy dragging his backpack and a hard plastic case out of the back seat.

"Thanks for the ride," Jeremy said, hoisting the backpack and slipping his arms through the nylon loops. The bug-splattered Thinker then caught his eye, reflecting light from the overhead bulb. Jeremy pointed to the hood ornament. "So, what's he reading?"

Percival reached through the open front window, felt around on the dash, and grabbed a dictionary. Fighting back another yawn, he held it out for Jeremy. "A dictionary, of course. Take this for a souvenir, a remembrance of our short time together on the long road."

Jeremy stuffed the dictionary into his backpack and again thanked Percival for the ride, a mad dash across three states that delivered him to the last leg of his pilgrimage.

Jeremy hiked five blocks down the frontage road and stopped before a spotlight mounted on a small trailer. Gnats and moths swarmed the bright beam, circling in a frenzy. The light was tilted upward at forty-five degrees, illuminating the shell of a long-nose Mack that was parked on the roof of the Fifth Wheel Truck Terminal across the street. Jeremy followed the beacon to the coffee shop. Deserted. He stashed his backpack and the hard plastic case in a booth and slid in beside the luggage. Jeremy rubbed his eyes, burying his fists into his sockets. He blinked several times, but his long eyelashes kept hanging up, wouldn't completely open. A few more winks, a little more rubbing, and his vision cleared. Before him sat a woman wearing a tan cowboy hat with a turquoise medallion attached to the front by a snakeskin headband. The straw brim was rolled up on both sides like a potato chip, and frizzy orange hair spilled out from underneath it. The stranger's elongated face featured a prominent chin. Jeremy blinked twice more, but the figure wouldn't go away. Then it smiled, revealing a small gap between two front teeth, and asked, "What are you doing here?"

Jeremy yawned twice. The first was uncontrolled. The second was stalling for an answer.

"I'm a trucker."

The woman plopped a bulky purse on the table. She opened it, extracted a pack of Winstons and a matchbook from Nick's motel, the lodge where Percival had just checked in. She tapped the Winston on the table, filter side down, compacting the tobacco so it would burn slow and even. "You're a trucker?"

"Yes, I am a trucker."

"Then I'm Dale Evans."

The woman dragged the match tip across the underside of the table and, cupping her hands around the blue flame, held it to the cigarette's tip. The sulfur smell made Jeremy's nose twitch and his eyes burn even more. "Whatcha hauling, trucker?"

"Ain't none of your beeswax. I'm just passing through. Stopped for coffee. That's all." Jeremy sat up straight and craned his neck, looking over the woman's hat crown toward the kitchen. "Where's the waitress?"

"She's probably got her head buried in a book." The woman inhaled, paused, leaned back and blew a funnel cloud over her left shoulder. "Says she's going to community college, studying something like biology. Or maybe they got a shift change. Bernice the bitch comes in about this time every morning."

"I just want a large coffee to go."

"Sure that's all you want?" The woman took another drag and slowly exhaled with a seductive sound. "Truck driver."

"Yeah, I'm sure," Jeremy muttered and waved a hand across his face. "Too early in the morning to be hungry."

"That depends on your appetite."

"I'm just not hungry. Period" Jeremy looked around the coffee shop.

The woman made a half-smile at Jeremy, lips parting just enough to reveal tobacco-stained teeth. "You're awful cute," she said, propping her elbows on the table, cigarette tip pointed upward. A trail of smoke drifted toward a slow-moving ceiling fan in the middle of the room.

Jeremy's eyes continued itching and burning. Now she's taking another drag, exhaling like the stacks on one of those rigs in the parking lot. Why won't she go away?

"Who are you?" Jeremy asked.

"I'm a girl."

"I know that," Jeremy said, "but what kind of girl?"

The woman leaned further across the tabletop, close enough for Jeremy to breathe in her tobacco breath. "For twenty bucks you can find out." She leaned back, rested the hand holding the Winston on the back of the booth, and anticipated the shocked look on this kid's face. Oooh, this should be good. Wonder if he's a virgin. That would be a first for both of them. On second thought, maybe twenty is a little high for a rookie. Maybe give him half off on account of his inexperience. He's kind of sexy, too, in a bony sort of way.

A waitress only a few years older than Jeremy appeared at the table holding a glass coffee pot. "You better get out of here," she whispered to the woman. "Shift change is in five minutes and you know what Bernice will do."

39

Without asking, the waitress took the inverted stone cup sitting before Jeremy, turned it over and filled it with a thick, black beverage that to Jeremy resembled motor oil.

In no apparent hurry to leave, the woman wearing the cowboy hat took another drag on her cigarette and watched Jeremy hold the cup to his lips. "That coffee'll put hair on your chest. Hair on other parts, too," she said with a wink and a low snicker.

Jeremy fingered the coffee cup handle. The waitress hovered above the table, apparently looking out for this wayward kid. "Look, there's Bernice's car," she said, pointing toward the window. A pair of headlights from an automobile silhouette shone across the parking lot. "She'll call the cops. Remember what happened last time."

Jeremy sipped the coffee, hot and stale. "Can I have a hot chocolate instead?"

"Okay, sure. You want to place an order, too?"

"He ain't hungry," the woman said, smashing and twisting her cigarette into an Oklahoma-shaped ashtray. "I already asked."

"Just hot chocolate," Jeremy said.

"There's Bernice," the waitress said, nodding toward a large figure looming at the front door. "Come on, you can sneak out the back."

Jeremy watched the two women disappear behind swinging kitchen doors. A minute later the waitress returned with a porcelain cup overflowing with frothy hot chocolate. What a beautiful smell— rich, sweet, fresh. He let the first sip linger on his tongue, then drank almost non-stop until the cup was empty.

Waiting for a refill, Jeremy noticed the sky outside had turned orange-blue, illuminating rows of cabovers and long-nose truck tractors pulling refrigerated vans, flatbeds with tarped loads, double-deck car carriers and livestock trailers teeming with meat on the hoof. The truckers in their sleeper compartments were now kicking back their sheets and blankets, shedding their cocoons. Morning sunlight filtered through the plate glass windows. Bernice took over the section where Jeremy sat.

"Can't you read?" Bernice said and pointed toward a sign shaped like a tractor-trailer rig that was hanging from the ceiling near the dining room entrance. Jeremy turned his head and looked up.

THIS SECTION RESERVED FOR TRUCKERS ONLY

"My drivers will be filling up all these booths, tables and stools in no time, son," Bernice waved a hand across her domain. "You have to move."

Jeremy heard someone across the dining room snort. He grabbed the check and noticed the Winstons and matches still on the table. He crammed them into his baggy jeans front pocket and headed toward the cash register.

Outside, Jeremy wrestled his backpack onto his shoulders, heavier now with the dictionary inside, gripped the hard plastic case, and trudged through the parking lot. He broke into a trot, backpack bouncing on his shoulders. He kept moving and didn't look back until he had made it to the frontage road.

This truck stop was no place for someone down on his luck, looking for a ride out West. What happened to that Southern hospitality? What happened to all those characters Grandpa Truck talked about in his stories? The brother and sisterhood of the road. Kindred souls. Too bad Flapjack wasn't in more of a hurry, could have rode with him. Too bad old Porcupine blew out that front tire, enjoyed his company just fine. And too bad Percival, kooky as he was, wasn't heading to Amarillo instead of OK City to sell dictionaries. Still, there was only one leg left to go. Almost there.

Ten

Jeremy trudged along, thumb pointed into the wind like a weathervane. The vortex from passing trucks shook the teenager's thin frame, yanked at his jeans, pulled on his T-shirt and blew his hair into a bird's nest. Cars swished by, too, but merely kicked up a little sand and gravel. Several miles of hiking since the truck stop. Why won't anybody stop? Turn around, try the backpedal method. Show my face. Maybe that'll do it.

Three, four, five more miles, walking, hiking, one thumb out, still nobody stopping. T-shirt wet under the armpits. Hair is moist, too. Greasy, messy, nasty. Looking back, Oklahoma City's downtown office buildings have faded into the morning haze. Sun climbing fast now. Burning off the cloud cover. Another mile. Traffic thinning. Can't buy a ride. Let's count white stripes, like Percival. One, two, three, hey, here comes a black Mustang convertible. Look at those fat tires and rear end jacked up with air shocks. The driver's dropping a gear. Car backfiring and hunkering down.

The Mustang driver nodded at the passenger riding beside him. Take a look at the scrawny-ass kid with the backpack, thumb sticking in the air.

Jeremy turned sideways, then spun completely around admiring the Mustang. Hey. Brake lights. And listen to that exhaust popping as the driver downshifts. Now they're waving to hurry up. Hope they don't ask why I'm hitchhiking because I'm not tellin' anyone else the truth. I'd rather die myself.

Jeremy squeezed the handle to the hard plastic case and hobbled toward the Mustang. Geez, now the sole on the right hiking boot is flapping, dragging. Be careful not to trip.

"Come on, kid." The driver turned around and waved. "We ain't got all day."

"Yeah, step it up." The passenger had spun around in the seat and was on his knees yelling between cupped hands. "Let's go."

Jeremy broke into a trot and closed the gap. And look at that—Texas plates. Grandpa said Texas was the friendliest state. Said that name, Texas, was taken from a Caddo Indian word, Tejas, meaning friends.

"Let's go. Times a-wasting."

Jeremy was about ten yards from the car when the passenger opened the curbside door. Jeremy arched his back, wiggled out of the shoulder straps and shed his backpack during the last few steps. Then the car lurched forward, just out of reach.

"Oops, sorry, foot slipped off the brake." The Mustang brake lights lit up and the car stopped again, dual mufflers rumbling.

Jeremy wrestled the backpack with his right arm, clutched the handle to the hard plastic case, and jogged the last few yards toward the Mustang. The car eased forward. Jeremy tripped on the loose hiking boot sole, stumbled, almost lost his balance.

"Aw shit, sorry. Happened again," the driver said as the car pulled away. "Look, I'm putting it in neutral this time." The driver turned around in the seat and held his hands up. "I'm not touching nothing."

Jeremy eyed the driver with suspicion. What kind of fool do they think—

"Come on and get in, kid, before you hurt yourself."

The driver then put the car in reverse, backed up to Jeremy. The passenger climbed into the back seat and reached out over the trunk to take the hard plastic case.

These guys were cool, after all, just having a little fun. It would sure be nice to get off these sore feet. The driver then dropped down in his seat and gripped the stick shift. He found first gear, popped the clutch and floored the accelerator. The passenger yelled, "Sucker." Spinning, squealing tires spewed white smoke. The Cherry Bomb mufflers exploded and discharged grey exhaust. The Mustang kicked sideways. The hard plastic case hit the ground, bounced and rolled several feet. The car's rear bumper edged out into the right lane. A passing tractor-trailer rig swerved and the truck driver yanked on the air horn—waaaaaaaaaa—hard and long.

Jeremy stood alone on the shoulder watching both vehicles disappear into the Oklahoma tableland. Bastards. He leaned over, picked up the hard plastic case and retreated to the frontage road. He started to cry at the futility, but the thought of those two assholes made him angry instead. His tears were better than that. Jeremy knelt in knee-high weeds before the hard plastic case. With shaking hands he opened the two latches and raised the lid. Thank God, everything was okay.

Walking again, about three or four miles. No thumb out, just picking 'em up and putting 'em down. Right boot flapping. Backpack bouncing. Then an old Subaru station wagon drives past, one like Mom and Dad drove about ten years ago. What the? That's Dad behind the wheel. Look at his olive skin and curly black hair. They're stopping on the shoulder. Mom's head is out the window. Her arm's waving, come on, Jeremy. She's got her favorite pink flowered scarf pulled over her head and tied under her chin. Sunglasses on. She's calling. Let's go, honey.

Jeremy broke into a sprint, hard plastic case slapping against his thigh. "Wait up! Wait up! I'm coming, Mom. I'm coming, Dad!"

An eighteen-wheeler blasted past Jeremy, swerving from the right lane into the left to miss some crazy hitchhiker running along the shoulder with a backpack and suitcase, zigzagging like a drunk. Jeremy tripped over an untied shoelace, staggered, and when he looked up—no Subaru. Just the silhouette of a big rig disappearing into the flat horizon.

Jeremy's stomach boiled over and he thought he was going to vomit. He stumbled through the ditch onto the frontage road. He bent over, head down, hands on his knees. Nothing came up. A minute later, the nausea subsided and Jeremy resumed walking on the frontage road. A gust of wind and the smell of something dead. Broken glass and a sun-faded Lite beer can. A discarded mattress in waist-high brush almost looked comfortable. Then a rusty sign swinging from a chain before a gas station. A closer look. It's a faded cowboy riding an animal that looks like Pegasus, the winged horse.

Jeremy cut through an open field. Weeds grabbed at his pants legs and sticker burrs hitched a ride on his shoelaces. Clumps of prairie grass made the ground uneven. Gotta watch your step or risk turning an ankle. Great, this place is closed, or should be. Let's slip out of this backpack, sit on this old bench under the sagging wooden eave for a minute. Oh, look, didn't see that faded billboard. Interesting name—Cimarron Station.

Tammy-Lu Rogers kept the lights on at Cimarron Station, a family-owned gas stop, cafe and convenience store, even after the children fled for big city jobs and she buried her husband, Bucky. Bucky died six years ago, heart attack. One minute he was stocking filters and hoses and fan belts in the garage. The next, slumped in a heap. By then, all four kids who grew up in the station had drifted away: Dallas, Tulsa, Denver, Wichita. They begged Mom to sell out, move in with them. But, oh, the history. Before the big war, this outpost was a jumping off point for families leaving their parched farms and weather-beaten homes for a California dream. For folks clinging to rattletrap cars and trucks, Cimarron Station was a chance to stock up on water, gas and groceries. And after the war, Route 66, the Mother Road, exploded with new Studebakers, Chevys and Fords rocketing across the country. Thirsty cars and thirsty drivers with fat wallets. They came from big modern cities like St. Louis and Chicago and Milwaukee, off to see the American West.

So how could Tammy-Lu leave this sandstone fortress? Bucky laid each stone his own self. Look at these walls, decorated with newspaper clippings from the glory days when this was a destination. And what about that small zoo out back? Bucky found a camel in West Texas, added some peacocks for color, and of course it all started with Goliath, a seven-foot rattler he found slithering onto the front porch one spring morning. Bucky pinned it to the concrete slab with a long-handled shovel blade and dragged it into a burlap bag. He added other reptiles—horned frogs and Gila monsters. Bought a parrot on a trip to Nuevo Laredo. Made a papier mache horn and fastened it to an old mare. Those big city kids from back East and California loved getting their picture took on an Oklahoma unicorn.

"You wanna come in?" The voice startled Jeremy. How long had he been sleeping? He turned his head east, then west, looking out on the empty highway. Oh, Oklahoma. He stood up and yawned, blinked at the wrinkled woman standing before him.

"Welcome to Cimarron Station," she said. "Looks like you got a case of THT."

"What the hell is that?" Jeremy blurted before he realized that wasn't the nicest way to greet someone.

"Tired, hungry and thirsty."

"I really could use something to drink."

"Well, come on in." Tammy-Lu leaned into the door with her shoulder and pushed it open. "Cold drinks are in that cooler," she said, pointing toward the back of the store.

Jeremy slipped down an aisle lined with half empty wooden shelves. But look here: Spam, Vienna sausages, sardines, bread, chips, saltines, a regular banquet for someone like Grandpa Truck; he carried stuff like this with him all the time. And look at this steel postcard rack, dusty pictures of oil derricks, cattle, cowboys, Will Rogers, a Jackalope. A couple of half-folded T-shirts; this one says, *Sit down mister and let Jesse rob the train*! Now the glass cooler door, dripping with condensation. Hmm, orange or grape, 7-Up, Coke and Big Red. Gotta try a Big Red in honor of Flapjack. Returning to the front counter, Jeremy limped down the hardware aisle. Wood planks squeaked under his hiking boots. More dusty old stuff. Tire gauges, tiny light bulbs for turn signals, pliers, screwdrivers and adjustable wrenches hanging from steel pegs. At the storefront, he plopped the can of Big Red onto the scratched and scarred glass counter top.

"That's it?" Tammy-Lu asked. "Not much for someone been hitchhiking all day." She pushed with a bony forefinger the number four and five knobs on the adding machine and pulled down the handle. "Forty-five cents."

Jeremy dug in his pants pocket. Only a few pennies and nickels. He handed her the last of his folding money—a twenty-dollar bill. Tammy-Lu counted the change and asked, "What brings you here, son? Ain't none my bidness, but . . ."

Jeremy took a deep breath. He felt obliged to reply; his parents raised him that way. "Thank you, ma'am," Jeremy answered. "I'm just taking a little vacation. That's all."

"Don't take no offense, young man, but if this is your idea of a vacation then you just arrived at Disneyland."

Jeremy peeled back the ring tab. Pinkish-red foam fizzed and oozed across the top of the can. He slurped it before the Big Red could overflow down the side. "Just taking a trip, a little, a little holiday," Jeremy stammered and turned away.

"Sure you are. That's why your eyes are red as that sody water you're drinking. Your hair looks like a tumbleweed, and your belly button rubs against your backbone each time you take a breath."

Jeremy took another swig of Big Red. Sweet and foamy. Tammy-Lu's gaze burned into the back of his head. He looked at the door. He wanted to bolt, to run outside and wave down the next westbound vehicle that happened by. He needed one good ride to reach Grandpa Truck. Maybe the first part of this trip came too easy. The rides seemed to flow one into the other. Now he would have to work harder, maybe make a cardboard sign. One thing for sure, this rundown store and this poor old lady don't look like the answer.

But Tammy-Lu wouldn't let it go. These days the customers trickled in so seldom. And this young 'un looked like he could use a friend.

"I know you got trouble back home, son. You ain't fooling nobody."

Jeremy stopped and scrunched up his face. You can't just walk away from a lonesome old lady when she's talking to you. He gulped the Big Red, felt the sweet, sticky soda wash across his tongue, down his throat. Okay, lady, you win. Jeremy slowly turned around and faced the stubborn woman.

"How can you be so sure I'm in trouble?"

"You forgot your change. Anybody who pays for a Big Red with a twenty dollar bill and leaves nineteen dollars and fitty-five cents on the counter, well it ain't too hard to figger his mind's on sumpin' else."

Jeremy took a long look at Tammy-Lu. What a face, lines and wrinkles and crevices like that topographic map of Oklahoma hanging on the wall. Whoa, and didn't notice at first, but she has no teeth and no dentures. Her lips disappear into her mouth.

"You can say it ain't none my business, but I wouldn't be able to sleep tonight wondering iffin you're all right," the woman smacked her gums. "Or not. I been running this store since, well, probably since your momma and daddy were about your age, I reckon, and I seen all kinds of down-on-their-luck folks coming through here. The old ones is hurtful sad, but it's the young uns like you that breaks my heart. You got yer whole life ahead and you come in here looking like a lost, whipped puppy. Hate to say it like that, but why don't you let someone help you?"

"Because I got run out of the truck stop at Oklahoma City," Jeremy snapped, "and was left in the dust this morning by two jerks who said they'd give me a ride. Who needs help like that?"

Jeremy squeezed the Big Red can, felt it begin to collapse. He swung around and yanked the doorknob. It came off in his hand. He turned around, held it up. Knowing how pathetic he must look, Jeremy smiled.

"I have to get to the Texas Panhandle, all the way up to the New Mexico line, see my grandfather, and back to Philadelphia in six days," Jeremy said, forcing a grin. "And I'll make it. But first let me, let me try and fix this doorknob for you."

Jeremy squatted before the door, closed one eye and looked through the keyhole. He spied a sign hanging from the awning outside. Didn't see that. A picture of a skinny dog, a greyhound, running with all fours stretched out so they're not touching the ground.

Tammy-Lu was now leaning over Jeremy, looking down on the poor kid that talked like he was from back East with the hard T and D sounds. "Don't worry about that door knob," she said. "Been that way a couple months. Just haven't had the gumption to fix it."

Jeremy turned and looked up at the furrowed face. "Is this a bus station?"

"Use to be. But they quit stopping in '87. Or was it '88? I still got the old schedule," Tammy-Lu said, pointing to the glass countertop she stood behind for so many years. "The bus stopped four times a day, two eastbound, two westbound. Now she just rolls past like this place is invisible."

"Can I see the schedule?" Jeremy said and chugged the last swallow of Big Red. Scrolling down the list of towns serviced by the bus line, Jeremy said, "Looks like they had a regular run to Amarillo."

"You do look awful sick," Tammy-Lu said. "I'll call them for an emergency stop."

The woman stepped behind the counter, bent over and muttered something unintelligible. She hefted a black, rotary-dial telephone and laid it on the countertop with a thump. Jeremy watched Tammy-Lu insert the eraser end of a pencil into one of the dial's ten finger holes, drag the disc in a circular motion and let go. It looked like it would take forever for the dial to spin back to the starting position. Jeremy had heard things moved slowly down South, listening to Grandpa spin his road stories with that Texas drawl was evidence of that. But out here, even the telephones worked at a snail's pace. Nine more times, the old lady dragged the dial around in a semi-circle. Nine more times, Jeremy waited for it to slowly retract. Then, a muffled voice on the other end and Tammy-Lu explaining she had an emergency.

"I understand you don't stop here anymore, but I got a sick kid needs to get to the Amarilla hospital. Cain't you make an exception?" Then a brief silence as Tammy-Lu's eyes narrowed. "Say what? He got a snake bite on his left laig. Got bit hitchhiking, walking in the ditch. Now you gonna help this kid or not?" Another pause and long frown on Tammy-Lu's face. "I know Oklahoma City is closer, but they got a special snake bite unit in Amarilla. Surprised you ain't heard about it." Another silent moment in the old store. Jeremy leaning across the counter. Finally, the old lady said, "He'll be okay here. I got it iced down, leg propped up, and he's sitting still. Bus will arrive at five o'clock? Okay. You know where Cimarron Station is? That's right. Thank you."

Tammy-Lu set the earpiece back in its cradle. "Guess you got a couple hours wait." She bent over, returned the phone to the shelf below, and rummaged around. A plastic first aid kid landed on the countertop. "Here ya go, son," she said, handing over a bandage, scissors and roll of white tape. "You better doctor up that snake bite 'afore you get an infection."

Eleven

A silver capsule skims the Oklahoma plains, droning diesel engine humming a lullaby to the restless and sleepless travelers squirming in their seats. The sun is a white-hot orb bearing down on the westbound pod, rendering the air conditioning unit useless. The captain and his passengers dab sweat from their foreheads, complain about this pitiful excuse of a cooling system.

Up front: Barry Rawlins, the driver, hiding behind a pair of wire-rimmed sunglasses that dims the landscape into an orange-yellow haze. Barry's velvety baritone comes across the bus speakers like top shelf bourbon. "Welcome to Blue Sky Bus Lines, bound for Amarillo, Albuquerque, Alamogordo." Makes those dusty towns sound like romantic Mexican resorts. Barry drove a limousine in Dallas for years but got the itch to move on. Lonely ladies love a smooth-talking, smooth-driving chauffer. Help with their bags, ask if they got plans for dinner, smile. One of the job perks that makes up for bad food, bad pay and bad roads.

Second row, driver side: A man about sixty-five, straw cowboy hat with brim turned up at a sharp curve, pearl snap long-sleeve shirt, starched jeans and tennis shoes. His carryon luggage—a plastic trash bag. Headed back to Clayton, New Mexico after attending his brother's funeral in Tulsa. Emphysema, that's what did it. Been strapped to an oxygen tank at least a year. Shoulda took time to visit. Now it's too late. Blood, you know, supposed to be thicker than oil, or beer, or water. No damn excuse for not going out there in fifteen years. Hope that Social Security check is waiting in the mailbox. Down to the bottom dollar. Bought sardines and can of V-8 at Cimarron Station. That's where that hollow-eyed kid got on.

Fourth row, street side: A woman, about nineteen, head leaning on a brown pillow with galloping horses embroidered on it. Flunked out at Oklahoma State. Too many drinking games at parties. Hope to get that waitress job back home. Work a couple months and get an apartment. Gonna be a tough stretch, though. Mom will be full of "I told you so." Dad, not so much. Wish this bus ride would last forever. And who is that baby-faced kid that got on at the stop outside Oklahoma City?

Three rows farther back, a family occupies four seats. Abuelita, thin, silver hair, bright red scarf, sits by the aisle. Stares. The daughter, hands throbbing from too many years cleaning motel rooms, consoles her son, about nine, sweating, complaining about the stuffy bus. Her husband runs stiff fingers through his moustache. The man stares at his reflection in the window, picks at his face. Another chocolate-colored sunspot appeared on his cheek last week. And who is this joven that straggled on at the old Cimarron Station? Pobrecito. Needs to put some meat on those bones or might be mistaken for a cabrito.

Second to last row, driver's side, Jeremy finds an open window seat. Crawls over a middle-aged man, legs spread apart, snoring. Jeremy unlaces his boots, leans back in the cushioned seat. How about these picture windows? Never seen the sky with this much purple and pink and orange and scarlet. At home, you get a glimpse of those colors between houses and office buildings, but out here there's nothing to block the view. And here's that familiar sound, that diesel engine purring under the floorboard. Peaceful. Tranquil. Hypnotic. Snakebite don't hurt too bad either. Can you believe that old woman making up that story? She's got spunk all right. Guess that's no surprise, surviving like she does, alone in that dusty old store. Tammy-Lu, you are the Angel of Oklahoma.

The sun hovered over the highway, glowing deep red, then landed on the interstate like a stop sign. It soon disappeared, lending a scarlet hue to the horizon. The bus exited the freeway and bounced down a side street in Elk City. The driver stopped at an old gas station that had been converted to a bus depot and announced a fifteen-minute break. Jeremy worked his way toward the front. Passengers' hands, legs, and feet were draped over seats and arm rests and dangled in the aisle. Jeremy walked sideways, picking his way past the body parts. Outside, he stretched his arms over his head and yawned. Then he slipped his hands in his pockets and arched his back. What's this? Oh, forgot about those cigarettes from the truck stop.

"Need a light, kid."

Jeremy looked up. The driver.

"I understand nicotine is good for snake bites," the driver said.

"The leg feels much better now," Jeremy stammered.

"You ain't gotta lie to me, kid."

"What are you talking about?"

"You ain't been bit by no snake."

"Is it that obvious?"

"Yep," the driver snapped. "You may be tired and hungry and sleep-deprived, running from boot camp or the law, or running after some gal, but you ain't no snake bite victim."

The driver lit a cigarette, shook the match until it expired.

"It used to bother me, seeing teenagers smoking, but I figger they're gonna try it sooner or later." The driver held out a matchbook from Memphis Motor Lodge—*Your home away from home in the Mississippi River Delta.*

Jeremy wiggled a cigarette out of the crumpled pack. Kinda flat, but looks like it'll burn. Okay, strike, inhale. Great. Match blew out. Awfully windy out here. Now the driver's watching. Act like you know what you're doing. Strike, cup the hands, and inhale short quick puffs like he did. Damnit, it won't stay lit.

"That your first pack?" The driver said with a smile.

"No," Jeremy answered, knowing that if he wasn't flat-out lying it was at least a stretch. He had gone in halves on a pack with Kevin Mumford back at school just a month ago. Only smoked about six or seven, though. Always left you feeling woozy. "This isn't my first cigarette."

"Then why you lighting the filter?"

Jeremy yanked the cigarette from his mouth, examined the burned filter.

"Here, try one of mine." The driver held out a pack of Marlboro Lights. "Don't worry, they're mild."

Jeremy inserted the filter into his mouth. Lit the tobacco end on the first try.

"Makes a difference, don't it?" the driver said. He then took a deep drag, exhaled and examined the Marlboro with curious eyes. "Cigarettes. They're like women. Too many of 'em can kill ya."

Jeremy took another drag, held back hacking up the smoke. The driver asked, "Where are you really getting off, Amarillo?"

"No, sir." Jeremy took another puff, but inhaled more slowly. "I'm riding up to Texicoma to visit a relative."

"Texicoma? Texicoma don't even have a stop sign, just a yellow blinking light. I never stop there."

"Well, my grandfather lives near there. So I was hoping to hop off real quick, if it's not too much trouble." The cigarette tasted bitter on Jeremy's tongue. He took another drag, but again inhaled slowly.

The driver took another hit and looked up at the western sky. "Venus. The first star each night. Named after the Roman goddess of love and beauty."

Jeremy followed the driver's gaze. "The sky seems bigger out here."

"Venus is just the beginning. Wait until midnight. That's when the fireworks begin." The driver took another hit and tilted his head back. He exhaled straight up and a funnel cloud drifted above. "That's how close the Milky Way looks," he said. "A cluster of stars so dense it looks just like smoke or fog. It'll be out in a few hours." The driver dropped the butt on the asphalt lot and extinguished it with his Dingo boot—polished black leather, square toe, silver buckle attached by a herring bone chain. Pushing down with the toe, he twisted and ground the embers and filter into the asphalt. "Time to move on. Driving a bus, if you want to keep a job, you got to keep a schedule."

Drop, stomp, swivel. Jeremy copied the driver's move. His hiking boots were no match for those suave Dingos. Especially the right foot, with that loose flap dangling. He held out the matchbook.

"You keep 'em. I got plenty," the driver said. "I'm going off duty in Amarillo. But we'll see what we can do about getting you dropped off in Texicoma."

Jeremy returned to his seat and the silver capsule glided across a glowing prairie. The riders dozed as the deep purple sky faded to black. Twenty miles later, the vehicle slowed and Jeremy was looking at Main Street in Hub City, a small community named for a once-thriving intersection between two county seats. Headlights cut through the darkness but found nothing. One cafe—closed. One gas station—closed. Laundromat, tiny grocery store, feed and hardware store—closed, closed and closed. Is this what it's like where Grandpa lives?

The driver pushed the bus through the hamlet in less than a minute. No one other than Jeremy bothered to look out, even acknowledge that Hub City existed. What kind of life was this? Lonely, that's what kind. Hit the gas, driver.

The bus made Amarillo about midnight. The driver announced a five-hour layover for passengers continuing to Pueblo and Denver. Jeremy walked three blocks in the direction that a clerk had pointed out and found a 24-hour hamburger joint. Any chance of a Philly cheesesteak sandwich? Don't laugh, just asking. Double meat burger with jalapenos and barbecue sauce? Sounds weird to someone from the East Coast, but okay here we go. Walking back, finishing off the French fries, another cigarette don't sound too bad.

Standing outside the bus terminal smoking one of the Oklahoma stogies, Jeremy watched the buses roll in. The drivers made it look easy, nosing the buses into those parking spots and coming to a smooth stop, big engines humming and air brakes hissing. But when the drivers opened the cargo bay doors it was a free-for-all for luggage. Look at the passengers, folks down on their luck, down on life, shoving and throwing other people's luggage around because it's in their way. And they say big city people are pushy.

After the passengers disappeared into the terminal, Jeremy focused on the silver bullets lined up and ready to roll. Illuminated destination signs above the windshields were tickets to the American Southwest: San Antonio, El Paso, Tucson, Santa Fe. People traveling on. Running to something. Or running away from something.

Jeremy lit the cigarette feeling much older than he was just three days ago. How many states? He counted on his fingers: Delaware, Maryland, Virginia, Tennessee, Arkansas, Oklahoma, Texas. How many miles? About 1,700. Jeremy took a drag and slowly exhaled. Yes, he felt much older.

Jeremy continued the people watching through the lonely hours. A thin man with a square jaw walked past. He was wearing slacks and a trim sport coat, patches on the elbows, clutching a tall paper bag tied with a ribbon and bow. A bottle of wine? A few minutes later, a bus from Topeka pulled in and the passengers spilled out, yawning, stretching, rubbing their eyes. The man watched the bus door with the eyes of a hawk.

And Jeremy watched the man.

He's waiting on someone special. Look how hard he's staring, so intense the skin around his eyes is stretched tight like that rawhide lampshade back at Cimarron Station. Who's he waiting for? Wife or girlfriend? Mother or daughter? The bus is almost empty. He's just standing there. Not even blinking. Only one person left. There she is, about the same age, tall, long black hair. Betcha this is a reunion. Hugs, tears and kisses. Oh, no. She's walking right on by. He's still staring at the bus. But there's nobody in it. Come on, somebody walk up to this man. Don't leave him standing there alone. Now everybody's got their luggage and they've all stumbled into the depot. But he's not leaving. Why doesn't he just give up? He's waiting on a ghost. Just go away, mister. She, he, it, whoever, they're not coming. This is too painful. I'm lighting another cigarette.

Jeremy burned four matches in the stiff breeze before he got the cigarette trailing smoke. Had to double up, strike two matches at once. The first hit was mostly sulfur taste and smell, but he kept puffing and got the red ember glowing like taillights.

The man finally turned and shuffled away, shoulders slumped, head dangling. He passed a steel drum with "garbage" stenciled on it and flicked the paper bag like he was shooing a fly. It landed inside with a clunk. Jeremy watched the man slip into a gray sedan and drive away.

55

What's in that bag? Gotta look. Uh oh, there's a line in front of the bus. Time to roll. Grab that paper bag, quick. Check it out when we're moving. Here's a window seat up front.

Barry Rawlins was back on duty, covering a run for a no-show. The bus slipped down Amarillo streets, spewing diesel exhaust into the early-morning air. The eastern sky glowed pink—a faint coat of lipstick on the horizon. Jeremy untied the ribbon from the top of the paper bag and slipped his hand inside. Soft tissue paper, then something made of glass, thin and tall. He tugged at the bag with his other hand, a little at a time, and pulled free a vase stuffed with daisies. Purple ones. An even dozen.

The driver now had the bus humming down the four-lane highway. He glanced in the mirror to check on his passengers. Everything nice and quiet. And would you look at this? That kid who don't know his ass from a cigarette filter has a bouquet of flowers. Looks like daisies.

The driver looked over his shoulder at Jeremy. "What's up with the flowers, Romeo?"

Jeremy climbed to his feet and grabbed a handrail. "Found 'em in the trash," he said in a dramatic whisper. "A man who looks like a private detective threw 'em in there. He was waiting on someone who didn't show. Maybe she missed her bus. Or it broke down."

"Kid, you tickle the shit out of me. Trying to smoke a cigarette ass-backwards and now you want to solve a mystery, a love story." The driver kept a steady hand on the wheel, glancing back and forth between the road ahead and this puppy dog teenager standing in the aisle, gripping a rail with one hand and a flower bouquet with the other. "I been running in and out of Amarillo for about eighteen months now. I've seen that man at least a dozen times, waiting on the bus from Topeka. He bought daisies this time, huh?"

"Yeah, look at 'em." Jeremy ran his fingers through the soft petals. "Aren't they pretty?"

"That person he's waiting for, she ain't never coming."

"What do you mean? How do you know?"

"Kid, your Yankee ass is something else. You come out West, out on the road, all naive, getting upset about something that don't even concern you. I thought you easterners were raised up street tough."

Jeremy ignored the man's remarks. "He must have some reason for waiting."

"The lady he's waiting on. She ain't never gonna climb off that inbound bus from Topeka because she's dead."

"What the . . . " The vase slipped out of Jeremy's hand and hit the floorboard.

"That man's crazy. Lost his mind when he lost his wife. She was riding on a bus north of Boise City when the driver hit an ice patch and crashed through a guardrail. Seven people died in that wreck."

Jeremy's skin tingled. "Life isn't fair." He bent over and picked up the vase and flowers.

"Don't take it too hard, kid. It happened six years ago."

Jeremy sniffed and wiped his nose with his shirtsleeve. One mile, two miles rolled by. He stood beside the driver and stared out the broad windshield, transfixed by headlights on the highway.

"Look. I know it's a sad story." The driver eased the bus around a soft curve, one of the few turns he would make on this straight highway. "But people die all the time, son. That's the cost of livin'. Nobody rides free. Not on this bus. Not on this Earth."

Barry pushed down on the accelerator and the bus surged. Jeremy rocked back and squeezed the handrail. After he regained his balance, he returned to his seat. What he felt like saying to the driver, what he wanted to say, he couldn't utter. *How would you like the school principal to come into your chemistry lab and take you into his office? Then you wait what seems like forever while someone gets your sister out of gym class. Then they tell you that your parents are in a hospital on life support and there's a grief counselor waiting in a car to take you there. Two days later, two days of no sleep and wrenching stomach, and they call you in from the waiting room, call you into some sort of lounge and tell you they didn't make it. But that don't mean you give up hoping, wishing, dreaming. So don't tell me about death mister bus driver. Don't tell me shit.*

Twelve

You ain't going to believe what happened on the bus up from Amarillo last night. This scrawny kid who climbed aboard in Oklahoma gave a bunch of folks a ride they won't never forget. He smelled like he hadn't touched a bar of soap since Christmas. Looked like he'd been sleeping in a dumpster. It would take sheep shears to cut his mop top hair. But it's not how he smelled and looked that I'll remember. While I was pushing the bus down Highway 87, he was walking up and down the aisle giving away flowers, purple daisies.

One woman, musta been eighty years old, nose in a magazine. She looked up at that boy, his face sprouting a few whiskers and smiling down as he held out the flower, and she grabbed that daisy like it was the winning ticket to a million-dollar Powerball game. Then her arms, flabby like chicken wings, they found the strength of Samson, yanked that boy by his T-shirt, pulled him down and kissed him on the cheek. The kid straightened up, and you could tell he was stunned, just stood there until the bus hit a bump and he almost fell on a sleeping man's lap.

Another lady, I felt bad for her, she was so big that nobody could sit in the seat next to her. Well, Mr. Toothpick here, he gives her a daisy, too. She tries to say no. I watch her wave him off. She looks at him like he's some sort of fool, a jester in crumpled clothes. But he wouldn't budge. Grabs the back of the seat and drops to one knee. And that fat lady, she breaks into a big old grin, takes that flower, breaks off the stem and puts it in her hair. And you know, I've seen her on this route before. She's always worn a long frown. For the first time ever, she smiled. And I'm telling you, she has a pretty smile.

Of course, no good deed goes unpunished, and sure enough one husband has to act the fool. After this anorexic Don Juan gives a flower to a young woman sitting in an aisle seat, her husband wakes up and demands to know where she got it. She won't tell, plays coy, but any idiot can figure it out. Just look at the kid standing in the aisle with a half-dozen daisies in his hand talking to that Asian-looking lady. So this guy's skin is turning greener than alga and he climbs over his wife and grabs the kid by his shoulder, spins him around and starts poking his chest. So you know what this kid does? He holds out a flower. And that asshole, he looks around and finally realizes every eye on the bus is watching him. He looks like he's been caught kicking a puppy. Finally, with everybody on the bus holding their breath, he accepts the daisy and sits down.

So this goes on for about fifty miles. The whole time, I'm trying to keep an eye on the road and what's going on in my bus. So I got a long straightaway, no traffic, and look back in the mirror and he's only got a couple flowers left. Guess who gets one? A woman wearing a black robe and habit. A nun. She's all absorbed praying the Rosary so he has to wait a couple miles for her to notice he's standing there. She takes the flower and smiles like it's Easter Sunday. Then she hands him the Rosary, shows him how to count the Hail Marys, one for each bead, and they pray together for another five miles.

By the time he gets down to one daisy, everyone, front to back, is watching. I'm doing my damnedest to keep one eye on the road and one on my mirror because I'm dying to know who gets the last daisy. There's several ladies left who haven't got one, so he's got a problem. I'm driving, thinking, counting the miles in my head. About ten more before he gets off. About ten minutes for the nun to pray that last daisy multiplies like the loaves and fishes.

So what does he come up with? He starts pulling off and handing out petals, one at a time, to the last of the women. They kiss them, smell them, and one young woman wearing an open-top blouse winks as her petal disappears down her dress.

Now, I've been herding these grey dogs for several years, drove charter for some filthy rich oil men, rock bands all hopped up on speed, and two-faced politicians bullshitting reporters and voters out on the campaign trail. But I swear to you on these broken white lines that nobody has held a busload of people in a spell like that. And he did it all with second-hand flowers.

When the kid gets off at the flashing yellow light in Texicoma, everyone scrambles to the left side of the bus to watch him cross the street to the post office. That's where he's going to get directions to his grandfather's place. And as we roll away, most of the passengers push their way to the back, watching through the rear window. He lights a cigarette, waves and ducks into the post office. Then I hear that nun say: "Someone should tell that nice boy he's too young to smoke."

Thirteen

The last leg of a two thousand mile journey. Move over, Ulysses. Maybe there weren't any Cyclops hiding in truck stops, or sirens sunning on the banks of the Mississippi River beckoning with golden voices; and four days on the road can't compare to ten years lost at sea, but a journey like this could change how you look at the world. It could change how you felt about everything. And it was only half over. Not even that.

The pocket-sized road atlas Sid gave to Jeremy had been a guiding light, had pointed him to this speck on the highway called Texicoma. But he still needed directions for the last few miles to Grandpa's hideout. At least that's what Molly called it when she learned he had bought twenty acres and built a barn to keep Old Ironsides, his 1956 Peterbilt, out of the weather. These days, Grandpa and a hired driver mostly haul grain across the open plains. Molly researched this region for a semester project. She said Grandpa must worship the wind and sun and have an antipathy toward people and trees.

Jeremy pushed open the sagging, wooden door to the Texicoma Post Office and stepped inside the tiny lobby. Look at this. A county map on the wall. Perfect. Jeremy set the hard plastic case on the floor and ran his hands across the top, brushing dust off the large J stenciled on it. He wiggled loose from the backpack. After a minute of careful study, he found County Road 17 where Grandpa lives. But which direction? Could be walking all day. He looked out a small window. Clouds drifting by. Feels like the floor is moving. Oooh, fuzzy head and churning stomach. Three nights on the road without much sleep or food, and those cigarettes, wow, need to sit down. Jeremy relaxed in a wooden chair. Closed his eyes. His mind wandered back to what that bus driver said about no free rides, in life or on the bus. But nobody had asked him for bus fare. So who paid? Maybe people looked out for each other after all.

"You must be lost." A shrill voice shot from behind the counter. "How long you been sitting there?"

Jeremy looked up. "What time is it?"

"Lunch time. That's when I drive in from Smith Corner for the afternoon shift."

Jeremy ran his fingers through his greasy hair and looked up to see a woman, about forty-five, turquoise earrings dangling from her lobes, wearing a hard hat. She says it's noon. That means a three-hour nap.

"I'm looking for a trucking company out on County Road 17," Jeremy said. He approached the counter. "I'm visiting my grandfather—Ubi Sunt."

"You must be one of the twins. One of Ahab's grandchildren." The woman made a pistol with her thumb and forefinger, pointed it at Jeremy. "He talks about you and Molly a lot. Saw him a week or two ago when he mailed a stack of invoices. But he don't come in much. Got a certified letter waiting on him from Philadelphia. Arrived today."

"I'll take it," Jeremy said, thrusting his hand forward.

"Oh no, you won't," the woman said, eyeing Jeremy with suspicion. "What a coincidence. A certified letter from a Philadelphia attorney and a grandson who ain't slept or et for days showing up at the same time? You in trouble, son?"

"Just visiting," Jeremy said in a low voice. "Summer vacation."

The woman hung her hard hat on a nail behind the counter. She ran her fingers through short brown hair. Maybe she should help old Ahab's grandson, regardless what trouble waited back East. Then again, it wadn't none her bidness.

"You musta come in on the bus," she said. "You're lucky to get it to slow down. It quit stopping here years ago. But if you can wait till five when my shift ends, I'll give you a ride."

"I'm kind of anxious. So if you don't mind, which way on 17?"

"North a couple miles, if you just got to walk. Wish you wouldn't though."

"I'll be all right. But wouldn't mind a glass of water."

The woman reached behind the counter and produced a plastic bottle of water. "Can you believe it? People buy water from the store these days?" Jeremy gulped twice and the bottle was empty. "You are as parched as ashes at the bottom of a bonfire," the woman said. "Two blocks down, across from the old junkyard, that's 17. You'll see the sign. Then take a right."

Jeremy thanked the woman and turned toward the door. He stopped and turned around. "Why are you wearing that hard hat?"

"When I was a little girl I saw my daddy pounded by hail stones big as peach pits. He tried to make it in from the barn, running, but got trapped under a tractor. He waited out the storm, clutching the ground under that old International. But he got bruised up real bad, cuts on his face, too. You be careful out there. Hail storms can rise up fast, out of nowhere."

Jeremy said good-bye and dragged the sagging door shut behind him. But the postmistress was suddenly standing beside him, holding out her hard hat.

"Take this," she said. "You need it more than I do."

Jeremy shrugged and looked up. No clouds. "Thanks, but I'm okay."

"I insist."

"Yes ma'am."

Fourteen

Jeremy trudged along the side of the dirt road for what would have been dozens of city blocks back home. Walking down the shoulder, this gravitational force, like a hand to the back, kept pushing him lower toward the ditch. Although it was dry and dusty at the top, the ditches on both sides were green with weeds and scattered shoots of volunteer corn, the children of seeds that had been blown, carried or washed from the fields and germinated. Jeremy let the incline steer him into the ditch. He was soon slogging through mushy brown mud that caked on his boots. Back on the road he climbed. Dragging and scraping the bottom of his soles, chunks of mud broke free like pieces of rubber from blown out tires on the interstate.

The post office lady said Grandpa's place was just a few miles down 17. But how do you measure a mile? Maybe they just seem longer out here because there are no landmarks. No bus stops. No office buildings. No apartment complexes like back home. Nothing but corn, cotton and cows. Been walking twenty minutes. Shoe won't stay tied and the loose sole is still flapping. Sore knee throbbing. Shouldn't have jumped off Porcupine's truck.

Jeremy drifted along, wind swirling in different directions. The cornfields yielded to a sea of blue-green grass. Now a chocolate-brown, shadowy figure about fifty yards away. Four legs, but larger than the deer in Pennsylvania. Jeremy crossed the ditch and stepped into knee-high prairie grass. The animal turned and faced west, offering its profile. Gigantic head with two short horns pointing upward. Low to the ground at the rear, but the backbone soars into a mighty hump. The face covered with hair, or fur, and a long goatee.

Jeremy stepped into the field to take a closer look. The massive creature stared at him across the open prairie. Other than swishing its tail, the animal didn't flinch. Jeremy's breathing was slow and relaxed. Why would anybody slaughter such magnificence? He stepped forward, two, three paces, over a high clump of bunch grass.

The loose flap on his hiking boot bent back and he stumbled. Jeremy caught his balance and looked up. The creature was gone. Jeremy blinked and rubbed his tired eyes. A trail of dust drifted up from behind a gentle slope and a thin brown cloud made its way across the horizon.

A rumble in the sky jarred Jeremy back into the present. Better get moving, could be a storm brewing. More hiking. Must be getting close. Okay, Grandpa's mailbox is supposed to be shaped like a big rig. Should see it soon. Unless someone decapitated it like that one a few miles back. That must be a pastime out here for teenagers, riding around smashing these old mailboxes with a baseball bat. Every one so far has had the stuffing knocked out of it, all dented and bent up. Living out here must get awful boring. Gotta find something to keep amused.

The dirt road was a maze, a labyrinth. Only way to tell you're getting anywhere, the grain elevators in town are growing smaller. Jeremy rounded another corner but stopped when he heard *swish, swish, swish* coming from an open field. Giant wagon wheels connected by a long, horizontal pipe were strolling across a green pasture. Streams of water soared and twinkled in the sunlight, watering the corn and cotton.

Now the dogs are barking, as Grandpa used to say after coming in from the road with tired feet. Take a break. Here in tall, soft weeds, plop this tired head on the backpack, hard plastic case safe at my side. Jeremy remembered the cigarettes, but thought again about smoking. He heard what sounded like thunder, adjusted the hard hat and looked up. A jet airliner was traversing the sky. Its contrail stretched from twelve o'clock high to about three-thirty. Staring, losing track of time, Jeremy watched the contrail break apart and drift away in pieces.

Jeremy dozed until he felt something crawling on his arm. A grasshopper, brown like the road and dust. He flicked it away. He climbed to his feet, hoisted the hard plastic case. Two steps later the sole on his shoe again bent back and he stumbled into prickly pear cactus. Needles pierced his toes and he hopped on one foot like he was walking on coals.

Walking again, a chalky-brown cloud appeared in a field maybe a quarter-mile ahead, growing larger, headed this way. It's a huge pickup. What's that sticking out the driver's window? A baseball bat, headed for a mailbox on the left side. Kapow! Did you see that post shake and rock? Better get out of the middle of the road. Fast as they're moving, swerving all over, looks like a little tornado coming this way.

The pickup truck swerved, fishtailed and whipped up white powder that coated the barbed wire fence and that lost fool walking in the ditch. Inside the truck cab, the young man driving looked at his girlfriend snuggled up next to him, soft legs straddling the stick shift. "You see that?" the driver asked, pointing to Jeremy. "Miss Carson's scarecrow done jumped the fence. It's making a break for the Oklahoma line."

Jeremy squinted into the dusty horizon and pushed on. Head down, he walked several hundred yards and stopped before a rural mailbox shaped like an eighteen-wheeler. The truck was parked atop a thick cedar post, hand-painted name on the side—Ubi Sunt Trucking. Texas flag flying above it. Yep, this is it. And wouldya look how the mailbox is flattened on the side?

A rumbling noise then drifted in with the south breeze. Another loud clap and the youngster looked up at black clouds blasting across the sky. Better find cover, quick. Jeremy jogged down the long gravel driveway and stopped under an awning that protected the side door to a tall, sheet metal garage. A quick glance at the sky told Jeremy he had a few minutes before all hell broke loose. He circled the small ranch-style house, banging on the front door, pounding on the back door, yelling.

"Grandpa, come out, it's me, Jeremy. Grandpa, it's Jeremy. Where are you?"

Lightning crackled across the sky and echoed throughout the prairie. Foreboding clouds swarmed low and swallowed the sun. The wind whipped the Texas flag and assaulted two small cottonwoods in the front yard, bending them horizontal. Jeremy hustled back to the small awning, one hand clutching the hard plastic case, the other pushing down on the hard hat.

Heavy drops peppered the driveway, carving small divots in the gravel. The rain grew heavier, and the idle landscape was now bursting with the storm's energy. The sheet metal roof barked and roared as rain beat down and gushed over the edges, digging a trench along the perimeter of the house and garage. Jeremy backed against the door, staying dry except for water splashing at his feet. But the rain blew sideways and soaked his jeans up to the knees. The howling on the little overhang grew louder. Hail stones bounced across the ground like ping pong balls. Broken glass, a window on the north side shattered. The yard turned white.

The storm raged and a hailstone caught Jeremy flush on the left cheek, slashing his skin. He turned his back toward the tempest, buried his face against the door and covered the back of his neck with his hands, arms folded around his ears. The hail and rain continued driving sideways, pummeling his back and legs.

Huddled under the overhang, Jeremy braved the fusillade. When the black clouds retreated southward, he squatted on the ground, closed his eyes and nodded off. First it was a dull pain, then something piercing like a needle buried in his thigh. Jeremy jumped to his feet, unzipped his pants and yanked his jeans to his knees. He slapped at a scorpion embedded in his flesh until it fell to the ground. Twisting and grinding with his hiking boot, Jeremy obliterated the evil creature into the gravel. He pulled up his pants and looked down the driveway.

"Grandpa, where are you?"

Fifteen

A helluva day, Ubi Sunt made four runs from the local grain elevator to the feed lot just across the Kansas state line. Rolling down County Road 17 in a tractor-trailer rig, he recognized the evidence of a brief and violent storm. Corn stalks bent over. Ditches with standing water. Little gullies where water had jumped the road. Ubi slowed the truck to a crawl, made a wide swing and eased down his driveway. Who is that standing by the garage? Is he buckling up his pants like he just took a leak? Ubi climbed down from the truck. "Jeremy, I almost didn't recognize you. How the hell did you get here?"

"It wasn't easy."

"But what? What's going on?"

"Grandpa," the teenager paused to catch his breath, chest heaving. He steadied his feet and looked straight into the old trucker's eyes. "Mom's dead. Dad, too."

Ubi's face went blank, an empty highway. His only daughter and her husband, both dead? That's all the family he has.

"What are you talking about?"

"They were killed in a wreck on the turnpike a few weeks ago," Jeremy whimpered, his voice cracking. "They sent you a certified letter, but I wanted to be the one to tell you. Mom and Dad are dead, Grandpa, they're dead. I hope I never have to say that again."

"When? How?"

"It's all in the certified letter," the teenager said in a high-pitched whine. "You have to pick it up at the post office."

"What about Molly?"

Jeremy tried to answer, but he choked up. The scorpion bite throbbed. A cactus needle pricked his foot. The gash on his cheek burned. His wet body shuddered. Desperate for an answer, Ubi grabbed his grandson by the shoulders and squeezed, their faces now inches apart.

"What about your sister? Is she okay?"

"It was just Mom and Dad in the car. We were at school. But you missed the chance to come to the hospital where the ambulance took them. They almost made it, Grandpa, but after three days . . . " Jeremy's voice trailed off as he looked down. "And we couldn't find you. We called and called, but no answer. Even sent a telegram. But no one was around to sign for it. You were probably on the road. Like always. And you missed the funeral, too, Grandpa, missed the chance to say goodbye."

Ubi clutched Jeremy and pulled him tight, closer than anyone he'd held since his wife died more than ten years ago. His eyelids clamped shut, blocked out all light, blocked out everything save that image of Jeremy huddled under that overhang like a stray calf.

"Let's get you inside and have a look at that gash on your cheek." Ubi ushered his grandson to the simple, wood-frame house adjacent to the garage. He pushed open the door.

"It's not locked?" Jeremy asked.

"What for?" Ubi said with a shrug. "Now, how'd you get here?"

"Flapjack, Porcupine, Sacajawea, Percival, purple daisies."

"I'm not sure what you're talking about, Jeremy, but sit here." In the tiny kitchen, Ubi opened a first aid kit and let Jeremy dab the gash with a dark red antiseptic. "Monkey blood," Ubi said. "Don't think you can find it any more."

"Is that stuff good for insect bites?" Jeremy asked.

"What the heck? You got bit, too?"

"On the leg, just before you pulled in. Burns like a hot needle."

After doctoring the scorpion bite, Jeremy declined his grandfather's supper invitation—pinto beans and cornbread.

"No offense, Grandpa, but I can't eat. My stomach, it's turned inside out."

The two sat at the kitchen table in silence. Ubi numb from shock. Jeremy numb from the trip. Jeremy slowly filled in the blanks, bits and pieces of the auto accident and his flight from the clutches of the Attorney General.

Ubi was unsure what to do next; there was no one to call, no arrangements to be made, everything had been taken of. Yet he had to act. But what?

"When do you have to be home?" Ubi asked.

"Monday, I got four days."

"Okay, let me think about this."

Ubi showed his grandson the spare room. Later that evening, with Jeremy sleeping, Ubi walked outside and faced east. How could it be? His daughter and son-in-law gone in a flash. How selfish and irresponsible he had been, living out here like a hermit, two thousand miles away from family. And all because the lure of this grand expanse. But hold on, he wasn't the one who chose to leave Texas. That was his daughter, Jeanne. Still, you got no excuse for being so reclusive. No damn excuse. Now they're gone and it's too late and you got a mountain of regret to deal with and a grandson who is hurting so bad; hell there's no telling how tough it must have been, all that pain and then bumming rides across the country. Looking at the shape he arrived in, bit up, cut up, skinny like a fence post, musta been one hell of a trip.

Ubi then saw headlights out on the county road and a compact pickup turning into the driveway. The sweet and kooky lady from the post office.

"Here you go, Ahab," the woman said, reaching through the driver's side window, holding out a certified letter from Philadelphia. "Sign here." Ubi scrawled his name on the back. The woman tore off her receipt and handed him the letter. "As often as you come into town, I figured I'd better make a special delivery."

Ubi nodded and said thanks.

"Did the boy make it okay? I found him passed out when I opened up this afternoon. He wouldn't wait for no ride, so I gave him directions and my hard hat."

"Yeah, he did. He's inside resting."

"Well, I'll let you get to it. But if I was you, I'd be ripping that envelope open before I hit the door. You can keep the hard hat. I got plenty."

Sixteen

Taylor, Malone & Jones
Attorneys at Law LLC 1300 E. Franklin Avenue
Philadelphia, PA 19148

June 5, 1992
Mr. Ubi Sunt
1205 Rural Route 17
Palo Alto County, Texas 79087

Dear Sir,

I regret to inform you of the death of your daughter, Jeanne Lynn Taylor, and her husband, Martin Jerome Taylor, on May 18, 1992, victims of a horrendous vehicular collision. Because you have no telephone answering machine, and Western Union would not deliver to your remote and desolate location, I regret that I could not disseminate the sad news in a more timely manner. Sadly, my last recourse is to send this certified letter.

Regarding the accident: The other driver was one of your ilk, Mr. Sunt, a truck driver. He walked away with minor scratches. The investigation is still underway, but as of today the authorities have yet to issue a citation. I plan to pursue this matter until justice is served.

About the grandchildren: Molly Jeanne Taylor and Jeremy Benton Taylor were not in the vehicle at the time of the accident. Because Molly and Jeremy are both 17 years of age, I am in the process of securing their legal and financial responsibilities. This means that you will not be allowed to participate in any decisions that affect their livelihood, such as health and medical procedures, education, and location of abode.

Although I doubt that you have any interest in your grandchildren's future, as evidenced by your inability to provide a stabile domicile in which you can be reached in case of emergency, I nevertheless extend to you the opportunity to visit on a semi-annual basis, by appointment, of course. Any more of your presence and itinerant lifestyle would only be a disturbing influence on impressionable young adults.

Eventually, Molly and Jeremy will make their own decisions regarding how and if they want to pursue a relationship with you. I wouldn't expect much.

Copies of death certificates will be forwarded soon.
Sincerely,
Donald Newton Taylor III

Ubi folded the letter and slid it back in the envelope. One hell of a stinging rebuke, dripping with sarcasm and condescension, just the way *Donald Newton Taylor the third* had always treated him, treated almost everyone.

At Jeanne's wedding, Donald complained the reception Ubi paid for was too small and the food lousy. Even the flowers he criticized. Not one to take things lying down, Ubi barked back. Some guests overheard Ubi raise his voice, which made him the bad guy.

But it was remarks after dinner that rankled Ubi to the point that he could not stand the sight of this man twenty years afterward. Donald had polished off several glasses of red wine. Ubi had made a significant contribution to floating the beer keg. That's when guests took turns toasting the couple. Donald stood and banged a spoon against his wine glass for quiet. When he had everyone's attention, he slipped in a remark that Ubi could not let go unchallenged.

"To Jeanne, my new daughter-in-law. Born in Texas, but that's not her fault. Jeanne, we welcome you to the enlightenment."

When Donald turned up his glass, Ubi stuck out his tongue and emitted a sound like a kid making a motorboat noise. Everyone, especially the beer drinkers, roared with laughter. Did you see the bride's father give the raspberry to super attorney Donald Newton Taylor III?

By all accounts, the two men were polar opposites: blue collar versus blue blood, country music versus country club, a trucker's logbooks versus an attorney's law books. They were two stubborn men from different worlds. But must they be adversaries? When they met on rare occasions such as holiday visits, they were cordial yet cold, polite but unapologetic.

Ubi ran all those thoughts of ill will around in his head. A better man would have let it drop long ago. He could have, and probably should have, tried to work things out for the sake of family relations. But in light of what happened on that turnpike outside Philadelphia, he would not be rendered insignificant.

Ubi stepped back outside to look at the night sky, something he often did when looking for answers. Big Dipper. Li'l Dipper. Mars glowing a dirty red. Ubi paced up and down the driveway, hands shaking.

In the guest room, Jeremy woke to strange surroundings. He rolled on his side. A clock radio illuminated the bedside table. A wedding photograph of Mom and Dad. He slammed it face down. *Those visions won't let me be.* And now, the aftermath. This flight from reality and images of them on the road looking content. Now this sojourn at Grandpa Truck's compound. What a terrifying, exhilarating, and unbelievable adventure the last four days had been. How can you return home, expect things to settle down after a journey like that?

Seventeen

Ubi Sunt yanked on the garage door chain. Clickety-clack, sheet metal rolled up and disappeared into ceiling rafters. Outside, the western sky was glowing with the reflection of a waning moon. Inside, a 1956 Peterbilt reflected morning sunlight slanting through a window. Ubi approached the passenger side and ran a hand across fresh red paint.

Circling the rig, Ubi examined everything: tires, rims, fuel tanks and vertical stacks that almost touched the rafters. He held out his left hand and stared at the busted knuckles, still scabbed from when a wrench slipped while reinstalling that muffler. Almost every nut and bolt had been sprayed with lubricant, loosened, soaked in rust remover or replaced altogether.

For months, the truck was nothing but a skeleton. Doors drying, hanging from overhead racks. Fenders stretched out on sawhorses for sandblasting and painting. After calling wrecking yards from Chicago to L.A. to Florida, the phone bill was thick as the Bible. And paying the freight to ship everything here wasn't cheap either. But it's authentic. None of the cheap and gaudy makeup and doodads and add-ons like some show trucks.

And don't forget that open heart surgery. Cat engine was a little gummed up inside. Pistons and push rods and bearings, took 'em all out, inspected 'em, soaked 'em, scrubbed 'em, took the pitted ones to the machine shop in Texline. Old Ironsides, you have been taken apart and put back together with the love of God. Ubi walked to the front of the rig and placed his hands on his hips. "We've been back and forth across this continent how many times?"

A wispy shadow appeared in the back of the shop, standing in a door. Grandpa's talking crazy. He's talking to Old Ironsides like a cowboy in one of those black-and-white movies he loves, muzzle to muzzle with his favorite horse. Sounds like he's saying goodbye. Jeremy stepped around the truck's rear bumper.

74

"How long you been there, Jeremy?"

Jeremy thought about saying, "long enough," but he avoided the question. "Just woke up."

Ubi reached for a light switch. "Shade your eyes," he said. Several fluorescent tubes hanging above blinked, flickered and hummed. Twenty seconds later, the garage was fully illuminated.

"Wow. Look at her. She's friggin' gorgeous, Grandpa." Jeremy circled the side of the truck. "Can I touch it?"

"Of course you can. You two are old friends, right?"

Jeremy ran a hand across the passenger side door. He flashed back to riding Old Ironsides through the neighborhood and around town when he was in grade school. "Booiful, Grandpa. She is booiful."

Ubi walked around the front bumper and faced Jeremy. What fortitude he showed, coming out here at seventeen years old. You wouldn't know it looking at him. Skin and bones and that wild hair and pimply face. You'd think this West Texas wind would blow him over like a dried out corn stalk. He's got grit, all right, and that's something they don't teach in a classroom. Bet he's got some stories to tell about his trip out here. Can't wait to hear 'em. And need to hear more about how Molly's taking things. From what Jeremy said yesterday, it sounds like there's some serious fence mending ahead.

"Grandpa?" Jeremy's voice and eyes turned from awe for Old Ironsides to trepidation. Focused only on the trip out, he hadn't thought of, or made plans, how to get home. Lying in bed half awake for the last twenty minutes, the reality of what he'd done and what lay ahead was a heavy load he had to figure out how to haul. "How am I getting back to Philadelphia? I've got to meet that bus when it returns from the Poconos."

"You talking about the soccer team's summer camp?"

"It's band camp, Grandpa."

"But you were crazy about soccer. Sent me a team picture every year. I remember a game when you kicked in a goal almost from half-court."

"It's called the center circle, not half-court. Anyway, the band director pushed me into choosing one or the other. So I gave up soccer for the saxophone."

"Well, you had a helluva right leg, way I remember."

"You may be having trouble remembering some things, Grandpa, but you got that right," Jeremy said and cracked a faint smile. "I was third in the league in goals the last year I played."

"Okay, I can't wait for you to look inside." Ubi pointed to the polished door handle. "Climb in."

The truck barely flinched as Jeremy gripped the handrail, scampered up the steps and slid into the passenger seat. Wow, new upholstery, too. Ubi limped around the front bumper, favoring a charley horse in his right calf. He took the steps up the driver's side deliberately, one at a time, and plopped into the seat.

"I was going to drive Old Ironsides to a truck museum in Iowa," Ubi said, running his right hand over the steering wheel. "Planned on leaving next week, but we can go to Philly first. I'll drop you off. Then double back"

"In this?"

"Yeah."

"Can she make it?"

"Yeah. Hell yeah."

"You sure, Grandpa?"

"Sure I'm sure."

"Well, she looks perfect, but what about the engine?"

Ubi turned the key to the ON position and with his thumb pushed the starter switch. The diesel engine sprang up, clattering and shaking the truck. Ubi tapped the accelerator and it felt like the whole cab rose up from the truck frame and leaned forward. Hovering at 900 rpms, the diesel settled into a smooth purring.

"Any more questions?"

Jeremy looked around. No mess of maps, logbooks, candy bar and cracker wrappers like the days when Ubi and Old Ironsides tumbled into town for an occasional visit. And the bunk, get outta town, instead of those scratchy old moving pads, he bought a comforter, new sheets and pillows.

"Well, any more questions, Jeremy?"

"Just one."

"What's that?"

"When do we leave?"

PART II

The Backhaul

"There ain't no surer way to find out whether you like people or hate them than to travel with them."

— *Mark Twain*

Eighteen

Before the sun, after the moon, the two travelers departed the lonesome compound. Ubi squinted into the darkness, hit the high beam switch and lifted his foot from the accelerator. Something on the shoulder ahead. A large, shadowy figure.

"Look out!" Jeremy shouted.

Ubi stomped the brakes and the rig skidded and bucked. Jeremy braced both hands on the dash but his head lurched forward and smacked the windshield with a thud. Ubi wrestled Old Ironsides onto the side of the road. Jeremy rubbed the red spot on his forehead.

"You all right?"

"I think so," Jeremy said, eyes watering. "Damn."

"What was that?" Ubi asked.

"That . . ." Jeremy said, still massaging his forehead, "I think, was another bison. I saw one yesterday when I was walking from the post office to your place."

Ubi nudged the gearshift into low and pulled back onto the dark highway. "Might be the same one I've seen pawing around the last couple of weeks."

"I thought bison had been hunted into extinction."

"They're about all gone," Ubi said. "But some ranchers keep a few around for old time's sake. This one must have escaped."

"Anybody who locks up a wild animal," Jeremy said, grimacing, "that's not right."

A few miles up the road, Ubi pulled into a small truck stop in Guymon, Oklahoma. The silhouette on the highway and the near miss had spooked the old trucker. He needed to splash some water on his face, settle the nerves. This was going to be a long haul.

Ubi hesitated just inside the truck stop door, glanced up at a small black-and-white monitor hanging on the wall. Messages about loads for truckers flickered across the screen. Hmmm, this one sounds interesting. Someone abandoned a trailer in Liberal, Kansas. That's just up the road. Need a driver who can haul it to New Jersey.

Ubi had expected to drive Jeremy home in Old Ironsides without pulling a trailer, then double back and deliver his trusty steed to the truck museum in Iowa. He could catch a bus home from there. But hauling this wagon would pay for fuel and expenses, and make a smoother ride.

For seven days, the trailer had rocked in the wind at Woody's Fuel and Food, catching dust stirred up by rigs pulling in and out of the dirt lot. The truck stop owner copied the toll-free phone number from the back of the unit and called the Patriot Van Lines home office. By the time the call from the Kansas truck stop owner came in, the operations manager at Patriot had already initiated termination papers for the driver who abandoned the trailer. Still, it was a relief to find the missing wagon. The shipment on it was now long overdue, so dispatch posted a request with a nationwide broker that matches drivers with loads.

Old Ironsides rolled into Woody's gravel lot with the sun still low in the eastern sky.

"Thar she blows," Jeremy said. "Patriot Van Lines. Look at the red, white and blue stripes wrapped around both sides like a flag."

The Patriot dispatcher had instructed Ubi not to worry about the load, just get the trailer to their Trenton yard and they would cut him a check. Ubi circled the trailer on foot. Tire bumper in his left hand, he banged it against the tread.

"We're not going anywhere yet," Ubi said. "We've got bubble trouble."

"Bubble trouble? What are you talking about, Grandpa?"

"The driver left us with two flats."

Ubi pulled the rig into the lube rack and tire bay. A gap-toothed man wearing greasy overalls rolled a hydraulic jack across the concrete floor and fired up his air compressor. The man squatted on his haunches. Wielding a tool that looked like a machine gun—rat-a-tat-tat—he soon had lug nuts spinning counterclockwise. He rolled the flat tires toward the automatic tire-mounting machine and slammed them onto the operating table. No split rims, thank God, Jeremy noticed.

Jeremy left the racket and slipped around the rear of the cafe. Already running behind. How are we going to meet the bus back home in time? Show up late riding in Old Ironsides with Grandpa Truck, boy that'll piss off the Attorney General. He'll probably sue Grandpa Truck into bankruptcy, send me to military school and close the borders for the whole state of Pennsylvania.

Jeremy dug in his jeans pocket and pulled out the crumpled pack of cigarettes. Several were torn and smashed, but he found three that were still whole and jammed one in his mouth. Jeremy gripped the matchbook the bus driver gave him and hunched over, back against the wind. After several tries, he was blowing smoke like Old Ironsides. Uh-oh. Now there's a long shadow on the gravel parking lot headed this way.

"Jeremy, where you at?"

Drop the stogie. Stomp it out. Look innocent. Then Grandpa Truck rounds the corner, takes a deep breath. Second-hand cigarette smoke. Boy, boy, boy, he smiled, looking at his grandson. Don't he know, you can't hide that aroma, even out here with the wind blowing ninety miles an hour? And there's the culprit on the ground. Sheesh, he snuffed out an entire cigarette. Must not know what a pack costs these days.

Ubi stooped over and picked up the cigarette. "Hey, look at this." he said, holding the Winston between two fingers. "Somebody wasted a perfectly good smoke. Got a light?"

Jeremy dug in his pocket for the matchbook and handed it over. Ubi smacked and sucked on the filter, gumming his lips, and lit the cigarette on his first try.

"Want a drag?"

"No, thanks," Jeremy said, again digging into his jeans pocket. "I got one of my own." Jeremy extracted another cigarette, and examined it carefully to ensure that he was inserting the filter end into his mouth.

Ubi held out his cigarette, red-hot ember glowing. Jeremy leaned forward, the Winston jutting out of his mouth. The cigarette tips touched and Jeremy puffed on it like he saw Grandpa just a few seconds ago. The cigarette immediately caught. Jeremy took a drag, careful not to cough and embarrass himself. What would Mom say? Grandpa Truck and me smoking together, out here in the middle of a desolate, run-down truck stop.

Ubi and Jeremy finished smoking and crushed the cigarette butts under their shoes. Ubi spied Jeremy's right boot with half its sole now torn off. "Looks like you've got a little bubble trouble of your own, Jeremy. You can't run across the country with a flat tire any more than I can."

"We don't have time," Jeremy said. "I'll be all right."

"What size you wear?"

"Eleven."

"I got an old pair of steel toe boots I keep in the cab," Ubi said. "Haven't worn them since, well that's a long story. Anyway, they might be a little big, but it beats what you got on."

Jeremy leaned against Old Ironsides and slipped on the heavy boots. He pulled the laces high and tight and took a test run around the rig. "A little heavy in the toe but I guess they'll do."

Nineteen

Looking onto the Kansas landscape, the two men passed a few minor landmarks that only seasoned travelers like Ubi Sunt and Old Ironsides would know. In the small community of Meade, the big rig purred past a wood-frame house with a sign that read: Dalton Gang Hideout. Ubi downshifted, tapped the brakes so Jeremy could get a good look.

"The Dalton boys had a sister who moved out here. Her husband built that place about a hundred years ago." Ubi pointed to the newly painted, yet modest building. "Legend has it, they dug a tunnel about one hundred feet long between the house and barn so the outlaws could sneak in and out undetected."

"Legend has it?" Jeremy said. "In school, we call that folklore, Grandpa."

"Aw, heck, Jeremy, most of that history you get in school, and just about anywhere else, is written by folks who weren't around when it happened. They're just going on second and third-hand evidence." Ubi pushed the pedal and cajoled the stick shift up to a higher gear. Old Ironsides gained speed. Jeremy leaned forward and looked in the rearview mirror, the old house growing smaller. Ubi said, "Folklore is the stuff that carries the weight of the truth without being bogged down in details."

"Details, Grandpa? You mean facts."

"You are a lot like Jeanne," Ubi said, "truly your mother's son."

Hearing his grandfather invoke Mom's name, well, Jeremy didn't know how to react. He wanted to talk about her, sure, but he didn't know what to say. And shouldn't that be where a grandfather would step in? Jeremy watched the prairie drift by but remained miffed with Grandpa Truck. How could he be so stoical? Sure, he'd always been a gnarled oak, but at one time there were green leaves on those branches. Now, well, he's petrified wood. Sixty miles down the road,

Old Ironsides rambled into the small town of Greenburg. Ubi narrated another odd story about pioneer antics on the Great Plains.

"The deepest hand dug well in America," Ubi said and pointed with his left hand toward what looked like a large gazebo. "Underneath that little building is where workers spent three years digging with nothing but shovels and picks, filling wooden barrels and pulling 'em out of the hole with ropes and pulleys. Didn't stop until they were more'n one hundred feet deep and thirty feet across." Ubi's face went suddenly blank, and to Jeremy it looked like he had lost his train of thought.

"You okay, Grandpa."

"Huh?" Ubi turned his gaze toward his grandson, blinked several times. "I was just remembering that I took your mom to this little museum there . . . long ago, when she was a kid. I can't believe she's gone."

Another awkward silence hung in the air. Jeremy took a heavy breath. Grandpa Truck wants to talk about her, but he can't bring himself to do it.

"They got a thousand pound meteorite on display there, too," Ubi said. "Fell from outer space maybe ten thousand years ago, something like that. I forget." Ubi frowned; the creases around his mouth turned downward. "I forget a lot of stuff."

"What was she like, Grandpa? When she was a girl?"

Ubi wrapped both hands around the big steering wheel and turned it to the left, pointing the rig due north. Old Ironsides rumbled along in the shadow of the long-legged water tower that advertised the world's largest hand dug well. Ubi again looked like he was daydreaming. And when the road took a hard jog to the right, it felt like Old Ironsides was driving itself.

"Well, she was . . . a girl, ponytail and tomboy and . . . we used to camp together." Ubi's voice trailed off. He bit his lip, jammed down the accelerator and threw the truck into the next higher gear.

Jeremy's stole a glance at Ubi. This was a different Grandpa Truck. Whenever he rambled into town, Grandpa was laughing and spinning yarns, wrestling and tickling, tossing us up in the air. He doesn't look like he could toss a balloon in the air right now. Maybe the news about Mom and Dad was weighing heavier than he let on. Maybe he was like Mom always said, unable to show what lies beneath that rawhide exterior.

"I gotta tell you something about what happened on the trip out West," Jeremy blurted, screwing up his courage. His chest filled with air and expanded. He exhaled slowly. "Two times—once in Delaware and once in Oklahoma—I saw Mom and Dad."

"What the?" Ubi shot a puzzled look at Jeremy.

"It scared the hell out of me, Grandpa. They were in that old Subaru wagon once and the other time in the Toyota, the one that, well you know."

"Damn it," Ubi said in a low voice. "You think that means you haven't accepted what happened?"

"Probably. I'm scared it might happen again. On the way home."

"You really saw them?"

"They looked just as alive as you do sitting next to me," Jeremy said. "Mom had on that scarf and pair of sunglasses she liked to wear on road trips. She was waving."

"I can close my eyes and see your grandma almost any time I want to," Ubi said. "But I've never seen her out on the road. That would scare the hell out of me, too."

"And I saw a photo of their wedding day on the night stand last night. I think I broke the glass when I slammed it facedown."

"That was no mirage, Jeremy."

"Huh."

"I've had their wedding photo on that night stand for years."

"Oh, well that makes me feel a little better. Anyway, I'm just warning you in case it happens again," Jeremy said.

"Okay. I got you, Jeremy. But when we get back to Pennsylvania you're going to have to do something about that."

"You make it sound like going to the dentist to get a cavity filled or something," Jeremy said. "I don't think it's that simple."

"Sorry, Jeremy. I didn't mean it like that."

"I know, Grandpa. I know."

Mercifully for Ubi, who was having trouble dealing with the uncomfortable conversation, the city limits sign to another small town popped up on the highway shoulder. It also had a landmark. A proud billboard proclaimed Kinsley "Midway, U.S.A." One arrow pointed west: San Francisco—1561 miles. Another pointed east: New York City—1561 miles. Ubi sidled Old Ironsides up against a concrete curb and climbed down from the rig. He walked across the street, stood under the sign, spread his arms in opposite directions. This is the heartbeat, the pulse, the nerve center of America. This is where time and space connect.

"What are we doing now?" Jeremy muttered from the shotgun seat. "At this rate, we'll be on the road until Thanksgiving." Grandpa Truck's gotten a little weird since his last visit several years ago. Maybe that remote life on the road, and now holed up in the far reaches of the Texas Panhandle, had turned his brain a little mushy.

Ubi slipped into a small café across the street and purchased a pack of Marlboro reds. He'd quit smoking numerous times, and it had been more than fourteen months since his last one. But a pack of cigarettes on a long trip, well, that was like an old friend at your side. And now, after enjoying just one cigarette with his grandson, he felt compelled to strike up the relationship.

Ubi returned with the smokes bulging from his shirt pocket. He pushed the starter button with this left thumb. The engine hummed below the floorboard. Jeremy draped an arm out the window and drummed his fingers on the door. Why is he stalling? We have to be home in three days. Maybe he doesn't want to deal with everything that's happened. Maybe he can't handle it.

As if Ubi could sense his grandson's anxiety, he pushed Old Ironsides along at a faster clip than normal, for him anyway, sixty-five miles an hour across Central Kansas. They caught the interstate just west of Salina. Rolling at a steady pace, Jeremy harkened back to that comment Ubi made in Texas, the comment about donating his beloved Peterbilt to a museum.

As a sensitive and romantic young boy, Jeremy sometimes thought about what would happen when Ubi died. Jeremy pictured a lengthy funeral procession. Coast to coast. Hundreds of big rigs led by Old Ironsides, Jeremy behind the wheel. Town to town, people would greet the convoy at the city limits, hats off, hands over their hearts. Jeremy would wave from the driver's seat, proud to carry the torch. It was a fantasy of course, but now that mom and dad were gone, death wasn't just something that happened to other families.

"Why are you putting Old Ironsides out to pasture, Grandpa," Jeremy asked. "She never looked better, sounded better, that I remember."

Ubi mulled the question. He itched for a cigarette. Quitting was hard. Picking up the habit was easy. And catching young Jeremy sneaking a smoke behind the tire bay brought him back to his early days when cigarettes didn't cause lung cancer and a pack of Lucky Strikes was the best friend you could have on a long and empty highway. Okay, let's wait awhile before we break open the pack. Anticipation, sometimes the best part.

"Who's going to look after Old Ironsides when I'm dead?" Ubi said. "You? Molly?"

"Why don't you put it in your will, donate it to the museum, after . . . you know?"

"I guess I could, but I'd rest easier knowing that it had been taken care of. Something that important, I won't leave to chance," Ubi said, stroking the stubble on his chin. "Or lawyers."

Twenty

Donald Newton Taylor III reached across his massive wooden desk, hit the intercom switch and ordered his secretary to call Blue Lake Camp. Time to check on the grandkids. A minute later, he was speaking to a volunteer holding down front desk duties.

"I want to leave a message for my two grandchildren," the attorney said, "Molly and Jeremy Taylor. I need them to call home and check in."

The teenage volunteer pushed her paperback face down on the counter and scanned the master list hanging on a clipboard.

"Hmmm, there's only one Taylor here, sir. Molly."

"Are you sure?"

"That's what it looks like. Molly is in cabin number seventeen. But no Jeremy Taylor is registered."

"No, no, no. That can't be correct."

The young lady opened several counter drawers, digging for notes or something about the missing Taylor. "I'm sorry, but there is no Jeremy Taylor here, sir."

The attorney tilted his head back, rolled his eyes toward the ceiling. Kids. "Are you stupid?" he said. "I took both Molly and Jeremy to the bus myself. Let me talk to someone who knows what he's doing."

"Everyone is out on the lake. Canoe races today, sir."

"Then take my number down," the attorney ordered. "Can you handle that?"

Two hours later, the Blue Lake manager called Donald at his downtown Philadelphia office. "The only Taylor who showed up is Molly from Liberty High School," the manager said, black swimsuit dripping on the lobby floor.

"Look, I paid good money for two Taylors. Molly and Jeremy."

"I am sorry, sir, but only one showed up," the man said. "We do have a lot of campers, and there's no way I can learn all their names, but I'm sure no Jeremy Taylor signed in."

87

The attorney ground his teeth. Imbeciles. "I dropped them both off at the high school. The buses were there, kids were loading their gear into the luggage bays. Parents were waving goodbye." Donald squeezed the telephone receiver like he was choking it. "You need to find my grandson. He's probably playing grab-ass with some girl in one of your cabins right now."

The camp manager held the receiver in front of his face, looked at it with disbelief.

"I'm giving you exactly sixty minutes to get my grandson on the phone," Donald barked. "Do you understand?"

"Yes, sir." The manager hung up the phone and stared at it. What an asshole.

Twenty-one

Midway between Topeka and Kansas City, Ubi and Jeremy and Old Ironsides rolled into a Kelsey Truck Stop. Kelsey was a chain of small fuel and food establishments that never seemed to have much business. And that was okay with Ubi. No crowd at the fuel desk. No jerks harassing the waitress or blowing smoke at the coffee counter. No wait for a shower, menu or coffee. Ubi preferred the little joints, places where a man could catch up on his logbook, make a few phone calls and top off the thermos without all the bullshit that was typical at travel plazas.

Two diesel pumps chugged along, pumping fresh fuel into Old Ironsides' twin saddle tanks. Ubi ambled around the rig with his tire bumper, banging sidewalls. No more bubble trouble.

Inside the truck stop, Jeremy ordered a cheeseburger and large order of fries while Ubi circled a long, narrow cart with stainless steel bins emitting steam. Several dishes were congealing underneath heat lamps. Jeremy had almost polished off his meal and emptied a large Coke mug before Ubi picked his way through the buffet line. Jeremy's straw hit bottom and a loud slurping sound echoed across the empty dining room. Ubi smiled. The boy's appetite is back.

Ubi eased into the booth and set down a plate overflowing with glazed carrots, mashed potatoes and some type of breaded meat cutlets. Brown gravy oozed from the mound of instant mashed potatoes like lava from a volcano.

"You going to eat that, Grandpa?"

"Road chow," Ubi muttered, unrolling his knife and fork from the paper napkin cocoon. Ubi mopped up the chow and wiped clean his plate with half a dinner roll. Five hundred miles already, a good start, especially considering two flat tires. He felt confident they could arrive at the high school parking lot before the bus from Camp Blue Lake arrived. Three days drive, less than 1,500 miles, should be no problem. Still a little daylight left, and it would be good to get past the Kansas and Missouri weigh stations today, before he ran out of legal driving hours. Sheesh, ten hours driving and you got to shut it down, rest eight before you can get back in the saddle. Whoever wrote that law needs to try and earn a living pushing eighteen wheels across the country. Oh, forgot, lawyers, that's who wrote the regulations. Lawyers like Donald Newton Taylor III.

"Let's get the hell out of here," Ubi stood up, irritated just thinking about that man. How could he have such a pleasant son, Martin? And Martin, sheesh, what a guy.

*　*　*　*　*

Martin Taylor caught a flight to Salt Lake City, rented a car, and checked in with dispatch to follow Ubi's trail, which wasn't hard, slow as he drives.

Coeur d'Alene, Idaho. Late July. A little after 10 p.m., but the orange-gold sun had just begun dropping into the coniferous forest on the horizon. Glowing pine and spruce trees looked like they were on fire. Martin pulled the rental car into the truck stop where he suspected Ubi was holed up, found Old Ironsides in the back row. He banged on the driver's door, asking if Ubi could use a hand loading furniture for a few days.

"Look, driver. I'll cut you a deal," Martin said. "Give a working man a break. I'm just trying to make an honest buck."

Ubi had seen his share of day laborers, men hustling the furniture haulers for cash. They'd climb on your steps, hang on the door before you could back in a parking spot. Some smelled like alcohol. Some settled with their fists who got the next driver. Some were skilled workmen, but it took a trained eye to pick one out.

Ubi looked down into the lot. This guy looks kind of familiar. Still, with sunlight slanting in like that, well, sheesh, can't really tell. Car has Utah plates. Must be a drifter. Hustler. Aw, hell, it's Jeanne's boyfriend—Martin.

"Whattaya say, driver? Help out a man down on his luck? I can load, unload, sweep the trailer, polish chrome."

"Then you'll wash my toes and give me a pedicure."

"Aw, come on, that's no way to treat a working man," Martin said, looking up at Ubi.

"Okay, hold on," Ubi said and stretched across the truck cab. He pulled up on the door lock. "Come around and get in."

The Peterbilt rocked to the right as the "stranger" grabbed a handrail and pulled himself into the shotgun seat. A closer look at Martin's face. He's nervous.

"What are you doing here, Martin?" Ubi asked. This was funny at first, but not so much any more. "What's the matter? Something happen to Jeanne?"

"She's fine," Martin said, his pulse racing. "She's wonderful and gorgeous and brilliant and funny and I want to spend the rest of my life with her. I have flown thousands of miles, driven hundreds more, swam mighty rivers, some teeming with crocodiles, and climbed majestic mountains to ask the honor and privilege of marrying your daughter."

Beads of sweat broke out on Martin's forehead. A long silence in the truck cab. Say something. Please.

Ubi smiled and shook his head. "Boy, what took you so long?"

"Well, for one thing," Martin said, exhaling and looking straight into Ubi's eyes. "You're not exactly an easy man to find."

Martin returned the rental car in town, spent the next week on the road with Ubi and Old Ironsides. Memories they both cherished.

*   *   *   *   *

Back on the road, Ubi handed the unopened pack of cigarettes to Jeremy. "My fingers are a little stiff these days."

Jeremy peeled away the cellophane strip and tore open the foil wrapper. He handed Ubi the pack. Ubi thumped it against the dash and up popped three cigarettes like on a '70s billboard. He held out the pack. Jeremy looked at Ubi. The Marlboro Man had traded his horse for a Peterbilt. Does Grandpa know that actor died of lung cancer? Jeremy took one anyway. He looked at it carefully and stuck it between his lips.

"A fella who has enough moxie to cross this country like the Pony Express is old enough to have a smoke now and then, in my book," Ubi said. "But don't let me be a bad influence. You already demonstrated you can make up your own mind."

The two smoked together in silence, watching the white lines slip away. Old Ironsides plowed head-on into Kansas City—KC—known for mouth-watering steaks, gangsters, barbecue, blues, jazz, and was once labeled the "Crossroads of the Country," the metropolis where railroads and waterways and highways converged, the city that sprawled across two states and blanketed two riverbanks.

Ubi used to enjoy loading and unloading at the downtown warehouse in Kansas City. Schedule permitting, he would arrive the evening before and visit the local drivers' hangout—Blue Daddy's Lounge, smoke-filled, pool balls cracking and B.B. King on the jukebox. Drop in, buy a round or two, trade war stories. Next morning it was steak and eggs sunny side up, white toast and coffee at Maude's Grill across the street. And Maude, boy was she something? With that big old smile, scratchy voice, baggy eyes, coffee pot and laminated menu she handed you soon as you sat down. Made you feel like the Prodigal Son coming home.

"How you been? Still driving that old war wagon? The Iron Curtain."

"Ironsides, Maude. Old Ironsides."

"You must have an iron ass, by now, Ubi. When you going to put the pedal up?"

"When you going to quit slinging hash?"

But the investment firm that bought Deaton Van Lines back in the early '80s sold the Kansas City warehouse. The new Deaton owners quickly liquidated the most valuable real estate—San Francisco, Chicago, Miami, Kansas City—to boost the bottom line. The company then leased warehouse space in suburban industrial parks. This left Maude without her customer base. Ubi reached for the Marlboros. Shook one free. Wonder what happened to her? Without Deaton across the street, her business probably dried up. He dug the matchbook out of his shirt pocket. These old ghosts won't let a man be.

Ubi checked his mirror for the sunset, always gotta pay your respects to that brilliant star. But the sun had lost its luster. It was shrouded in a haze and fading into the Kansas prairie.

Burrowing into the network of loops and bypasses and through-routes, the road deteriorated until it felt like driving on a concrete washboard. Jeremy clutched the door handle with his right hand and sat on the edge of the seat. The nuts and bolts and sheet metal below squealed and groaned, yet Old Ironsides rumbled on, low beams cutting a swath of light through the darkness. An hour later, the rig crested a hill. Kansas City lights twinkled in the rear view mirror. Dashboard gauges glowed in the truck cab. And a pair of red-tipped Marlboros radiated in the hands of the two travelers.

"How far we going tonight, Grandpa?"

No answer. Better not ask again. Sometimes, Grandpa Truck seems to get lost. Not lost on the road—for him, that's impossible—but lost somewhere in his past.

Twenty-two

The long-distance telephone line between Traverse City and Philadelphia was sizzling like a freshly lit stick of dynamite.

"What? You're kidding. Daddy, you're going to miss the rehearsal dinner?"

"I'm sorry, Sweetums, this trip seems to drag on and on. If everything had gone as planned, I would have been there this morning."

"Well . . . if it's that much trouble, Daddy, I'll find somebody else to walk me down the aisle."

"Sweetums, please don't say that. I'll be there first thing on the wedding day. I promise."

"Does Mom know?"

"Not yet. I haven't been able to reach her. She should be on the plane to Philadelphia right now. Honey, I'm sorry. I really am."

"Don't worry about me. I'll be all right, but you're going to break Mom's heart. Again."

"I'll call tonight, when she's in town. She'll understand."

"Sure she will, like all the times before. She always forgives, but that doesn't mean she forgets."

Ubi shook his head, forcing himself back into the present. Regrets. Damned regrets.

Twenty-three

Reclining in the sleeper berth, Jeremy rolled onto his side and yanked the comforter over his head. It was warm, but it kept out light and road noise and CB radio chatter. Below the bunk, the diesel engine droned and massaged the truck cab. Jeremy slipped into a daze. Could lie here all morning. Wonder when Grandpa got up? Last thing Jeremy remembered, Ubi was sprawled across both front seats, on his back, snoring and mumbling about a piece of road in Wyoming where it looked like you could drive the truck straight up into the sky. Now an aroma, coffee, like Mom and Dad in the kitchen every morning. A few more minutes roll by but you can't stop thinking about them. Had their lives taken away just like that. Enough to make you feel guilty for being alive. Maybe this trip was a bad idea. It's not going to bring back Mom and Dad. It's not going to make that aching inside the head and the heart stop. It's not going to make the Attorney General lighten up. Now, cigarette smoke, almost like a campfire. Grandpa's burning through that pack like the chain-smoking waitress at the Kelsey truck stop yesterday.

On the other side of the sleeper curtain, Ubi lit another Marlboro, his third that morning. Compound that with black coffee from the little store on the frontage road and you got a great morning road kick. Caffeine. Nicotine. Sun peering just above that hay field. Morning dew glistening on bronze bales. Now that's trucking.

But back in the bunk, Jeremy's bladder was about to explode. He rolled on his stomach, no use. Then, KABAM! The truck smashed into a cavernous pothole. Jeremy's body launched several inches into the air. The sleeper shook like it was breaking apart. And Grandpa cursing.

"Goddammit, Missouri. The Show Me State. Show me some pavement for once."

Jeremy landed on his side, palms clasped between his legs, thighs squeezing together. He reached up with his left arm and pushed back the sleeper curtain.

95

"Grandpa, I gotta piss like a racehorse. Can you pull over?"

Before Ubi could answer, Old Ironsides crested another hill. A flashing, yellow arrow atop a billboard pointed toward Lucky's, a roadside chain store with dozens of locations across the South and Midwest. Ubi eased the rig down the exit ramp. Jeremy scrambled out of the bunk and into the passenger seat. He was leaning forward tying the steel-toed boots when Ubi swung the rig wide to the left so the rear trailer wheels would clear a culvert and a four-foot drop.

"You're blocking the mirror," Ubi snapped. "Lean back."

Jeremy sat up straight. Ubi craned his neck forward and sat on the edge of his seat. Looking past Jeremy's chin, he could see in the mirror that the rear trailer tires had sunk into soft mud and were about to drop into the ditch. That would hang up the truck for sure.

"Sheesh. Need to back up," Ubi said. "But we got a caravan waiting behind us. You're going to have to play traffic cop, Jeremy."

"But, Grandpa, I gotta go. Bad."

"You need to wave those cars around," Ubi said, dismissing his grandson's complaint.

Jeremy's eyes looked like they were about to explode out of his head. Why couldn't Grandpa take care of the problem himself? How long had he been driving? Forty years? Now he gets stuck. Sheesh.

"Whatever you do," Jeremy said, "don't back up until I give you the signal."

Jeremy flung back the truck door, hit the ground and slipped into the space between the back of the cab and front of the trailer. Hidden from the line of cars, he took a whiz right there, splashing the steel-toed boots. Then he directed traffic while Ubi negotiated the tight curve, and scrambled back in the rig.

A few miles down the road, a voice on the CB howled injustice. How could that jury let those LA cops who beat hell out of Rodney King get off scot-free? A different voice raged, said that don't make it right to riot and burn. Ubi turned down the volume. The travelers looked at each other across the cab. Had the whole world gone to hell?

Jeremy wiggled and crawled into the sleeper, grabbed his backpack and unzipped it. Digging around inside, looking for a clean T-shirt, he dragged out the dictionary and set it on the upholstered engine shroud that sits between the two front seats. Jeremy was pulling his high school band T-shirt over his head when Old Ironsides slammed into another break in the pavement. The dictionary popped open. A white envelope sat in the crook between the pages like a bookmark. On the envelope, elaborate red script spelled "Percival."

Ubi looked down at the envelope. "Who the hell is Percival?"

Twenty-four

My dear and perky Percival,

Listen up you longwinded purveyor of tomes, because I have great news. Last trip through Portland I found in my post office box a contract from a London publisher. Frustrated with the dismal and slow response from the Yankee publishing houses, I had sent my proposal across the Atlantic. Turns out, the Brits have a keen interest for oddball Americans, you know, like this dictionary salesman I met on the road to Ruidoso who lives out of a Ford Galaxie with a modified statue of The Thinker for a hood ornament. What a loveable kook he was, rather, is! Regrettably, I digress again, my literary Achilles heel, as you say. So, I courted a small publishing house that claims to operate outside the stuffy mainstream and per your suggestion submitted a few writing samples. The acquisitions editor said she went cuckoo over the South Texas woman who had built 1,693 birdhouses, including the one she lives in. And oh, my stars, the editor loved the Montana rancher who built a replica of the Big Dipper. Looking down from a granite outcropping onto an expansive valley, you could see aglow these lights twinkling from energy captured by solar panels. Imagine two Big Dippers, the original up in the sky, and a mirror of it sprawled across the prairie below. Heavenly! The publisher also salivated over the Root Beer Boys Museum in Madison. Four brothers had collected classic root beer bottles, cans, signs—Frostie, Hires, Barq's, Dad's, A&W, Triple X, dozens of smaller brands, too—and developed their own recipe through a decade of experimentation. That frothy drink would make you swear off that hideous diet cola habit that hangs around your neck like a concrete collar. (Sorry about that bit of chiding, Percy, but you know how that cheap diet cola turns you into a run-on sentence that spreads from state line to state line. God bless any hitchhikers you may have picked up.) Now back to the Root Beer Brothers. They bought a small bottling machine from a defunct outfit in California, trucked it in and rebuilt it. On Tuesdays and Thursdays, it shakes, rattles and rolls out several cases an hour. Tastes so good, makes you want to lapse into a string of adjectives and adverbs.

So, my bearded boy, after three years traversing the U.S.A, the last chapter of my homage to the American imagination is underway. It is a compilation of Ma and Pa Truck Stops. You know them well, those greasy spoons, dives and dumps that have managed to hang on despite the proliferation of those god-awful travel plazas. Next time you are in the Philadelphia area, stop at Sid's, look for the giant pancake on the roof. The pancakes are so fluffy they float off the platter and levitate. (I arrived the day after a light dusting of snow had blanketed the city, and Sid explained that he mixed melted snow in the batter.)

Alas, my dear Percy, grandiloquent one, I now must close and point my vehicle south toward Mississippi. I am looking for the truck stop with a fifteen-foot catfish on the roof, hitchhiking, complete with a Waltzing Matilda. But oh how I ache to feel your lithe body against mine, your beard trailing like a great cloud. With that said, I have reserved a cabin at the Ebb and Flow Lodges on the Current River for our annual three-week summer retreat. *Beginning the second week of June.* We can map out next year's schedule, the appointed, monthly drop-off locations. At the Ebb and Flow, we can linger in each other's arms and you may rail again about my excessive use of parentheses. (I just love them and can't help myself.) Until then, may your Ford fly like a magic carpet to the Ebb and Flow, and to me.

Yours truly, Jostlin' Josephena

After he had read the letter aloud, Jeremy folded the pages and slipped them back in the envelope, careful not to wrinkle the stationery. "We got a problem. Josephena is waiting for Percival right now," Jeremy said. "And Percival is probably going nuts looking for this letter. He's already half off his rocker."

"Who is this Percival character?" Ubi said.

"Percival is the man who gave me this dictionary." Jeremy climbed out of the sleeper into the front seat. "I rode with him from Tennessee to Oklahoma."

"Must have been one wild trip."

"I won't ever forget it," Jeremy said. "Where's the Marlboros?"

Ubi slid the cigarettes across the engine shroud, known as the doghouse to truckers. "So Josephena, obviously, is waiting alone at Ebb and Flow."

"Waiting for her beloved Percival."

Ubi pushed the accelerator almost to the floor. The diesel engine growled. Old Ironsides surged. "She's going to get stood up."

Jeremy reached for the dog-eared road atlas. "I've never heard of the Current River. What state does it flow through?"

"I know of only one Current River," Ubi said. "It's in central and south Missouri, about one hundred-twenty miles southwest of St. Louis. It flows through the Ozarks, down into Arkansas."

Several miles later, Jeremy found the trickling blue line that represents the Current River.

"Here's a tiny town called Ebb and Flow. It's right on the river." Jeremy had the map pinned flat on his lap. "Not that far out of the way, Grandpa."

"You're not going to get a big rig down those goat trails through the Ozarks," Ubi said and flipped the headlight toggle switch, signaling a passing tanker truck to merge back into the right lane.

"He didn't blink his tail lights in response to you flashing him over," Jeremy said. "You taught Molly and me that was the code of the road."

"That code is about dead, Jeremy."

"Wish I coulda' rode with you twenty years ago."

"I wish it, too."

"That era may be gone," Jeremy said, "but that spirit, looking out for each other, doesn't have to die too." A quiet mile rolled by. The only sound: diesel engine humming, wind whistling through the cab. Then, like a mandate, Jeremy blurted, "We gotta go to Ebb and Flow."

"What about our deadline?" Ubi asked. "We have to get you back before the band returns from summer camp. Your grandfather will blow a gasket if we show up late and he finds out you were out on the road with me."

Jeremy looked out the passenger window. Telephone poles and wooden fence posts clicked by. Then he stared at the dotted white lines vanishing under Old Ironsides. "Why don't we rent a car, zip down there, find Josephine, drop off the letter and hustle back? I'll drive."

"That might work," Ubi said. "It would solve our problem with wrestling Old Ironsides through that forest." A smile then stole across Ubi's face. He shook his head, slowly back and forth. "Sheesh, I can't believe you're talking me into this. You sure?"

Jeremy leaned across the doghouse. "The guy who is supposed to get this letter, he's a free spirit like you. And so is the family living out of a rig that gave me a ride and Flapjack and the lady hanging on with no hope at Cimarron Station and the bus driver I smoked cigarettes with under Venus. I'm doing it for folks like them." Jeremy looked away from his grandfather and back at the road rushing under the rig. "It's a different world out here. And Percival with his long-distance love affair with Josephena, that's all he's got. Am I sure? Yes, I'm sure. I'm damn sure."

Ubi took a long breath. "Okay, then," he said in a worried tone. "We're almost to the St. Louis suburbs. Should be able to find a Hertz or Avis without much trouble. How far out of our way?" Ubi nodded at the atlas resting on Jeremy's lap.

Jeremy studied the map. Old Ironsides hummed a few more miles toward the Mississippi River and the Illinois state line. "With me driving, maybe six, seven hours, round trip. With you behind the wheel, be back home for Christmas."

Ubi looked away, out the driver's side window so Jeremy couldn't see him wipe his misty eyes. Damn, this kid is growing up fast.

"We got St. Louis traffic to deal with," Ubi said. "Twice."

"Add an hour."

"Got to track down a rental car, sign in, sign out, too." Ubi raised his eyebrows.

"One more hour." Jeremy held out his hands and looked at his Grandfather with a puzzled look. "If we're late getting back, so what?" The atlas pages rustled in the breeze that poured through open windows.

"Aren't you forgetting about your other grandfather?"

Jeremy set the atlas on the doghouse, away from the wind tunnel blowing through the window. He again stared ahead at the white lines disappearing under the rig.

"What about him?"

Twenty-six

"Molly, you have a visitor," a camp counselor said, banging on the cabin screen door. "Your grandfather."

Molly was stretched out on the top bunk. Upon hearing the messenger at the door, she rolled over and pulled back the window blinds. Morning sunlight trickled through the towering hemlock trees and splashed the lake with flickering shadows. It's almost a three-hour drive from Philadelphia. He must have left before sunup. What could be so important that he would show up unannounced at the crack of dawn? Something must be wrong with Grandmother. Or Jeremy. That's it, Jeremy. Maybe he found out Jeremy never checked in at camp. Maybe he found out Jeremy went to find Grandpa Truck. Maybe he knows that I know.

"I'm getting dressed," Molly yelled, hand cupped around the side of her face. She slid down from the top mattress. "Tell him I'll meet him in the lobby in a few minutes."

"Molly," the counselor said in a low voice, barely audible from outside.

"Yes."

"He doesn't look too happy."

Ten minutes later, wearing a two-piece swimsuit with a baggy, yellow T-shirt over it, Molly circled the back of the log cabin that was the main lodge, a tactical advantage. Approaching from the left flank, she spied the man that Jeremy dubbed AG for Attorney General. He was standing on the front porch behind a rough timber railing, arms crossed, right foot tapping.

Molly's flip-flops had just hit the wooden steps when the AG barked, "Where the hell is Jeremy? He never checked in, did he? What is he trying to pull? And you ... you ... why didn't you tell me?"

"Morning, Grandfather." Molly reached up and pecked him on the cheek. "What a nice surprise. How was the drive up? Where's Grandmother?"

103

"She's fine. The drive was fine," the AG said in an annoyed tone. "Molly, don't play coy with me. Where is he? I've already called the highway patrol. I have connections, you know. We'll find him."

Molly plopped into a wooden Adirondack chair that was damp from a fresh coat of dew. "Then why are you asking me?" she said, legs crossed.

"You are his sister," the AG said, leaning over her chair. "His *twin* sister. You know where he is."

Molly pulled her feet onto the chair seat and wrapped her arms around her bent legs, chin resting on her knees. "He got on the bus at the stadium and that's the last I saw of him. He didn't tell me what he was doing and I didn't ask."

"An accomplice. You are a co-conspirator. An abettor." The AG paused to let the levity of his charges sink in, then lashed out at the absent lad responsible for causing him all this inconvenience, causing him to leave the law practice for a day and drive up here.

"I knew that boy was headed for trouble. I smelled tobacco on his breath one day, and he's been snooping around my office." The AG paused and caught his breath. "When we find him, he's going to straighten up and fly right, or it's military school."

Molly buried her head in her knees and closed her eyes. Barely a month ago Mom and Dad were gone in the blink of an eye. Had to move in with Daddy's parents. Grandmother was okay, but Grandfather was insufferable. Early curfews, even on weekends. Wake up calls like reveille every morning. Calling teachers and the band director. Constantly meddling. Now Jeremy may have made his way to Texas. So what. Good for him.

Molly looked up and peeled her hands away from her face. "You're only worried about getting Jeremy back so you can punish him," she said. "Don't you care about his safety?"

"Of course I do, Molly," the AG answered, softening his harsh tone. "I love you both, and that's why I'm here. I'm worried sick."

"Could have fooled me," Molly said. She had never before stood up to her grandfather, but now she was firing back like her grandmother sometimes did.

"So this is the thanks I get. After everything I've done for you and Jeremy."

The AG turned his back to Molly. He rested his hands on the cedar railing and looked out on the campground. Kayaks and canoes resting on the beach. Roped swimming area. He turned slowly and looked down at Molly. She was using the back of her hand to wipe away the tears that had trickled down her face.

After Mom and Dad died, Molly wept behind her bedroom door for several days. Grandmother had brought hot soup for lunch and casseroles for dinner, but the food turned hard and cold on the TV tray beside her bed. Molly finally promised herself that she would never let anything hurt her bad enough to make her feel like that again. But now she was sniffing and sobbing and it was her own grandfather who had got to her. Bastard. What a horrible thought, calling your Grandfather a bastard, but that's how she felt right now. Bastard.

"I'm sorry if I was too harsh, Molly," the AG said.

Molly looked up. Huh? The AG apologizing? For real?

"Why don't you come home with us? Go back to your cabin and pack up. We'll have a nice meal on the way home."

"Pack up now?"

"It's for the best."

"I'm staying."

"Molly, your brother is a missing person."

Molly held her breath, trying to comprehend what had happened in the last half hour. She climbed to her feet and crossed her arms. "I'm not leaving."

Camping in the Poconos had been a respite from living with the AG and a narcotic for her grief. Sure, only three days were left. But that was seventy-two hours of freedom from *him*. "I'll ride the bus back like we planned." Molly looked up and met her grandfather's eyes.

"Molly, you're not listening."

"I heard every word you said, Grandfather. I'm staying."

"You need to get up, get your stuff and get in the car."

"How is me leaving camp early going to help you find Jeremy?"

"Just do as I say, young lady."

"I'm not leaving. You can find him on your own."

Molly felt hot blood pulsating, warming her skin, turning her face scarlet. Her arms, legs and face tingled. Pointing a shaky finger at her grandfather's chest, she said, "You don't own me."

"Molly, don't be ridiculous."

"I'm not leaving camp to come home and help you find Jeremy," Molly said, her lower lip quivering. "Besides, you don't need me. *You've* got connections."

"You sarcastic snip. That is enough!"

The AG grabbed at Molly's left arm. She pulled back and his right hand caught nothing but air. Molly vaulted the porch railing and hit the ground at full stride. She kicked out of her flip-flops, flung her hair back and raced toward the beach. Before the AG could descend the porch steps, Molly was at the shore wading into the cool lake water. Her feet tingled and almost went numb. In one fluid motion she raised her hands over her head and disappeared beneath the glass surface. Twenty feet from where she dove in, Molly's arms and legs surfaced, stroking and kicking with precision like yesterday when she took a silver ribbon in the hundred-meter freestyle. She sailed past docks and swimming platforms and disappeared into the hemlock shadows.

Back in the Jaguar purchased only three months earlier, the award-winning and respected attorney, Donald Newton Taylor III, squeezed the steering wheel. An insurrection. These kids were acting like insurgents. He looked across the front seat at his wife, Katherine, and tried to explain what had just happened.

"She just took off," he said, raising his hands in frustration. "Swam out of sight like a duck. Just disappeared around a bend."

"Ducks aren't graceful swimmers," Katherine said. "Maybe you meant a salmon or brown trout."

"Whatever. She just fucking swam away without looking back, all right? I don't need a marine biology lesson right now. We have two grandchildren gone wild."

Katherine leveled her eyes at her husband. The creases running across her forehead and the crow's feet around her eyes that she treated every day with layers of lotion and makeup grew wide and deep.

"Did you provoke her?" Katherine asked in a calm voice.

"No, I did not provoke her. I just said we needed her to come home."

"I shouldn't have let you talk me into staying in the car," Katherine said. "*Everything will be fine. Let me handle it*," she mocked. "Now you've run them both off. Nice work, dear."

"Oh, don't overreact," Donald said. "She'll be back after she blows off a little steam. Let's go into town and grab some breakfast. Come back in an hour."

Katherine shook her head. "You will do no such thing. Start this car, now, and point it toward Philadelphia."

"Come on, Kat. Molly will snap out of it. She'll come around like a good girl."

"Staying will only make things worse."

"I'm not letting a couple of teenagers push me around."

"No one's pushing you around," Katherine said as she reached across her husband's right thigh. She turned the key to the starter switch. "No one but me."

Donald thrust the Jaguar down the country road toward the state highway, snaking around corkscrew curves. The Jag shot past two cyclists, peppered them with pebbles and forced them onto the shoulder. One mile later, at a hairpin turn, Donald spun the car sideways and it slid to a halt blocking both lanes.

"If you don't slow down, you are going to get us killed," Katherine scolded. "Remember, you didn't buy a Jeep, you bought a Jaguar. A four-door sedan."

Donald turned the wheel hard to the right and hit the gas. The car hugged the next curve at a reasonable speed. "It's not a Jag-wire, dear, as you say, but a Jag-u-are."

"Well," Katherine snapped, "what a jag-off you are."

Another S-curve and Kat fingered her seatbelt to ensure it was still stretched across her chest and snapped tightly into the latch. "This was a bad idea, coming up here. We didn't need to drag Molly into this. Obviously Jeremy is going through an adjustment. We just have to figure out how to handle it."

"First, we must catch him."

"*Find* him," Katherine corrected.

"When we do catch him, I mean find him," Donald said, closing in on a slow-moving van, "here are the conditions of surrender. No use of any vehicles for the summer. Come fall, straight to school, straight home. Except band."

"Don't make rules you can't enforce, dear. Besides, you can't stop him from attending things like homecoming dance and senior prom. If you try, he'll probably run away again," Katherine said. "And please slow down. You're making me nervous."

After a long, tense silence, the Jaguar hit the state highway and shot into the left lane. The speedometer arced higher until it reached eighty, then leveled off. Katherine stared out the passenger window, cold left shoulder pointed at her husband, and watched cars in the outside rear view mirror peel away behind them.

Donald had been such a charming young corporate attorney when they met. Ambitious and confident, sure, but there was a sweet disposition hidden beneath those custom-tailored suits. But something over the years had hardened him. Maybe it was the workload, arguing before a judge that this company had not operated in good faith, or this CEO deserved a golden parachute. Maybe it was just part of his DNA, but somehow he had grown cold and distant and impatient.

Although Donald didn't want children, he was a good father to Martin. Oh sure, he hadn't exactly showered their only child with affection ("That's not how you raise boys."), but he seldom missed a soccer game, band concert or chance to take Martin to their favorite ice cream parlor.

When grandchildren finally came, Donald had already grown stiff and distant. Kat explained to Martin that his father's indifference was no measure of his love. And it's not fair to compare him with the other grandfather who lived in Texas—actually he lived out of an eighteen-wheeler—who bonded with Molly and Jeremy in a way Donald could not.

Maybe Donald was envious how they worshipped their rambling Grandpa Truck, adorning their room with his postcards from the road. And it irked Donald how the grandchildren loved retelling his tall tales, those corny stories about dragons living in ditches like trolls along the highways, ghost trucks flying across the sky, lightning striking his CB radio antennae and lighting up the rig like a neon sign. Standing the two grandfathers side-by-side was unfair—different men from different worlds. And it irked Donald when Martin spent a week on the road with Grandpa Truck to gain approval to marry Jeanne.

Martin's career path did little to help family relations, too. Shortly after Martin earned a master's in journalism, Donald groused to Katherine one night, within earshot of his son, that Martin would be nothing more than a working stiff.

Katherine watched the white lines fly by so fast they disappeared into a blur like the lost years. And now, since the tragedy out on the turnpike, Donald was ruling the grandchildren with an iron fist, gaveling down all dissent. Why couldn't he understand that Jeremy was reaching out for someone, something? Who or where, Kat wasn't sure, but she had her suspicions.

Twenty-seven

The Ford Maverick started spewing steam on a two-lane state highway southwest of St. Louis. Vapors gushed through the crack between the hood and front grill and soaked the windshield. The needle on the dashboard temperature gauge soared into the red. Jeremy jabbed Ubi in the ribs.

"Wake up, hey, wake up. The car's on fire."

Jeremy eased the Maverick onto the gravel shoulder and hit the four-way flashers. The two travelers spilled out of the front seat. Ubi raised the hood. The pulsating radiator cap glowed green and gold. "Sheesh, she's about to blow her top," Ubi said. Boiling engine coolant dripped and oozed down the radiator onto the ground. "These old Mavericks are good little cars, if you take care of 'em. But this poor old girl's been neglected. From the looks of the garbage spewing out of the radiator, no one's changed the anti-freeze since the car rolled off the assembly line."

Ubi then rolled onto his back and slithered under the car, careful to lie uphill from the molten lava. Using a greasy rag he found under the front seat, he wiped the bottom of the water pump. Yellowish coolant oozed from the unit like pus from an infected flesh wound. Ubi yelled from underneath the car, "Hey, Jeremy, get the tools, wouldya?"

*   *   *   *   *

Back in the St. Louis suburb of Black Jack, Ubi had rented the Maverick from a small garage owner he knew from his days on the road. Lucky to find a rental car at all on short notice. After reminiscing with Stu, the garage owner, Ubi handed Jeremy the car keys. Jeremy dropped the Maverick's transmission into drive and pointed the car south, toward St. Louis. Merging with interstate highway traffic, he glanced at Ubi. Grandpa Truck looks, well,

110

comical, sitting in the passenger seat, all buckled in, atlas resting on his lap. Never saw him anywhere but the driver's seat of his old Peterbilt.

"Hey, Grandpa, you going to dangle your *right* arm out the window?"

"Huh?"

"You always drove with your left arm hanging out the window. Molly and I laughed at how you had one arm tan and one white. Are you going to work on that other wing now?"

Ubi rolled his shirt sleeve up to his shoulder. "Maybe I will."

Jeremy exited onto a ramp that Ubi pointed out. They were headed into the heart of St. Louis, the Gateway, launching point of Lewis and Clark, two men who shared with Grandpa Truck a lust for exploration. "Hey, wasn't Sacajawea the Indian woman who showed Lewis and Clark the path across the Rocky Mountains?"

"I think so," Ubi said. "Why do you ask?"

"No reason," Jeremy said with a pensive smile. "Just thinking."

Swinging the Maverick onto another freeway, Jeremy snuck a glance at his grandfather. He looks strange—and old, come to think of it—riding shotgun. Never in a thousand years would Jeremy have imagined this scenario. But not in a *million* years would he have guessed Mom and Dad would exit this world how they did. Let's just take it easy and not think about that right now. Okay? Let the road do the talking. Let the road do the healing.

Ubi recognized that painful look on his grandson's face. He'd seen it in Texas and Kansas and now here in Missouri. Maybe it's time to talk about it, face up to reality. On second thought, maybe not. But if not now, when? You can't keep ducking it, hiding from the truth. Ubi's chest heaved and his tongue felt like sandpaper. He turned toward Jeremy. A voice inside his head said you have to talk about it. But the voice in the Maverick front seat, his voice, said something completely different.

"Back at Stu's Garage we were only a few miles from the confluence of America's two great rivers—the Missouri and the Mississippi," Ubi said. "I love running a highway that hugs a riverbank. Meandering. Winding and weaving."

Jeremy easily imagined his grandfather a riverboat man from the 1840s. White beard hanging to his chest, standing at the keel of a flat bottom boat loaded with furs from Montana and Idaho territories, peering downriver with narrow eyes the way he looks through the windshield onto the open road today.

Stuck behind a slow-moving city bus, Jeremy pushed the accelerator almost to the floor and changed lanes. The car choked, coughed and sputtered.

"Maverick could use a tune-up," Ubi said. "Guess old Stu don't keep up his equipment like he used to. Hope we don't break down."

* * * * *

On the highway shoulder where the Maverick overheated, Jeremy opened the car trunk. He looked down at Ubi's canvas bag, his backpack and the hard plastic case, now a little beat up. A couple times, Grandpa had asked about it, made comments. "Sure got a fancy letter stenciled on the lid, that capital J with a little tail on it. Is it new? A gift? How did it get that gouge on top?" Jeremy wouldn't answer, just said "nothing."

Next to Jeremy's luggage sat Grandpa's tool box. Using both hands, Jeremy wrestled it out of the trunk. He walked around the passenger side of the car like a man with one leg shorter than the other, tool box banging against his thigh.

"What's in here, granite?"

"Better to have it and not need it," Ubi said, "than need it and not have it."

Jeremy and Ubi sat in thick grass on the shoulder and waited for the engine to cool down. Ubi yanked up a tall seed head and examined it. Again, he felt the need to reach out, to console his grandson. Instead, he climbed to his feet and leaned over the fender. Standing on his tool box to extend his reach, Ubi pawed at the water pump with a socket wrench. He broke loose several bolts and disconnected two hoses. Using a soiled rag like a hot pad, he wiggled free the water pump and held the dripping component in his hand.

"That's the easy part," Ubi said. "Now we have to get a ride into town, find a parts house." Warm and rusty coolant trickled down Ubi's forearm. "I need another rag," he said and circled around the Maverick. Leaning over the trunk, the hard plastic case stood out like a rose blooming in the snow. What was Jeremy hiding? Why so secretive? Maybe it's stolen. No, not my grandson. And that don't explain the J stenciled on top. Ubi's bent fingers twitched as he stared at the mysterious piece of luggage. His hands were shaking, but they worked both latches. Then the lid popped open. On its own. Just peeled back. And inside wouldya look at the shiny. . .

"What are you doing?" Jeremy's shrill and outraged voice startled Ubi. Jeremy was now standing behind his grandfather, looking over his shoulder. "You got your greasy paws all over it." Jeremy grabbed the bag of rags and found a relatively clean one. He nudged Ubi out of the way. "If I wanted you to know what's inside, I would have told you," Jeremy said in an angry tone. He closed the lid and latched it tight, wiping off the smudges that bore his grandfather's greasy fingerprints.

"Sorry, Jeremy," Ubi stammered.

"Keep your hands off my stuff, Grandpa." Jeremy's face was flushed.

"What's the big deal, anyway?" Ubi asked.

"Big deal?" Jeremy wadded up the greasy rag, and flung it to the ground. "What's the big deal?" He kicked at the gravel on the highway shoulder. Pebbles shot out onto the road. Jeremy looked around for something to throw or hit. Nothing, so he raised his hands high over his head.

"Take it easy, Jeremy," Ubi said, his eyes wide-open with surprise.

"Take it easy?" Jeremy threw his hands down. "You invade my privacy and you want me to take it easy? You're just like *him*."

"What are you talking about?" Ubi said, his voice at a high pitch. "I'm just like who?"

Jeremy waved his arms back and forth like he was swatting mosquitoes. He was done arguing. "Can you leave my stuff alone, please, until we get home?"

During the roadside family argument, a couple of cars had slowed and passed. Then a pineapple-yellow convertible approached from the opposite direction. The car grew closer and the driver lifted her foot from the gas pedal. That Maverick could use a coat of paint. Hood up. Must be broke down. Old man and a kid on the shoulder.

The driver turned and looked at her sister riding shotgun. "Are those two fighting?"

The driver stopped the car on the shoulder across the road from the Maverick. She looked to be in her mid-twenties, wearing a black and orange baseball cap. The woman cupped her hands around her mouth.

"What's the problem, guys?"

"We need a frigging water pump," Jeremy yelled across the two-lane highway.

Ubi walked across the road, water pump dripping in his left hand. "We need a ride into town to get one of these." He held up the rusty piece of steel. "And a radiator cap."

"What do you think, Sister?" The driver said, turning to the young woman riding shotgun. "We got time to make a run into town for auto parts?"

"Up to you," the woman in the passenger seat answered. Her face was dotted with freckles. Reddish-orange hair was all in a frizz from the humidity and riding in the open car. She wore a blue halter top and blue jeans shorts with a frayed hem.

"We only have room for one. See." The driver turned and pointed toward the back seat piled high with suitcases, a tent, duffel bag and sleeping bags.

"So we'll take *him*," the passenger said and pointed to Jeremy.

The driver climbed out of the car and held the door open. The redhead patted the middle of the bench seat. She smiled across the road at the youngster with hair wild as hers. Jeremy waited for a motorcycle to pass, then crossed the road. Still angry with his grandfather, Jeremy threw a casual glance at him and said, "See you in a bit," and slipped into the front seat.

Jeremy was sandwiched between Terri and Kelli McKinley, sisters from South Bend, Indiana. Terri was the older sister, the driver. It was her car they were riding in, a '57 Studebaker Silver Hawk. Nineteen fifty-seven was one of the last profitable years for Studebaker Motor Company in South Bend. The girls' grandfather, during his long career at the assembly plant, had worked his way up from installing doors and dashboards to shift manager. He fed and clothed four boys and two girls on union wages. Only one year from retirement, the plant closed. The settlement from Studebaker amounted to six months pay. After that ran out, Bob McKinley bounced around, worked as a mechanic at various car dealers. Then he opened a garage that specialized in Studebakers, a niche he exploited until he died in his eighties.

Mr. McKinley had bought the Hawk—wrecked— from a friend of a friend. The driver had buried the front end in an elm tree south of town on a rainy April morning. Working countless evenings, nights and weekends, Terri helped her beloved Poppy restore the sports car. At first, Terri handed the wrenches to Poppy when he was bent and twisted underneath, inside and on top of the vehicle. But as the restoration progressed, her grandfather's health regressed and Terri often turned the wrenches herself. While sister Kelli painted her fingernails, Terri often went to high school with grease under hers.

When Bob McKinley died, his legacy was a collection of six Studebakers, maintained like show cars and housed in a large barn that protected them from bitter Indiana winters. A dozen grandchildren had to decide among themselves who got what: a '51 Champion with a Cyclops-looking eye in the middle of the grill; a '59 Lark with compact European styling but no shark fins like the big boys in Detroit; a futuristic Avanti; a low-slung Commander Starliner with long sloping hood; a baby-blue pickup truck. And the Hawk that Terri had labored over as a teenager.

Terri claimed the Hawk. No one challenged her. Her siblings and numerous cousins may have been secretly jealous of the special relationship Terri had cultivated with her Poppy, but they didn't show it. Sure, you can have the Hawk, Terri. We understand how much it meant to you, restoring it with Poppy.

Terri stomped the gas pedal and the Hawk took flight. A few hundred yards down the road she saw in her rearview mirror Ubi looking like her grandfather, standing in the middle of the road holding up the water pump.

"Oops." Terri hit the brake pedal and dropped the transmission into reverse. Romping the accelerator, driving backward, she smoked the tires and left a black patch in the road.

Ubi handed over the water pump and a fifty-dollar bill. "Don't forget the gasket and a tube of sealer and the radiator cap," he said.

The Hawk soared off, wind whipping the trio's hair all around.

Twenty-eight

Ubi was a silhouette in the rearview mirror when Jeremy asked where the girls were headed. Kelli pushed her red hair out of her eyes, reached under the front seat and pulled out a scrapbook bulging with photographs. The plastic pages kept the pictures neat and clean.

"Before we talk about where we're going, let's look back to where we've been," she said, opening the string-bound portfolio on her lap at an angle for Jeremy to see. She flipped to page one. Kelli and Terri stood on a set of concrete steps before a domed building. And Kelli was holding close to her chest a Jack Russell Terrier puppy with droopy ears. "This is Madison last fall," Kelli said. "Wisconsin has the only state capitol built on an isthmus. Sits on a narrow strip of land between two lakes. And look at the beautiful white granite. The dome is almost as high as the capitol building in Washington. That was our first one, right, Sis?"

"Other than Indianapolis," Terri replied, watching the speedometer needle lean far to the right. "But that's our home state so it don't really count."

Another page and another state capitol, St. Paul, Minnesota, with the sisters standing arm-in-arm on the front steps, another white dome backdrop, and the same puppy held firmly in Kelli's grasp. Kelli explained that she had taken a photography class at a community college and carried a tripod and camera in which she had mastered setting the focus, aperture and timer so she could rush back into the picture before the shutter clicked.

More miles and more plastic pages and more capitol buildings flew past in a blur. Westward to the Dakotas, Bismarck and Pierre. "It's pronounced peer, like peering into a window," Kelli said, again pushing her orange-red hair out of her eyes. Jeremy was sitting so close that their legs rubbed. She wasn't pulling back, so he wasn't either. Besides, they were sandwiched so close together, he had no choice.

116

Kelli reached in the glove box for a hair band. She turned her head to the side, toward Jeremy. Jeremy noticed that Kelli had different color eyes. One blue. One green.

"You have two eyes," Jeremy blurted.

Terri slapped the steering wheel at twelve o'clock high. "You are hilarious," she said with a grin as wide as the front grill. "You hear that, sister, *'you have two eyes.'*"

Kelli smiled at the innocent remark. She thought she'd heard it all, growing up with different colored eyes, all the teasing and comparison to cats' eyes, so this naive comment was more endearing than off-putting.

"The scientific term is hetero-chro-matic," Kelli said, slowly enunciating the syllables over the screaming Hawk engine and swirling wind. She'd spent most of her life explaining this phenomenon to the curious and cruel and had learned to take it in stride. "But I call it diversity of color."

Behind the steering wheel, Terri was still grinning and shaking her head. "You have two eyes," she said again.

Kelli gripped her wayward mane with one hand, and with the other deftly wrapped the hair band around the ponytail she had just made. "We call this the northern tier," Kelli said, resuming where she had left off. "We've covered almost all the capitols in states that border Canada, from Helena to Albany. But we had to turn back when the Hawk got sick."

"The what?" Jeremy looked up from the scrapbook and into Kelli's eyes. Wow, they're hypnotic. Never seen anything like it. So far, he liked the green one best. And her skin, so white, but freckles on her face and arms and legs. Clusters of 'em. And her bare leg, it's touching, rubbing.

"The Hawk," Kelli said, aware Jeremy had lost the thread. "That's the car you're riding in. We limped home with a cracked something-or-other."

"Cracked piston," Terri said. "When we got back home, I figured might as well rebuild the whole thing while I was at it. That took three weeks, but now she flies like a hawk, all right." Terri romped the gas pedal to prove her point. Jeremy's head tipped back. The engine sounded tight and firm, as if it was capable of running like this all day and all night.

117

Kelli flipped through more pages. Sisters smiling, standing before an Abraham Lincoln statue and looking up at the silver capitol dome in Springfield, Illinois. Sisters in Topeka, Kansas, squatting with the puppy at their feet before a tarnished green dome topped with an archer pointing his bow and arrow toward the heavens.

"Right now, we're focusing on the central states," Terri said. "We just left Jeff City."

The photograph of the statehouse in Jefferson City was fresh from the one-hour photo lab there. Jeremy noticed that the puppy was missing. The sisters were grinning, all right, but not like when the dog was with them. The smiles that gleamed like polished chrome and pushed their cheekbones high on their face had been reduced to a stiff pose.

"Hey, where's the puppy?" Jeremy said.

Kelli frowned and closed the scrapbook like it was the Bible, reverently, and tucked it back under the front seat. The trio rode in silence for a mile; white lines zipped under the hood, much faster and closer compared to riding in Old Ironsides. Another quick and quiet mile passed. Then Terri took her eyes off the road and looked at Jeremy.

"He's in the trunk."

Jeremy sat stone-faced, unsure whether the sisters were serious or not. Afraid he would embarrass himself again, he held back. But he couldn't hold out long. The Hawk flew around a tight curve and past a field dotted with large, round hay bales.

"You can't keep a dog in the trunk," Jeremy said, his voice squeaking like an adolescent. "How's he going to breathe?"

"He's not breathing," Kelli said. "He's dead. Somebody poisoned him when we were camping in a state park the other night. So we iced him down in the cooler, dry ice, and we're heading home to bury him in the woods behind the barn."

"After we visit Frankfort," Terri added, eyes fixed on the road.

"Geez. Sorry about that," Jeremy mumbled. "What kind of person would kill a dog?"

"Two jackasses from Arkansas," Terri said. "We had a few beers with them, a few laughs, but when we left their campsite to go to sleep they got nasty."

118

"Vulgar," Kelli said. "Then Terri told them to fuck off and we thought that was the last of it. But Mellencamp slipped out of the tent. Next morning, the Arkansas assholes were gone and our puppy was lying dead near where they had camped. An empty dog bowl was turned upside down at the base of a tree. Smelled like antifreeze."

"Did you take her to a vet?"

"For what? She's already dead."

"For an autopsy, maybe."

Terri shook her head no and gripped the wheel with two hands. Kelli gazed at the pine trees whizzing by.

"I'm sorry," Jeremy stammered in an uncomfortable way. "Some people."

While the girls were telling the sad story, the Hawk had closed in on a Jeep. Terri waited for a straight piece of road and then eased into the oncoming lane. She punched the pedal. The Hawk flew past the rumbling Jeep and Terri merged back into the right lane.

"Boy, she runs don't she," Jeremy said, hoping to change the subject.

Terri leaned forward, looked past Jeremy at her sister and smiled. This kid was something. Naive don't begin to explain it. Maybe he never lost anything or felt real pain in his life. That'll happen soon enough.

"Hey, what are you and your grandfather doing out here anyway?"

"Just riding."

"Okay." Terri winked at her sister. "Hey, Kelli. They're just riding."

"Maybe they stole a car," Kelli said, trying to snap out of her gloomy mood.

Unsure how to read the two sisters from Indiana—wisecracking and free-spirited—Jeremy rode in silence, praying a town and a parts house would soon appear. A few more miles down the winding two-lane highway, the Leadville city limit sign greeted them.

Terri sniffed out a parts house like only a true mechanic could and parked the Hawk in the gravel lot. The man behind the counter tried to sell Jeremy the wrong water pump. Terri caught the mistake. Just look at it. The bolt holes don't line up. The parts man returned to the back room for another try and the second one was a perfect match. The group was on its way out of town when Terri pulled up to a stoplight behind a Ford pickup. Hood, doors and fenders painted with gray primer. Tailgate missing. Knobby tires looking like they belong on a tractor.

And Arkansas plates.

"That's the same truck," Terri said. "Those A-holes."

The light turned green and the pickup peeled out, squealing and smoking tires. Terri nailed the gas pedal to the floorboard. Although the Ford had a head start, the Hawk caught it within several blocks. The two vehicles raced down the main drag, doors nearly scraping, Terri yelling from the driver's seat.

"Pull over, damnit, pull over!"

The vehicles slowed in traffic, but when the road cleared the pickup driver again stomped the accelerator. The engine gasped for air. The tailpipe coughed up grey-black smoke. There was no chance of shaking the feisty Hawk. Only one way to lose 'em. The driver yanked the wheel hard to the right and the pickup bounced over a curb. The truck disappeared into dense woods. Terri drove past, took a hard look at the point where the truck left the pavement, then spun the Hawk around. She eased the car at an angle over the curb and headed down the trail.

"Let 'em go, sister," Kelli urged, her right hand gripping the windshield. "You're going to tear up the car and it won't bring Mellencamp back."

Jeremy was bouncing inside the convertible, observing, taking it all in. A simple run to get a water pump had gone awry. But it didn't really matter. Everything else was off kilter. Why should this side trip be any different? Maybe nothing mattered at all anymore. Still, you wouldn't trade a moment of these last few days for anything. Anything except to have, well, let's just catch these creeps and move on.

Terri pushed the convertible around a bend and it fishtailed and threw Jeremy's head into the rearview mirror. But the Hawk straightened out and once again gave chase, zipping through dense pine trees. Another curve and an opening in the forest. There they are, those sonofabitches. Hey, they're stuck. Big mud hole. Pickup sunk to its axles. Terri locked the brakes and the Hawk skidded to a soft landing.

"There they go," Kelli said as she climbed on the front seat and pointed into the woods. Two figures slipped through the shadows. "Bastards are going to get away."

Both girls climbed down from the car and gave chase. Jeremy followed in a trot, working the stiff knee loose until it felt like it could take his full weight. A sharp twinge. Keep running. It'll loosen up like in all those soccer games and marching band practices. The girls are already slowing down. All right, the knee is warming up. But geez, these steel toed boots weigh a ton.

Jeremy ran past the girls at a steady gait. Knee was loose and warm and limber.

Terri looked at Kelli. "What's his skinny ass going to do if he catches a couple of Arkansas hillbillies in the woods?" The sisters returned to the car, panting.

"Maybe we should quit smoking," Kelli said.

"That's not happening. At least not today," Terri said and dug the cigarettes out of the glove box. She pushed in the pop-up dashboard lighter.

Kelli paced at the edge of the clearing. Who was this kid? Why did he interject himself into their fight? Although he was standing on the side of the road arguing with his grandfather, he didn't seem the angry type. Guess everybody has issues. Still, something about the boy is not quite right.

The lighter popped out of the dash like a little jack-in-the-box. Terri held it against a Winston and pursed her lips. She leaned against the trunk, blew a funnel of gray smoke and handed the cigarette to her sister. Kelli took a long drag. To cut back on their tobacco use, the sisters shared cigarettes. They developed an unspoken pact to never smoke alone. One smokes, they both smoke. One tries to quit, so does the other. But if there ever was a situation that called for the soothing calm of nicotine, well, this had to be it.

Passing the cigarette back and forth, Terri said, "I hope those hillbillies don't hurt your new friend."

"*My* new friend?"

"Aw come on, Sister. You had him eating out of the palm of your hand. You lost one puppy dog, but gained another."

Jeremy jogged through the humid and dim woods, picking his way down a path that deer had beaten down. Sweat dripped down his forehead into his eyes, stinging and burning. Jeremy stretched and dragged his T-shirt sleeve across his forehead to wipe away the perspiration. The boots had picked up a layer of mud, felt clumsy and heavy. He didn't see the pine tree that must have fallen during a recent thunderstorm. Ugh! Jeremy plunged head first over it. Sprawled facedown in the forest floor, Jeremy felt like he was always tripping over something.

He climbed to his feet and wiped the dirt and mud from his pants knees. Then he heard someone behind him. Someone laughing. One of the hillbillies must have circled around. Jeremy turned and looked back across the log. A chubby man with a fleshy face, about twenty-one, heavy blue jeans and work boots, western shirt with the sleeves torn off, but flabby arms. "Look who the girls sent to defend their honor. A fence post."

"Dog killer," Jeremy said, wiping his hands on his jeans. "You have to answer for what you've done."

"Oooh, don't be so bad, scarecrow man."

"Tell you what I'm going to do," Jeremy said, his voice a little shaky. "I'm taking you back to your truck, and you're going to do whatever those girls say to make things right."

The hillbilly snorted. "Now I'm telling you, pimple-faced, pencil dick, what I'm going to do. I'm coming across this log, and if you're still standing there when I get to the other side, I'm marching *you* back to the girls with both your skinny arms pinned behind your back."

Jeremy froze. Fists clenched, dangling at his sides. The hillbilly took a high step and straddled the log. Leaning on it with one hand, he looked down to steady himself. The events of the last thirty days agitated and churned and swirled inside Jeremy: The newspaper story about the truck driver walking away unhurt from his parents' accident. The AG trying to force him into a new school. The awful letter he found in the study. Sleeping in a rat-infested trailer at Sid's. Those jerks in the Mustang in Oklahoma. Now this threat from a pudgy hillbilly. How much can a person take? Jeremy's radiator was boiling over, about to explode. The hillbilly swung his back leg over the log, but his boot heel dragged the bark and slowed his progress.

The steel-toed boot caught the hillbilly flush in the nose. The head snapped back and blood spewed forth like it was gushing from a faucet. The shocked hillbilly screamed, "You bastard." He looked down at his blood-splattered shirt. Jeremy backed up and measured the distance between them. The hillbilly stood frozen in place, clutching his nose with both hands.

"Next one's right between the balls. And don't think I won't cause I got nothing to lose. Now let's get moving."

The sisters were on their second cigarette when two figures appeared at the edge of the clearing. Jeremy was walking with a stiff leg behind a man wearing muddy and baggy blue jeans. The hillbilly's eyes looked blank, like he wasn't sure where he was. His bloodstained, plaid sleeveless shirt was now unbuttoned and hanging at his sides, belly sagging over his belt buckle. He drew short breaths from a nose that whistled.

"Nice work," Terri yelled across the open field. "One out of two, not bad."

"You apologize to these ladies for what you've done," Jeremy barked.

Holding his nose between thumb and forefinger, the man staggered forward. "Sorry about the pooch," he said.

"You ain't sorry," Terri sneered, imagining how that cigarette would look planted in this guy's face.

"You can't do any better than that?" Jeremy said. "You killed their dog."

"How do I know they ain't lying? I ain't seen no dead dog."

Moving quickly, Terri popped open the trunk and pulled on a pair of rubber gloves. She threw back the lid on a large, steel ice chest. "What's this?" She held up a big plastic bag.

Jeremy recognized the puppy, now frozen stiff and entombed in the transparent bag. The same droopy ears he saw in the scrapbook. Looked like a stuffed animal now. Terri pushed the frozen puppy into the man's chest. He shivered and pulled back.

"Look. It was an accident. That truck uses antifreeze, all right? Got a slow leak. So we topped off the radiator, but forgot to put the jug away. Forgot to put the lid back on."

"Lying sack of shit," Terri yelled into the hillbilly's face. "You knew what you were doing. Dog killer."

Jeremy watched the tense situation, wanting to do something. Best to stay out of it now. "Put the puppy away, Sis," Kelli said, tears welling up. "This loser is not worth any more of our time."

Terri returned the frozen dog to the ice chest. "Have fun getting that piece of shit out of the mud hole," she said. "Wrecker driver ought to tow it straight to the junkyard. Only a sorry-ass dog killer would drive a piece of crap like that."

Back on the road, Kelli lit a cigarette. After two long drags, she reached out and held it up for her sister. But Jeremy intercepted the Winston on its way across the front seat.

"Okay to share?"

Twenty-nine

When the Hawk approached the disabled Maverick on the little state route, Ubi's head and shoulders were buried under the hood. He heard the Hawk land with Terri's typical sliding stop. Then two doors slammed.

"Sheesh." Ubi turned around and leaned against the front grill. "Where did y'all go to get parts? Detroit?"

"We made a little detour," Terri said. "Had to see a man about a dog."

Ubi went straight to work. Jeremy and Kelli watched for a while, grew bored and retreated into the thick shade of a burr oak. But Terri glued herself to the fender. The old-timer knows his way around an engine. He wrestled that water pump past the alternator and into position like dropping a peg in a hole. He would have gotten along well with Poppy.

"Maybe we should . . . aw never mind," Terri said.

"Maybe what?" Ubi said without looking up. He had the socket wrench singing.

"Well, I was thinking when you overheat an engine and have to replace the water pump."

Ubi stopped working, turned his neck and head sideways. That girl was leaning over the engine, almost close enough to be turning wrenches herself. Obviously, she likes cars. And she wears a baseball cap. Drives like Richard Petty.

"Aw hell, a thermostat," Ubi mused. "Shoulda had you pick up a thermostat, too."

"I'm not telling you how to do your job," Terri said. "It's your car."

"Naw, it's okay," Ubi said, going back to work. "You're right. A thermostat is cheap insurance. But it's not my car. It's a rental. Poor old Ford hasn't had much affection."

125

Back under the shade tree, Kelli and Jeremy overhead the conversation. "My sister will be in a good mood after this. She found someone to talk cars with."

"Grandpa, he loves fixing stuff. Used to drive Mom crazy when he visited. Couldn't sit still. One time he replaced the garbage disposal and water heater. After that, he installed an electric garage door opener for a lady across the street."

"Where was that?" Kelli asked.

"Huh?"

"When he visits you guys. Your mother and father—"

"Never mind. It's not important," Jeremy said and jumped to his feet. "Let's see if they need any help."

Kelli remained seated on the soft grass. She frowned and watched Jeremy walk away. Something's bothering that boy.

Then Ubi threw his hands up in disgust and launched a loud "Damnit," into the ether. "We got no water to fill the radiator. Why didn't I tell y'all to pick up a few gallons of coolant?"

"I didn't think about it either," Terri said. "Something that simple, just forgot."

Jeremy remembered a clear-running creek they had crossed just before the Maverick overheated. "We got water. About three miles back, at the bottom of a sharp curve."

"What are we waiting on?" Terri said. "We got a five-gallon plastic jug in the trunk."

Jeremy was headed toward the Hawk when he overhead Kelli talking to her sister. "Why don't you stay here?" Kelli asked. "Keep Jeremy's grandfather company."

"Okay," Terri smiled and winked. "Don't get lost."

With Kelli at the wheel, the Hawk no longer bore down like a predator. Rather, it floated like riding a thermal. And Jeremy now had ample legroom. He leaned back and ran his fingers through his hair. This had been a wild day, yet fulfilling in some way he couldn't explain. And he didn't want it to end. He didn't want to say good-bye to Kelli and Terri and the Hawk and the stiff pooch in its frozen tomb in the trunk. And it bothered him how he had abruptly avoided Kelli's innocent question a moment ago. She didn't know.

"We're going to the Ebb and Flow Campground," Jeremy announced. "To deliver a letter."

"That sounds kinda weird," Kelli answered.

Riding to the creek, then filling up the plastic jug, Jeremy explained the history of the two letters. One he had discovered in his other grandfather's study—the hateful missive from the Attorney General. Of course, Jeremy had to explain the reason for the letter as well. Telling only the bare minimum, he offered few details about the horrific crash. And before Kelli could ask any questions, he segued into the second half of his story. A love letter, inadvertently captured in a dictionary, which was a gift from a man who gave him a ride in Tennessee. It was a lot of ground to cover in a short trip to fetch water, but Jeremy found himself talking to Kelli like he had known her much longer than a few hours. Upon their return, Grandpa Truck was standing on the shoulder, hands on his hips. Maybe he and Kelli had lingered near the shady creek longer than he had thought.

"Where'd you go for that water?" Ubi asked. "Lake Huron?"

Terri laughed at the old man's sense of humor. "You like geography, don't you?"

"And old cars," Jeremy said.

The thirsty Maverick gulped down every drop of creek water and was still a quart low. Ubi and Terri agree that would do. The Maverick wouldn't overheat on their way to Ebb and Flow.

Ubi rubbed his greasy fingers and forearms with Gojo, a cream-colored, slimy hand cleaner that he always carried in the toolbox. Jeremy picked up scattered screwdrivers and wrenches. With Ubi slamming shut the hood and Jeremy slamming shut the trunk, Terri and Kelli huddled under the burr oak, then approached with a smile.

"We want to go see the Current River, the Ebb and Flow Lodge, with you guys," Kelli said. "Jeremy, from how you described the letter and Percival and his yearning for the woman, uh, what's her name?"

"Josephena."

"Yeah, Josephena. We want to see that beautiful hideout on the river. It sounds romantic and . . . and . . . " Kelli suddenly felt self-conscious and lost her nerve. Her last few words trailed off, so her sister picked up the slack.

"And we want to make sure that water pump doesn't start leaking," Terri said with a cocky grin. "I was part of the pit crew and I stand behind my work."

Jeremy's pulse quickened. He felt like he could backflip six feet in the air and land in the shotgun seat next to Kelli. Riding with her to the Ebb and Flow, well, that would be unbelievable. Jeremy looked at his grandfather for a reaction. He expected Grandpa Truck to answer with his usual deadpan style, say something like, "Suit yourself," or "It's a free country." But it was Grandpa who was looking at him, waiting for an answer.

"Okay, then, why don't the mechanics ride together in the Maverick so you can keep an eye on the water temperature," Jeremy said. "Kelli and me will follow in the convertible."

The two cars then slipped thirty miles through the national forest. A green highway sign with an arrow pointing to the right popped up in a clearing: *Ebb and Flow 15 miles*. The Maverick and Hawk rolled along at a moderate pace. Although the sun was eclipsed by swaying treetops, soft rays filtered through the heavy woods and danced across the road and forest floor. Deep in the forest, the two cars trickled down corkscrew curves. Limestone and dolomite outcroppings straddled the road alternately on each side. Water seeped through fissures and moistened drooping ferns and deep purple lichens that clawed at the vertical rock, clinging to stone, clinging to life.

Thirty

This is certainly unexpected. Percival late for our rendezvous. What to do? Notify authorities? He could be laid up in a hospital somewhere. A traffic accident? He drives like a madman from hell. A medical emergency? I warned him about his high blood pressure. Too many diet colas. But looking for him would be like looking for that pebble the little boy skipped into the river this morning. So, what to do? Sit and wait. Sit and cry. Maybe this is it. Maybe we've come to the end of our road. Living this fantasy life with no home, just random correspondence hidden across the country. A silly game. Can't blame him for growing weary of it. What a fool I have been.

Now here come two cars, crunching gravel, parking in front of the lodge. Oh my, what a snappy, yellow convertible. Makes that Ford Maverick look like an equestrian dropping. Four folks. Must be a grandfather and grandson. They favor each other. But the girls. Too young for the old man. Too old for the youngster. Well, on second thought, maybe the one in the halter top. Hope they have reservations. This place stays booked weeks in advance.

Thinking of my Percival makes me want to roll up in a ball and cry myself to sleep. And I think I will. Here in this one-room log cabin, I can close my eyes and see you, my lost love. Maybe I can't touch and feel and hold you. But I can still hear your rapid-fire monologue and envision your crooked, toothy grin, eyes squinting, forehead wrinkled, beard flowing like a silver river. Oh, sweet slumber, have mercy, bring my Percival to me, even if it's in a dream.

Thirty-one

The short man behind the wooden counter snapped at the nosy kid with the big city accent. "This is a private lodge, son. We can't give out information about our guests to any Tom, Dick or Harry that waltzes in. You a relative?"

"No, sir."

"Friend?"

"Not exactly," Jeremy replied. He had been in the lodge office just long enough to pick up a few brochures and ask a simple question when he found himself on the defensive. "Sir, I have an important letter to deliver." Jeremy reached in his back pocket, pulled out an envelope. "It's a long story. I'm looking for a woman named Josephena. She's a travel writer, so she probably has out-of-state plates."

"Oh, that narrows it down a lot," The lodge proprietor said. "Look in the parking lot. Oklahoma, Kansas, Iowa plates." With an air of disdain, the man examined the skinny kid. "Maybe I can hold your *secret letter* at the desk. Do you have a last name?"

"Well, not exactly," Jeremy said, looking at the floor. "But how many Josephenas could there be? You have only eighteen cabins."

"And there could be eighteen Josephenas registered, for all you know," the man said. "People don't always give their real name here. Folks like privacy."

The man dipped under the countertop with little effort. He looked to be about forty, no hair anywhere, arms, scalp, eyebrows. A cancer survivor? Naw, way too heavy. Jeremy took a step back. "I appreciate anything you can do, sir."

"Here's what I'll do," the man said. "You get out of here right now and I won't call the sheriff." The man pushed open the wood-plank door, cocked his head at a slight angle, and looked up at the young smart-aleck who thinks he can come in here like a cannon and demand to see someone.

In the parking lot, Jeremy explained to the trio that "things didn't go too good."

"We're too close to give up now," Kelli said.

The proprietor remained standing on the front deck, arms folded, staring.

"He looks like a first-class, certified A-hole to me," Terri said.

"Let's get off his property," Ubi said. "Then we'll regroup."

Back on the county road, Kelli, still driving the Hawk, and Ubi, still behind the wheel of the Maverick, found a wide spot with a river view and pulled over. Winter rains had recharged the aquifers and springs that feed the river. People in kayaks, canoes and inner tubes from truck tires like Old Ironsides floated past. A woman's giddy laugh drifted in on the breeze, made the four travelers smile.

Jeremy remembered the brochures he had picked up at the lodge and retrieved them from the Hawk's dashboard. "Look, you can rent a canoe or kayak and drift right past the lodges," he said, pointing to a map inset.

"That's it," Kelli said, looking over Jeremy's shoulder. "We'll approach her cabin from the water."

The group agreed on Paint Rock Outfitter & Campground. They could put in three miles upstream. At the end of the short cruise, a van would pick them up at a crossing called Pine Point. And on the way—a surreptitious landing at Ebb and Flow Lodge.

Twenty minutes later, Terri and Kelli strapped on life jackets. They were already wearing shorts so it didn't bother them to get wet. But Ubi hadn't owned a pair of shorts since, well, who knows when. He was happy to stay with the cars. Maybe tinker a little with the Maverick.

But what about Jeremy?

"You can't go like that," Kelli said. "Those jeans will get wet and weigh thirty pounds."

"You need shorts," Terri said, adjusting the strap on her orange life jacket.

Ubi reached in his pocket and pulled out a folding knife that he had carried for years. He sharpened it often with a small whetstone he kept in the truck sleeper.

"We can fix that," Ubi said, opening the knife. "Hold still, and I'll be careful not to amputate a leg." Ubi bent over and slipped the knife through the denim, just above the right knee. The knife sliced into the thick cotton with ease. Ubi severed the right pants leg. Jeremy kicked out of it and Ubi went to work on the left. He cut that one free in half a minute. Terri held up the scraps.

"I'll take those," Ubi said and folded the knife. "Make good grease rags."

The threesome waded into waist high water and slipped into rented kayaks. The water felt frigid and refreshing. "I've got goose bumps," Kelli said, laughing.

Jeremy bent over the side of his kayak, splashed his face several times and drank from cupped hands. He wanted more. More of these healing waters so far away from home. He paddled up beside Kelli. He again found himself transfixed by her eyes. One green. One blue. Mesmerizing. And those freckles were like a dot-to-dot puzzle. The kind you connected back in kindergarten to draw a picture of a unicorn or giraffe. As Kelli paddled, the ponytail that she had tied while riding in the Hawk bounced along and slapped at her back and shoulders.

Jeremy pulled his T-shirt over his head and stashed it in a well on the inside wall. He paddled past the sisters and was soon several yards ahead of them. But Kelli was stroking hard, catching up. Jeremy dipped his paddle in the water and used it to slow the kayak. He waited until Kelli was broadside and then flicked the paddle across the water, splashing Kelli in her face.

"You're going to pay for that," she said.

Jeremy stroked the water several times in an attempt to escape—left, right, left, right—but Kelli was suddenly beside him. She raised her paddle and skipped it across the surface. A rooster tail of cool water rose up and swamped Jeremy's kayak. Wiping his face, he braced for a second salvo. But when he wiped his eyes, Kelli was several kayak lengths downstream. Down the river they glided, splashing and chasing each other, darting past slow-moving folks on inner tubes. Big sister Terri followed at a distance.

The river flowed at a brisk pace. Sunlight glinted through the sycamores that lined both banks. It took only a half hour for the kayakers to reach the Ebb and Flow Lodge. The wood cabins were easy to spot. Jeremy and Kelli dragged their craft onto shore and were waiting and talking about the steep cliffs and sharp bends in the river when Terri floated up.

"You guys look like you had fun," Terri said, climbing out of the kayak into knee-deep water. "You're soaked."

Then it hit Jeremy like a splash of frigid river water. "Oh no, the letter." He pulled the damp envelope out of his pants pocket.

"Open it and put it on this boulder to dry," Kelli said, pointing to a large rock on the shore. "We'll stay here while you go find Josephina."

Jeremy wandered the campgrounds with a careful eye for the angry manager. Maybe he wouldn't recognize him, cutoff shorts, soaking wet hair. By process of elimination, Jeremy felt he had a good guess that Josephina was in number eleven. Most of the other cabins showed signs of vacationers enjoying their stay. Swimsuits and towels hanging from makeshift clotheslines on porches. Hamburger meat and hot dogs sizzling over charcoal grills. Kids riding bikes, laughing. But number eleven was closed up tight. Curtains drawn. A solitary car sat out front and the back seat was full of binders and satchels. Then the final clue, a dictionary on the floorboard.

Jeremy returned to the river to fetch the letter. All three pages had dried somewhat, but smeared blue ink had bled down the pages. The sisters stood on the rocky bank wearing long faces.

"It's not that big a deal," Kelli said. "Josephina is the one who wrote the letter. She knows what she said, right?"

Jeremy nodded. "Still, just look at it." He held up the limp pages. "Percival will never get to read it. And it was a beautiful letter."

"Jeremy, that woman will be so relieved when she learns what you've done she won't care about a few smeared lines," Kelli said. "She'll know why Percival is a no-show."

"It's up to her to find Percival now," Terri sad. "Deliver the message. It's all you can do."

"But still," Jeremy said, his bare chest heaving. "Percival is somewhere out on the road, broken-hearted. He's probably going crazy looking for the lost letter."

"You can't change that. Give Josephena the letter, tell her your story like you told me, the midnight ride in that car loaded with dictionaries, Percival driving one hundred miles an hour, talking one hundred twenty miles an hour," Kelli said, walking up to Jeremy. She took his hands and squeezed them. Her heterochromatic eyes pierced like a laser. "Let Josephina figure out a way to find Percival," she said in a whisper.

"I know," Jeremy said. "I guess it just hit me that I'll never know how things turn out between them."

"Life's full of unanswered questions," Terri said, matter of factly.

Jeremy bit his lip. He didn't need to hear that.

Kelli squeezed Jeremy's hands tighter. "Give her the letter. Give her a hug. Wish her Godspeed. That will have to be enough."

"We'll wait here," Terri said.

Jeremy knocked on the door until his knuckles turned red. Still, no answer. Worried about making a disturbance, he surveyed the grounds. All clear. Jeremy walked around back and tapped on the bedroom window. Nothing moving. Out of desperation, he returned to the front porch and turned the door knob. Unlocked. His stomach pitched. He poked his head in and looked around. There was a woman lying on a daybed. A thin blanket covered all but her face and feet. Josephena?

Jeremy banged on the door and said in a loud voice, "Josephena, my name is Jeremy and I'm a friend of Percival's."

The woman's eyes flickered. She held the blanket tight to her body and sat up. "What's wrong? What's happened? Where is he?"

"I don't know," Jeremy said, standing half in and half out of the doorway. "But I can tell you why he's not here. He never got your letter. The one you hid at the rest area in Oklahoma."

"How do you know?"

Jeremy held up the letter. "It's right here."

Josephena continued clutching the blanket. Who is this wet kid, dripping, standing in the door talking nonsense? She climbed to her feet and took baby steps until she was at the door, looking directly at Jeremy. One hand held the blanket to her body like a cloak and the other one, shaking, reached for the damp pages. The smeared blue ink had almost dried.

"You're a good writer," Jeremy said, his voice unsteady.

Josephena looked down at page one. "You read this?"

"Well, yes. Percival gave me a ride from Tennessee to Oklahoma, and a dictionary, and that's where I found the letter." Jeremy saw that Josephina was still suspicious so he looked down at the floor, avoiding eye contact. "So he's not here because he never got the word where to meet."

"What happened?" Josephena held up the limp pages. "Why is it wet?"

"The lodge owner kicked us off the property, so we kayaked in."

"We?"

"Me and two girls from Indiana."

Josephena blinked several times and ran a hand through her ruffled, silver hair. "This is all too much. Maybe you should come in and sit down."

Jeremy balked at the door, held out his hands to emphasize he was shirtless, barefoot, and dripping wet. "You sure?"

"Don't be ridiculous. It's a lodge on a river. Everyone runs around half naked and soaking wet," Josephena said as she folded the blanket and tossed it on the daybed. Her cotton nightgown dragged the floor. "So that long-winded, absent-minded, lovable oaf never read my letter?"

"That's right. I found it in the dictionary he gave me. And it was unopened."

"So that explains it." Josephena's narrow lips formed a wistful smile. "You were there at the roadside park when he found it?"

"I was half asleep and stayed in the car, but yes, I was there."

"He likes to read my missives in private. Probably meant to stash it away until later."

"He stashed it away a little too good."

"And he gave you a dictionary as a souvenir?"

"That's right."

"Talk your ear off, too?"

"All the way across three states." Jeremy smiled and bobbed his head. "He's probably going nuts, looking for the letter."

135

"He wouldn't have far to go," Josephena said and chuckled, her mood growing a little brighter. "Well, let me think about this. I may have to call his sales manager and leave a message. He checks in about once a week. Hate to do that, takes the romance out of the thing, the mystery, the fanciful element we thought we had cultivated, if you catch my drift."

"What about the annual secret rendezvous?"

"Not this year," Josephena said, walking into the kitchen. She sipped white wine from a small plastic glass. An almost-empty bottle sat on the tile kitchen counter. "Not this year."

Josephena slipped on a pair of shorts and a baggy T-shirt imprinted with a likeness of William Shakespeare (a gift from Percival) and walked Jeremy down to the riverside. Jeremy introduced her to the sisters. Then she gave Jeremy a loud kiss on the forehead.

"Thank you. Thank you, very much."

"Give Percival my best," Jeremy said. "Whenever, wherever, you see him."

Paddling downstream, Jeremy looked over his shoulder. Josephena was leaning against a maple tree. The water trickled past, bubbling and gurgling as it lapped against the shoreline.

Thirty-two

The sun had just dipped behind the river canyon when a white van carrying wet rats eased down the gravel driveway that led into Paint Rock Outfitters. Ubi was sitting on the ground scrubbing with a wire brush spark plugs he extracted from the Maverick. "Would you look at that?" Jeremy said, peering through smudged window glass. "Grandpa's not happy unless he's got grease under his fingernails."

The van pulled up beside the Maverick, but Ubi continued working, flashlight perched on his toolbox. A dozen kayakers and tubers tumbled out of the van. "Mission accomplished," Jeremy said, grinning. "We found Josephena, dropped off the letter and sailed away."

"Good work," Ubi said, wiping greasy hands with a piece of rag cut from Jeremy's blue jeans. While Ubi installed the spark plugs, he explained that he had rented two small bungalows for the night. Trundle bed, ceiling fan, small dressing table and nightstand. Not much, but you can roll down the shades for a little privacy.

"We're going to hit the road hard the next few days," Ubi said. "We need a good night's sleep. I figured you girls been such good company that I got you a spot, too. They got showers at the bathhouse."

For supper, the foursome slapped smoked ham and American cheese between slices of white bread they had bought at the little store located inside the office. No mayo or mustard. But a jar of locally made pickles and a six-pack of Busch beer made the meal complete. The youngsters were still buzzing from the kayak ride and visit with Josephena and confrontation with the two jackasses over the poisoned puppy. They seemed content with the meager meal.

That night, Ubi sat at the small table inside the bungalow and studied the road atlas. He opened his tattered wallet and pulled out a calendar printed on the backside of a business card from an Amarillo truck dealer. No time for any more side trips. Have to get back to

Old Ironsides and make it to the East Coast in just two days. Doable. But that's cutting it close.

Ubi yawned and stood up and pushed back the screen door. Looking across the campground, he found no sign of Jeremy and the girls. Oh well, he's a big boy. And those girls were something else. They can take care of themselves. Wait a minute; here comes the older one, Terri, the one who knows her way around an engine blindfolded.

"I've got first shift driving tomorrow," Terri said. "So I'm calling it a night."

Ubi watched her shadow disappear around the little cabin and heard the screen door slam.

Thirty-three

Gushing and sluicing water for eons had sculpted the limestone hillside across the river from the campground into a sheer cliff. Swirling currents had worked patiently and methodically, pounding and massaging the stone, and built a beach out of gravel and polished pebbles ideal for lounging and wading. The beach had been a gathering place for the Osage Indians until European immigrants chased them into Oklahoma Territory. In the early twentieth century, a St. Louis banker wrangled clear title and kept it for a private retreat. Now part of an investment portfolio for an absentee owner out of Dallas, it's managed by two brothers, Vietnam War veterans who embrace the secluded location and laid-back lifestyle.

Jeremy sat beside Kelli on a fallen maple tree trunk that someone had trimmed with a chainsaw and carved into a bench. Sitting on a front row seat to Mother Nature and Father Time, they baptized their feet in the chilly water below. The river murmured. Tree leaves sighed in the soft breeze. Something splashed in the water. A barred owl asked the age-old question, "Who?" And the Big Dipper hung overhead like a cosmic kite, immortal stars tethered by invisible string. Back in Philadelphia or South Bend, you don't get this close to eternity, to creation. Instead, you're embedded in a metropolis of round-the-clock shrieking sirens and rumbling trains and buses. And light isn't a gift from the heavens, it's manufactured. Bright bulbs clinging to steel poles are fed by pulsating kilowatts that race down a network of wires stretching across the city from the transfer station. And those transmission lines connect to coal-fired power plants spewing emissions that choke out what little sky there is and transform cloudbursts into an acidic solution that poisons trees and animals, and your dreams and aspirations.

The campground behind Jeremy and Kelli had gone to bed. Fires burned low. Lights dimmed. The couple now had this sacred place, this temple, to themselves. Kelli pulled her frozen feet from the water and placed them against Jeremy's warm calves. He shivered so hard they both giggled.

"Was it hard when your grandfather died?" Jeremy asked.

"Oh, of course. Especially for Terri. They loved working on cars together," Kelli said, folding her legs and turning sideways on the large log, facing Jeremy.

"How long does it take? You know, to get over something like that?"

Kelli felt something strange in Jeremy's voice. The questions seemed to come out of the depths of the river, from the caverns and sink holes and springs hundreds of feet below, or from the black sky punctuated with stars that lined the narrow passageway between the tree lines. What was he getting at?

"First, you have to accept it," she said. "Then you can learn to live with it. And someday you'll get over it." She then realized that Jeremy never fully explained what he was doing out on the road with his grandfather. "Why do you ask?"

Jeremy's throat felt like a river rock was wedged in it. He couldn't bear to look back into that pair of eyes—one green, one blue—that had intoxicated him all day. So he spied a cottonwood leaf floating past and followed it downstream. Kelli scooted closer and ran a hand along Jeremy's bare chest. She felt the hard pectoral muscles still developing. At seventeen, he was no longer an adolescent.

"What's the matter, Jeremy?"

"Nothing."

"You're not a very good liar."

The barred owl apparently felt the need to move on; it raised its wings and swooshed upstream. Kelli continued. "You asked what it was like after my grandfather died, but I left out one important thing. The first step in getting over something like that," Kelli said, her hand falling on Jeremy's thigh. "You have to grieve. You have to let the tears flow. Like this river."

Jeremy stood up in ankle-deep water. He raised one leg over the log. Now facing Kelli, he swallowed the river stone.

140

"My parents were killed in a car wreck last month," Jeremy said without emotion. "And I have been avoiding the pain. Whenever I have to tell someone, I get angry, bark at them like it's their fault. Like they did something wrong, or who the hell are they to . . . " Jeremy took a long breath and slowly exhaled. "See, I'm doing it again," he said, frustrated. "But then, later, I feel bad."

Jeremy suddenly grabbed Kelli by the shoulders, as if he was falling off the log, and pulled her up close. Their cheeks met, flesh on flesh. He ran one hand through her damp hair; the other found a depression in the small of her back. Kelli remained balanced on the wide and heavy timber.

"You'll grieve when you're ready," Kelli said, her eyes watering. "Do you think this is the time?"

Jeremy shook his head violently up and down and blurted out "yes" before he lost his voice. Then he squeezed this beautiful creature—orange-red hair, different-colored eyes, freckles covering her arms and legs like grains of sand. He clutched her harder and closer than he thought possible, like he was holding on to life itself. Her tight breasts pushed against his chest and he felt thump, thump, thump, emanating from deep insider her.

Jeremy tried to muffle the sobs in Kelli's arms and neck and face, but suddenly he no longer cared who or what heard the wailing. He raised his head toward the sky and let go. Out came the poison that had been choking him for weeks. Out it came, in loud bursts like a wounded black bear, foot caught in a steel trap. Jeremy did not give a damn if he woke everyone in the camp and shook the whole forest, deer and raccoons and turkey, fish slumbering in deep pools. The poison had been torturing him, killing him, and it had to be expelled.

Kelli gripped Jeremy's shoulders and held on so they wouldn't crash from their perch on the maple log. She felt tears dribbling down her face. But she couldn't tell whose. His? Hers? Both? It didn't matter. This was a magnificent young man she had just met. No stranger to heartache herself, she was honored to help him grieve, to help him ford that river in the journey to understanding that we all eventually pay a price for this adventure through time and space.

"Why did it have to happen so soon?" Jeremy said, finding his voice. "They were still young."

"I don't know. I don't think anyone does," Kelli said. "And if they say they do, well, I'm telling you they're full of it."

Jeremy was breathing easier, but his diaphragm ached as it expanded and contracted. "There's more."

Kelli's mismatched eyes said, *go on.*

"After Mom and Dad died, I was living with my grandparents. But I ran away from home, hitchhiked from Philly to the Texas Panhandle. My other grandfather, the one you met, he lives on the backside of nowhere and hadn't heard the news. I had to be the one to tell him."

Kelli listened, surprised with the details of the tragedy, but not taken aback that Jeremy had been harboring something. Then, a soft rumble in the distance. In the Ozarks, early summer showers often pop up unannounced. A mighty gust of cool night air rushed down the passageway that the river had cut through the hills. Spindly sycamores bent low and clung to the shore. Another thunderclap. Closer.

"Maybe that's your answer," Kelli said, wiping Jeremy's face with her fingers.

"Just like that, they're gone. Both of them. They should have more time. It's not fair."

"I know it's not fair," Kelli said, still clutching Jeremy. "I know it's not."

Jeremy peered at the dark water for what seemed like a long time. The tears had stopped running down his face, but the river kept rolling on. Jeremy ran a finger under his nose, pinched his nostrils together. A flash of light in the sky suddenly illuminated the river. And what sounded like distant cannon fire echoed in the hills. Cottonwood and pine and maple tree limbs shivered in the breeze.

"Maybe," Jeremy said, stammering, "maybe the answer is . . . there is no answer."

Thirty-four

Dense clouds swollen with moisture swirled across the sky and smothered the Big Dipper. Jeremy and Kelli stood in the darkness and confronted the stone steps rising from the river to the campground. They quickly established two rules: arms must remain firmly around each other's waist and no grabbing the iron handrail.

Up two or three steps they would climb, gaining ground and maintaining balance until one of them leaned the wrong way and pulled the other back down a step or two. Laughing and crying, whoa, hold on, they negotiated their way up the bluff like Siamese twins.

In the parking lot, the wind paused and a high cloud peeled away, revealing stars that winked down at the couple below. Jeremy and Kelli stood at the crest of the hill and surveyed the campground. All theirs.

"Uh-oh," Kelli said, "I forgot to put the top up on the Hawk."

Kelli walked toward the convertible and was reaching for the accordion-like canvas cover when she felt Jeremy's long, slender fingers wrapping around her forearm.

"Not yet," Jeremy whispered. "I know it's late, but I'm not sleepy."

"Okaaay," Kelli said, slowly. "You want to talk?"

Jeremy shook his head no. "I want to . . . well, I don't know what I want."

Jeremy then reached for the driver's door and placed his hand on it like he was about to get in the front seat.

"No, wait," Kelli said, holding up her left hand. She approached the passenger side and placed a hand on the door. "You have to *climb* in, otherwise you'll be too loud and wake up somebody. Kelli then raised her left leg like a gymnast and plopped it on the passenger seat. She gripped the windshield with her right hand and pulled herself into the car. Sitting on the backrest, she looked over at Jeremy.

Jeremy grabbed the steering wheel and pulled his right leg over the door. Performing an awkward scissor kick, he managed to get the other leg in the car, but not before banging his foot on the sport mirror attached to the door.

"Ouch," he said, laughing as his momentum carried him across the front seat where he bumped shoulders with Kelli. "Am I graceful or what?"

"That was actually pretty good," Kelli said with a wide smile. "For your first time."

Sitting on top of the front seat, the couple looked over the windshield toward the river. "Hey, watch this," Kelli said, raising her bare left foot toward the dash. Her big toe then pushed a cassette into the tape deck that her sister had installed especially for their adventures.

"You're talented," Jeremy said. "Can you turn it up a little?"

Using her toe, Kelli twisted the chrome volume knob to the right. A sultry tenor saxophone rose up from the door speakers. "Clarence Clemons," she said. "He plays with Springsteen."

"I know," Jeremy said. "I play sax in the school band. Clemons and Springsteen are from just across the Delaware River, over in Jersey. Where I'm from, they're like gods."

At the end of the song, Jeremy asked to hear it again. So Kelli put her big toe into action and tapped the rewind button.

"You are amazing," Jeremy said.

"So, are you a good sax player?"

"Well, I'm no John Coltrane, but I saw Bill Clinton playing sax on late night TV and I can do better than that."

"Okay. If you say so."

"You don't believe me?"

"I didn't say that."

"I can prove it."

"How?"

Jeremy swung his long legs over the door and pushed off with his hands, landing upright on the ground. "I'll be right back," he said and scurried toward the cabin. Inside, his grandfather was making a nasal sound like a train whistle. Don't have to worry about disturbing him. Jeremy pawed around in the dark looking for the car keys. Can't see. He then opened the small refrigerator door. The light bulb inside the fridge illuminated the kitchenette. Eureka, Grandpa left the keys right there by the sink, next to a half-empty beer can.

Jeremy tiptoed outside and held back on the screen door so it closed without a peep. He approached the Maverick parked around back and popped open the trunk. There she be, been through hell and back. Jeremy's pulse raced and his throat grew dry and tight. What are you afraid of? Pick it up. You heard what Kelli said down by the river. Pick it up, Jeremy, pick it up.

With a shaking right hand, Jeremy reached down and grabbed the handle. His free hand pushed the trunk down with a soft click. Walking toward the Studebaker, he looked up and saw Kelli sitting on top of the seat, hands clasped together under her chin.

Jeremy handed Kelli the hard plastic case and he climbed into the car. They both sat on top of the backrest, bare feet on the seat below, knees propped up. Jeremy balanced the hard plastic case on his lap. Kelli reached down to help steady it.

"It's heavier than it looks," Kelli said.

Jeremy popped open two latches and raised the lid. A shiny brass reflection beamed up at him. A lump settled in his throat.

"Oh, Jeremy. It's beautiful," Kelli said in a soft whisper.

"It's a Yamaha tenor saxophone. Gift from my parents the night before they were killed."

Kelli cocked her head in surprise. She let go her hold on the case and it tipped forward.

"Hey, hey," Jeremy said and grabbed hold of it. "Be careful. It's never been played."

Jeremy reached into the case and pulled out a thin piece of wood shaped like a long fingernail. He popped the thin end into his mouth and made a sucking noise. "Ith called the reed. Goth to weth it down good," Jeremy said, lisping and smacking. "Wanna helpth?" Jeremy leaned forward and pressed his face close to Kelli's.

"Am I gonna get splinters?" Kelli asked with a giggle. Then she nibbled the reed and pulled it with her teeth "Let go," she said, taking the reed into her mouth.

Jeremy reached into the case and picked up the neck, an elbow-shaped section of hollow brass. He slipped a cork sleeve over the narrow end. Kelli then handed over the moistened reed and Jeremy finished assembling the sax. He tightened a small clamp that holds the reed and mouthpiece in place and inserted the whole crook into the body of the instrument.

Jeremy slipped over his head the strap attached to the sax and sat with his back straight. He wrapped his lips around the mouthpiece and depressed his cheeks so it looked like he had two large dimples. He blew a few soft and low notes, licked his lips, then said, "It's all about the embouchure. How you hold your mouth. Don't puff your cheeks full of air. That's wrong technique." He raised a mischievous eye at Kelli. "What do you want to hear?"

"Oh, I don't know," Kelli said. "I'm not much into jazz. All I know is what I hear on top forty radio."

"Nothing wrong with that," Jeremy said. "There's some great saxophone solos in pop music. Here's a little medley I put together just for fun." Jeremy's cheeks sucked in tight and his fingers went to work, tapping and pushing white buttons that opened and closed numerous air vents.

The rich, brassy notes soared from the instrument into the night sky for the next ten minutes. Jeremy seamlessly segued from one song to another. Drawing from deep inside his diaphragm and blowing into the mouthpiece with steady rhythm, he launched into "*Urgent*," with its quick beat, by Foreigner. He then played the haunting melody, "*Baker Street*," by Gerry Rafferty, the one about someone like Grandpa Truck: "*You know he's going to keep moving, 'cause he's a rolling, he's a rolling stone.*" The next one struck a chord with Kelli because she had recently attended a Bob Seeger concert. With the house lights dimmed, a saxophonist appeared in the balcony, then down on the floor, then the mezzanine, each time playing a spooky solo with the spotlight glaring down on the musician and his shimmering instrument. Jeremy leaned back and pointed the sax toward the sky coaxing it into a low moan, then making it wail, sending shivers down Kelli's neck and arms. Jeremy's body swayed and his shoulders hunched up. His head moved side to side. Kelli mouthed the words: "*Here I am, on the road again. Here I am up on a stage. Here I go playing star again. Turn the page.*"

Unnoticed to Jeremy and Kelli, flashlights and lanterns and cabin lights had flickered on during the concert. Campers crawled out of sleeping bags, tents, cots, cabins. They stood outside listening with interest and intrigue. Who cares if it's the middle of the night? Whoever that is, he can really play. Blow that thing, man. Play it like you live.

"Here's a real crowd favorite," Jeremy said, pausing to take a breath. "But you have to help. When I pause, you say the name of an alcoholic beverage from Mexico that you drink in shots with lime and salt."

Jeremy again arched his back and wrapped his lips around the mouthpiece. The sax exploded into a quick and bouncy beat. Right on cue, when he paused, Kelli sang out, "Tequila!" Commencing the sax solo, Jeremy coaxed the instrument into a sultry low sound, almost making it growl. Finishing with a flourish, he raised his eyes toward Kelli to ensure she was ready. Jeremy closed with an abrupt but emphatic note, and Kelli shouted, "Tequila!"

Breathing hard, Jeremy let the sax dangle from the strap and they both laughed and rocked on the car seat, bumping shoulders, looking into each other's eyes.

"What was that growling sound you made, Jeremy?"

"You mean this," Jeremy quickly raised the sax and again coaxed it into an earthy, sensual sound. "It's called the flutter tongue. You have to sort of roll your tongue, think about making a sound like a purring cat."

Then a loud voice from a nearby cabin. "Turn that racket off. People are trying to sleep."

"There's always a critic," Jeremy said and lifted the strap over his head.

Jeremy let the sax rest on his lap and reached his arm around Kelli's shoulder. After a little nervous and awkward fidgeting, they disassembled the instrument and placed it in the back seat. Cabins dimmed and the campers returned to their slumber. Kelli looked up into Jeremy's face and pulled his mouth against hers. "Show me again your embouchure," she said. Their bodies floated down from the top of the front seat and nested on the passenger side of the car.

Kelli leaned back against the door and scooted down, pulling Jeremy on top of her. Jeremy's long limbs and feet spilled out onto the floorboard. One bare foot pushed against the brake pedal, the other against the accelerator.

Kelli wiggled deep into the seat, plush upholstery soft on her back. The top of her head rubbed the passenger door. She guided Jeremy's face toward her breasts. Emboldened and terrified at the same time, Jeremy slipped an arm under Kelli's back. His fingers fiddled with the clasp on her halter top. The cramped conditions made it difficult for him to wiggle his fingers like he wanted, like he could playing sax, but Kelli arched her back and Jeremy felt the tight elastic grow slack. He pulled the halter top free and it fell on the floor mat.

Jeremy buried his face in her breasts. Kelli moaned softly and wrapped a leg around Jeremy's back. She turned her head to one side and said, "Mmm, your flutter tongue is amazing."

Heavy drops began splashing on the back of Jeremy's neck. A few more peppered the windshield and hood, making a tapping sound. Kelli whispered, "Jeremy, stop," and pushed him back. They both sat up. Raindrops falling harder.

Kelli wiped cold water from her forehead. "We've got to put the top up."

"Which one?" Jeremy said, feeling clever and poised.

"Aren't you funny? Come on and get out of the car and help me out," she said. "Terri will freak out if the new upholstery gets soaked. I promised that I'd batten down the hatch before I went to bed."

Under direction of Kelli's precise orders, the couple neatly covered the Hawk in a minute. The pitter-patter of raindrops continued a steady drumbeat on the hood, roof and trunk. Jeremy was standing behind the car when a stealthy lightning flash illuminated the whole campground. For a millisecond, he had a clear view of Kelli. Her long mane frizzy and full of electricity. Tight shorts clung to thighs and hips. Flat tummy. Bare breasts and nipples, firm and wet. Freckles scattered down her face and chest and arms and legs. And those heterochromatic eyes—one blue, one green—lit up like a fawn's eyes in morning light.

Jeremy promised himself that he would never forget that image, regardless how long he lived, no matter where life took him. That visage would remain forever burned into his brain, indelible. Regardless what great works of art he would see firsthand—Venus de Milo, Mona Lisa—that flash of light illuminating the speckled seraph from Indiana would remain vivid in his mind and accompany him to road's end.

"Hey, Jeremy," a voice startled the youth. It was Kelli, standing with the car door open. The rain was now peppering them both and bouncing harder on the hood and trunk, sliding down the wax sheen. "Are you getting back in?"

Thirty-five

Like a banjo solo ripping through a bluegrass melody, Missouri back roads dip and dart and pick their way through lush, pine-covered hills. Don't fight the curves; accelerate and hug and embrace them. Then open it up on the straightway, but don't get carried away, and be sure to back it down a little before the next bend. And never, *never* let yourself get caught braking halfway into a sharp curve. That's a good way to kiss a guardrail or land greasy side up in the ditch.

Although the sun had broken though early morning clouds and dried the road, small puddles remained in the shadows and low spots at the bottom of embankments. The Sky Hawk caressed the road on the tight switchbacks and splashed through the shallow standing water, kicking up a misty spray. The clumsy Maverick followed at a respectful distance. It couldn't handle the corkscrew curves, but on straight sections it would close the gap. At the crest of a long and rocky hill, limestone cliffs lining both sides of the road, the highway unfolded into four lanes.

Ubi spurred the Maverick up to seventy. He pulled beside the Hawk, top down, Terri at the wheel. Her baseball cap was pulled on tight and backward. Riding side-by-side, the two motorists eyed each other. In each back seat, their passengers slept, heads thrown back in awkward positions that would later make their necks pop and crack. Terri eased the Hawk to her left, tires singing and engine humming. The cars' fenders were only a foot or two from rubbing. With a tight grip on the wheel, Terri turned her head toward the Maverick and yelled, "How's she running?"

Ubi smiled, punched the gas pedal. The Maverick's hood reared slightly and the vehicle started to walk away from the Hawk. But Terri throttled the convertible and they were soon rolling neck and neck. The two cars rushed downhill for a half-mile. But the road soon twisted uphill and slowed the old Maverick. The highway squeezed into two lanes. The Hawk took flight. It crested the hill a tenth of a mile ahead of the Maverick, and just before disappearing over the ridge, Terri shook her baseball cap high overhead, back and forth. When the Maverick topped the hill, the narrow and winding road ahead was empty.

Back at Stu's Garage, the rusty water pump hit the counter top with a wet smack. Green-yellow sludge oozed from the cast-iron housing. Ubi pulled the receipt from his front shirt pocket and held it out.

"You need to reimburse me for this," Ubi said. "And be glad I'm not charging you labor. My assistant and I had to perform an emergency roadside appendectomy."

"Sorry, Ubi, but that old Maverick is all I had on short notice," Stu said.

"I understand," Ubi said. "But I still have to give you a hard time. We do appreciate it."

"You will never know how much we appreciate it," Jeremy said, extending his arm across the counter.

A few minutes after a vigorous hand-pumping session, Old Ironsides rattled and coughed and spit out the soot that had accumulated in the twin stacks from last night's rain. Ubi cajoled the Peterbilt through an industrial area, heavy with tall fences topped by barbed wire. Jeremy spotted a convenience store with wrought iron bars guarding the windows and door.

"Can you pull over right quick? Maybe they have hot chocolate," Jeremy said in a voice thick with hope and desperation.

"You're plain goofy about hot chocolate, Jeremy."

"You want a coffee, Grandpa?"

"Sure."

"Who's goofy?"

Up on the interstate loop that skirts the north side of St. Louis, Jeremy looked down on the Mississippi River. Muddy and murky. Speedboats zipped around the slow and heavy barges the way four-wheelers dart before big rigs on the interstate.

"Makes the Current River look like a little creek," Ubi said.

Jeremy smiled a wistful smile. He looked at his grandfather for a second and then back into the chocolate-colored water far below.

Old Ironsides pitched and bucked and bounded across the bridge. Thump-thump, thump-thump, Jeremy bounced in the hard vinyl seat. Shortly, the river was in the rearview mirror, and the rig made the gradual climb out of the valley through the Illinois suburbs and into hazy hills covered with chest-high cornstalks. Back in the Ozarks, the sun had played peek-a-boo, darting in and out of the forest. It was cool and shady in the river canyon there. But out here in the open, a hot wind blasted across the landscape. The temperature crept into the mid-nineties.

Old Ironsides cut through the Illinois countryside past the relics of yesteryear—tractors, plows and discs, grain trucks—their once-bright paint corroding and oxidizing in pastures and behind barns. American agricultural history forsaken, rusting and flaking and fading away. Still, the endless cornfields marched down both sides of the road. Haze and humidity hovered on the highway, shimmered on the interstate like glass. Rolling on, both windows down, a zephyr swirled in the cab, tossed back the sleeper curtain. Logbook and road atlas pages fluttered. After that cool and misty morning on the river, the hot breeze felt like it was launched from an oven. It would be a sweaty, muggy ride across the nation's breadbasket.

Two hours later, the truck crossed the Indiana line. Jeremy had been nodding off in the front seat much of the way, but that red, white and blue sign—*Welcome to Indiana. Crossroads of America*—made his pulse skip a beat. He was crossing Kelli's and Terri's homeland—the Hoosier State. No matter. They were probably in Kentucky by now, on their way to Frankfort.

Jeremy reached in his back pocket, pulled out his damp, cloth wallet and peeled back the Velcro strip. Tucked deep inside, carefully folded into fourths, was a gasoline receipt from South Bend. Jeremy read the phone number and address scribbled on the back, already composing in his mind the letter he would write when he got home. It would be an invitation to show the girls around Harrisburg, the proud Pennsylvania state capitol, just one hundred miles from where he lived. He'd been there twice, once on an eighth-grade field trip, and once with the family. But the third time would be . . . well . . . right now there were no words.

Indiana looked about the same as Illinois, far as Jeremy could see from his perch riding shotgun in Old Ironsides. Tired as he was, staying up almost all night, he willed himself awake. He felt obligated, for a reason he couldn't explain but had everything to do with Kelli, to keep his eyes peeled in Indiana, not missing anything that he could associate with her and their brief encounter.

Ubi pushed the rig along faster than normal. Indianapolis, called the Brickyard on the CB, was bustling but not congested. Ubi chose a loop around the city's south side. He encountered a few brake checks—places where motorists had to suddenly slow and creep along for a mile or two—but otherwise made good time. A little more than an hour later, Old Ironsides rolled into Ohio, the Buckeye State.

East of Dayton, Ubi fueled the rig at Fast Eddie's Truck Plaza, named for Ohio native Eddie Rickenbacker. The walls inside were covered with paintings and photographs that chronicled the life of the World War I ace and his long career in aviation and transportation. Jeremy stocked up on snack food: mixed nuts, sugar-coated fried pies, salty potato chips, beef jerky and peanut butter cracker sandwiches. Ubi nodded his approval at the cash register, dropping a can of sardines and a roll of paper towels onto the pile of staples.

"That's how you make up time," he said. "Forget all that sit-down dining. We gotta get you home."

At that comment, Jeremy forced an awkward smile; but he felt a groan in the pit of his stomach. *Home.* Why did he have to say that word? In a remote corner of his subconscious, Jeremy had pushed aside the inevitable, the inescapable confrontation with the Attorney General. Had the AG deduced that Jeremy had skipped out on band camp? And what about Molly? Would he drag her into the mix, into whatever firestorm erupted over his absence? The trip had seemed like it would never end. Like he was suspended in time. The duo rode in relative silence, through Columbus at evening rush hour, until Ubi peeled back the lid on the sardine can.

"Oh my, God," Jeremy said, pinching his nose. "You stunk up the whole truck, Grandpa."

Unfazed, Ubi stabbed with his pocket knife one of the small fish swimming in mustard sauce. One hand on the wheel. One eye on the road. He dropped the sardine on a cracker and shoved it into his mouth. Jeremy looked away and shivered.

"Mmm, mm, mmm." Ubi smacked and licked his lips. "Want one?"

Jeremy shook his head and smiled at his grandfather who was clearly enjoying himself. "Should have bought some air freshener back at Fast Eddie's."

About thirty miles later, the pungent aroma had cleared the cab. The sun disappeared behind low-hanging wispy clouds in the West. The sky ahead turned a deep and heavy blue. Oncoming truckers had yet to flip on their headlights, but they were burning their clearance lights, an amber outline that illuminated the perimeter of their rigs. Twilight. Sweet light.

Jeremy had stayed awake much of the day, so he didn't feel bad about crawling in the bunk and leaving Grandpa and Old Ironsides alone together as they neared the Ohio River at the West Virginia line.

The Ohio fascinated and haunted Ubi like America's two other great rivers—the Missouri and the Mississippi. These historic waterways had carved wide valleys through hundreds and hundreds of miles of forests, plains and hills. They drained the land and fed and provided transportation to Native Americans long before the white man's steamboats and barges lugged the lumber, the cotton and the coal, the cast iron, the wants and needs of a burgeoning country up and down it.

It thrilled Ubi that he was crossing all three—the Holy Trinity of American rivers—in one day. And it disturbed Ubi because he felt like he had somehow, somewhere, floated or paddled, or at least shoveled coal in a steamboat on these rivers. Ubi didn't believe in reincarnation, that concept was too far-fetched to seriously consider. But why did he feel this spiritual connection to unknown ancestors who lived one hundred or one thousand years ago?

Approaching Wheeling and the mighty Ohio, Ubi lost his bearings. Signs ushered all the big rigs onto a new bypass. When did this happen? Before he could realize what was going on, Old Ironsides was swept downhill in a sea of headlights and tail lights; then a stiff crosswind buffeted the cab and the trailer drifted almost into the next lane. Ubi subconsciously eased off the accelerator and the truck slowed as it hit a slight grade. A line of cars and trucks backed up behind him. Some swerved and changed lanes, passed and cut back in front, annoyed at this antique tractor-trailer poking along like it was in a Thanksgiving Day parade. Ubi's recollections were cloudy. Where did the river go? Where is that old tunnel? And what happened to those road signs, *Welcome to Wild and Wonderful Wheeling.*

Before Ubi could finish his thoughts about the highway changes in the West Virginia Panhandle, Old Ironsides crossed the state line into Pennsylvania. Sheesh, that was quick. Oh, forgot, it's only about twenty miles across this fingerling wedged between Ohio and Pennsylvania. Ubi felt like yanking back the curtain and teasing Jeremy for sleeping halfway across Ohio and completely through West Virginia. Never mind. Let him be. He's been running hard for a week. And, damn it, what a treat it was to see him come out of his shell with that gal, Kelli. Hope she didn't break his heart. But, on second thought, that's already happened. Need to have that sit down talk with him, soon. Need to have that sit down with myself, too. Spent my whole life running. But . . . but me and Old Ironsides were always traveling with purpose— pick up a load, drop a load, beat it over that mountain pass before the road freezes, beat it back home. Sheesh, maybe I'm running from the truth. Maybe I'm running from myself. Maybe I'm running just to be running. No, wait. That ain't right. Sure, I like to keep moving, but it's not like I'm evading responsibility or the law. Just looking over the other side of the mountain to see what's out there, that's enough. Don't want to ever grow out of that. Damn, it's getting dark out here, and getting late, and suddenly I'm feeling like a foolish old man.

A few more miles passed with Ubi ruminating on life's choices, crossroads, forks in roads, roads taken, roads not taken. Old Ironsides peeled off the freeway and into a truck stop. What a day, from the river lodge in the Ozarks, to the big city of St. Louis, driving across three more breadbasket states. But now, time to put the pedal up.

Thirty-six

Molly zipped up the soft-sided travel bag and dropped it by the cabin door. She crawled into the bottom bunk and slipped her hands under the back of her head. The bus wasn't leaving Blue Lake Camp until mid-afternoon, but she was ready. Ready to face whatever the Attorney General had planned, schemed, plotted since she had last seen him. That was an awful day when he barged into camp. Tried to seize her like a runaway slave that had to be returned to the plantation. Molly rolled onto her side and looked out the window. Another week of camp would be nice. But that wasn't possible. Let's just get on the bus and get back to Philadelphia. Get it over with.

Molly dozed until a soft knock on the door woke her. A camp counselor's voice drifted through the window screen. "Molly, you had a phone call."

"Who is it?" Molly said, lying still.

"Your brother."

Startled, Molly sat up and banged her head against the wooden slats in the bunk above. "Ouch! Damnit." She pressed an open palm on her forehead but blood had already trickled down into her eyebrows. She rolled onto the floor, kneeling.

"Molly, are you all right?" The counselor was suddenly squatting beside her. "Let's get some ice on that."

Molly climbed to her feet, pulled her T-shirt up over her face and dabbed the blood. "I'll be okay," she said and pushed past the counselor. She threw open the screen door and darted across the campground. In the main lodge, she found the telephone receiver hanging on the wall, resting in its cradle. Who hung up the phone?

The counselor climbed the lodge front steps, panting. He handed Molly a note pad, phone number scrawled in pencil. "I didn't say he was still on the line," the counselor said with a calm voice. "I said, you *had* a phone call. Why don't you use the phone in my office? And don't worry about the long distance charges."

157

Molly tore the top sheet from the scratch pad and looked at the director. Mid-twenties with a kind face and peaceful eyes. How do you get to that point in life?

Sitting in the counselor's hardback chair, Molly's shaky index finger pecked out the number on the phone keypad. A woman's voice said something about a travel plaza. Molly asked to have Jeremy Taylor paged.

Jeremy was sitting in the smoky truckers' lounge staring at a fuzzy big screen TV when he heard his name announced on a speaker hanging from the ceiling. Up at the fuel desk, the attendant plopped on the counter a black telephone with a flashing red light. "Line three," she said. "And make it quick, please."

"What is going on?" Molly's voice sounded desperate and worried. "Are you okay?"

"I'm all right," Jeremy said. "I'm with Grandpa Truck somewhere in western Pennsylvania. We're on schedule to meet the bus this evening. Isn't this the day?"

"It's the right day," Molly said. "But don't think you're fooling anybody. The AG has been here. He knows."

"Knows what?"

"Knows that you went AWOL. And he thinks I'm covering for you. So I caught hell."

"Sorry, sister. I didn't mean to drag you into this."

"Well, you did and it's going to get ugly this evening when . . ." Molly paused. "How are you and Grandpa Truck getting back to town?"

"Molly, you should see Old Ironsides," Jeremy said. "It looks brand new. He spent six months rebuilding it."

"So you went to Texas, found Grandpa Truck, and he's taking you home in Old Ironsides. That's crazy. You don't really think everything is going to be okay with the Attorney General, do you? Just a plea for amnesty and that'll do it, huh?"

"Come on, Molly, don't talk to me like I'm your baby brother," Jeremy said. "You're only a few minutes older than me."

"When you act like a little kid, I'll talk to you like one."

"Now *you're* sounding like the AG."

"Well, you took off on some mad adventure and, and . . . " Molly balled up her fist and softly pounded it on the desktop. "And

I'm caught in the middle. You can bet he's called all his policemen and highway patrol friends, sent out a missing person bulletin, or whatever, all across the country."

"And my picture is probably hanging up in the post office, too."

"Very funny," Molly said. "Look, brother, just be prepared for the worst when you get to school and meet the buses. I assume that was your plan, to somehow sneak up with your backpack and act like you had been to camp."

"It was, but, since he already found out, I guess there's no reason—"

"To continue the charade," Molly said. "Look, I understand you wanted to find Grandpa Truck and tell him personally, but running away like a chicken with your head cut off was stupid. And now we're both boiling in hot water."

"I know, I know, and I'm sorry for dragging you into this, but I'd do it again."

Jeremy heard a hand tapping the glass countertop by the phone. He looked up at the attendant, a silver-haired woman. She mouthed the words "one minute" and held up an index finger.

"What's Grandpa Truck going to do after he drops you off?" Molly asked.

"I don't know," Jeremy said, shrugging his shoulders. "We haven't even talked about that. I hope he sticks around."

"He never stuck around before. What makes you think this time will be different."

"Because this time, you have no idea," Jeremy said through clenched teeth, his face red. The attendant stopped counting change and turned her head to look at this kid who was obviously no truck driver and apparently in some sort of trouble. Jeremy took a breath and continued. "Give Grandpa a chance."

"Well, it's Grandfather Taylor who holds all the cards," Molly said. "Your fairy tale road trip is going to hit a dead end this evening."

"Look, Molly, I understand that. And I don't want to fight with you," Jeremy said. "But I think Grandpa Truck offers some things that the Attorney General can't."

"Okay, okay. It's just that." Molly paused and blinked back tears. "Well, it's just that everything is so messed up." Molly rubbed her forehead. The counselor standing in the doorway held out an ice pack.

"We'll get through this together, sis."

The woman at the truck stop made a throat-slashing hand motion. "That's it, kiddo."

Jeremy said, "Gotta go, Molly. Love you."

Riding the bus home that afternoon, Molly sat alone in a window seat near the back. Campers' shoulders and heads bobbed left and right as the bus squirmed its way through the hills. Molly was dozing when she felt the upholstered seat gently sag and a warm body move in next to her—Miss Ketchum, the tiny, young band director, shorter than the shortest freshman. Miss Ketchum knew Molly's parents through various concerts, fundraisers and banquets.

"What happened to your forehead?"

Molly forced a flat smile. "Head shot from a bunk bed," she said and looked out the window.

After several miles of cold silence, Miss Ketchum said, "I'm worried about you, Molly. I saw your grandfather storming across the parking lot the other day. And you haven't said more than a couple words to anyone all week." Molly continued staring out the window, as if she hadn't heard. "And why didn't Jeremy join us?"

The bus driver pushed the clumsy vehicle around a curve and everybody had to grab something—the back of a seat, a handrail, each other—to keep from bumping heads or sliding off their seat.

"Wouldn't want to bother you," Molly said, her voice cracking. "It's a long story."

"That's okay," Miss Ketchum said. "It's a three hour ride home."

Thirty-seven

Pennsylvania Turnpike. What a mess. Whoever sells these orange barrels to the state highway department must own a Caribbean island. Just look at 'em. Lined up for dozens and dozens of miles, up and down hills, around curves. And nothing ever seems to get finished. This road's been under construction since Ben Franklin was flying kites. These fifty-five gallon drums stretch on forever. Maybe the state legislature should adopt the orange construction barrel for the state bird. Sheesh.

Old Ironsides poked along at about forty miles an hour until the road opened up and a four-lane highway beckoned. Ubi romped the accelerator, but the Cat diesel engine sputtered and choked. The rig limped uphill. Cars and trucks and buses zipped past. Ubi steered the Peterbilt down an exit ramp, paid the toll at the booth, bit his lip.

"I think we got bad fuel," Ubi said, looking at Jeremy with a look of concern and disgust. "Had a bad feeling back at that truck stop in Ohio, at Fast Eddies. Don't know why, just didn't seem right, the smell, maybe, was a little too strong, or the color was a little cloudy, or something."

"What are we gonna do?" Jeremy said. "The bus is due at six p.m."

Ubi nursed the sick truck into a gravel lot behind a pancake house and set the air brakes. A flashing yellow sign welcomed travelers.

Best food between here and there is here and now.

Jeremy was sitting on the edge of his seat. "The AG knows I'm not going to be on that bus. He went up to the camp and I wasn't there. So even if the cat's out of the bag, I need to be there when Molly returns from camp," Jeremy said. "For Molly, if nothing else. And I want to finish this trip right. I left when the band left and I returned when the band returned. I didn't hurt anybody. I just did what I had to do. And that's that."

"From what you told me about your conversation with Molly back at the truck stop, she caught hell for something she didn't do."

"That's right. She caught hell for me," Jeremy said. "For what I did."

"For what *we* did," Ubi said, correcting his grandson. "I coulda' sent you home on a plane, called Mr. Taylor and explained what happened. Naw, Jeremy, I'm in this just as deep as you are." Ubi fidgeted with the black knob on the stick shift and said, "I think the fuel filters might be clogged and need replacing."

"You got one?"

"Got a couple."

"Then what are we waiting on?"

Under Ubi's close supervision, Jeremy inserted a short iron bar into the hydraulic cab jack mounted on the frame and began pumping up and down. The steel shell creaked and groaned and tilted upward to a forty-five degree angle, exposing the dark yellow Caterpillar diesel engine. Ubi smiled at the sight of the beautiful beast.

The fuel filters were about the size and shape of a coffee can. Ubi had always wrapped a small strap around them for leverage and tugged until the seal broke free. But with long fingers and a youthful grip, Jeremy removed them both barehanded. One was half empty and the other, three-quarters full.

Ubi and Jeremy carried the used filters to a small gas station next door. It was a red-brick relic from an era before interstates crisscrossed the country. Modern toll plazas and sprawling travel centers had rendered this four-pump operation obsolete. The business now survived on local customers. The manager on duty pointed to a twenty-gallon steel barrel behind the garage. Ubi and Jeremy turned the slippery filters upside down and shook them. Sludge and dirt and gunk dripped out.

"Where'd you buy fuel?" the manager asked. "That crap musta took a bypass on its way through the refinery."

The little gas station kept a diesel pump out back that supplied fuel to local farmers' trucks and tractors. Jeremy and Ubi each held one new filter as the manager filled them with clean diesel. Back at the truck, Ubi gave Jeremy the honors and the youngster spun both filters into place.

Ubi decided it was best to top off the tanks. Dilute that bad fuel as much as possible with clean diesel from the little station. But the long Patriot Van Line trailer wouldn't track around the tight corner behind the station. They would have to unhook the trailer. Under his grandfather's watchful eye, Jeremy cranked down the trailer's landing gear, round and round with a steel handle. Next, he pulled a lever that released steel jaws that connected Old Ironsides to the trailer. Ubi pushed the starter button and the engine groaned and shook the cab. CB antennas wobbled. Grey-white smoked belched from twin stacks. An ornery giant with a nasty hangover had been roused.

Ubi nursed Old Ironsides forward. Two air hoses and an electrical line dangling between the back of the truck and the front of the trailer stretched as tight as guitar strings.

Jeremy rushed up to the driver's window. "Grandpa, you forgot to unhook the hoses."

Ubi shook his head back and forth. Forgetful old fart. Who are you fooling? He slipped the stick shift into reverse and backed up. The lines slackened and Jeremy disconnected them. Ubi eased the Peterbilt across the street and up to the diesel pumps behind the gas station. The manager had watched the air hose incident and decided to have a little fun.

"Hey, I was wondering what you were up to. Thought maybe you was going to hang out some laundry," he said, laughing at his own joke.

The slow pump chugged along and had just finished topping off both tanks when a voice from the restaurant parking lot caught everyone's attention.

"You get this damn trailer off my property," yelled a pot-bellied man, white apron tied loosely around his waist. "Or I call and have it towed. I'm tired of you truckers tearing up my lot."

Jeremy and Ubi looked at each other and both lifted their eyes at the same time. "I'll talk to him, Grandpa," Jeremy said and jogged toward the angry man.

Ubi paid for the fuel, drove back to the trailer and backed under it. The truck's steel jaws snapped shut around the trailer kingpin. He was standing on the truck frame, behind the cab reattaching the air hoses, when Jeremy walked out with a paper sack in his hand.

"Hot chocolate for me, coffee for you, and donuts for both of us," Jeremy said, smiling. "Had to buy him off."

"Maybe I should have told him what we were doing," Ubi said. "You really like that cocoa, huh?"

"Better than coffee, Grandpa. Eight days a week."

Climbing down from the truck frame, Ubi lost his grip and tried to jump free. His left foot landed in a pothole and he went down on one knee. Ubi rolled onto his back, groaning and gripping his left shin with two hands.

"Jeremy, come here," Ubi said through clenched teeth, rolling around on his back. He reached down to his ankle, rolled his khakis almost up to his knee and unlatched two boot buckles. "Grab my left boot and yank it hard," he ordered.

Jeremy bent over and pulled on the black work boot. It let go with just one tug. He staggered back several steps and almost hit the ground himself.

Jeremy regained his balance and stood both feet firm in the parking lot. Now, what is Grandpa Truck doing? He's standing up, balanced on his right foot, holding on to Old Ironsides. Jeremy gawked at the stump at the bottom of his grandfather's left shin. He looked down at the boot in his hands. A prosthetic foot. Plastic. One that you obviously could take off and put back on.

"Geez, Grandpa," Jeremy said, a baffled look on his face. "When did this happen?"

Thirty-eight

Jeremiah Fisher for several years had wintered at his Montana retreat on Old Onion Top, elevation—10,800 feet. Not a measly mile high, like Denver, but more than two miles above the oceans. Jeremiah first explored the Gallatin National Forest at age 28, looking for a respite, a place to hibernate like the grizzly. He had hit the mother lode—silicon—in the nascent computer chip industry in California, then sold his business for several million. Young and virile with coifed hair like James Dean, he suddenly had enough money to live a life of debauchery. And he did a good job of it. But after a few years of indulging in all of the seven deadly seven sins, he matured and began a quest for something more meaningful.

It took a summer of hiking, backpacking and camping to find the perfect lookout where he would build a granite fieldstone cabin. You could see fifty miles south and east across the windswept Montana prairie. On clear nights, the Milky Way was close enough to sweep up in a butterfly net. When the storms blew in from Saskatchewan and Manitoba, you had a close encounter with the fury and beauty of those blizzards, weather that humbled you regardless the number of zeros in your bank account.

Although the winter shows were breathtaking with their stark beauty, they were sometimes deadly. Snowdrifts entombed cars and trucks caught in the path of nature's pitiless, yet magnificent, wrath. Every winter, the blizzards stranded dozens of motorists out on the interstate, twelve miles distant yet clearly visible from Old Onion Top. During one of those early winter storms, after a viscous blizzard blasted across the valley, Jeremiah watched through his binoculars a man trudging along the side of the road. His sedan had slipped down an embankment and buried its nose in a snow bank. Jeremiah lost sight of the man after he disappeared around a bend and assumed he would be okay. After all, the wind had stopped. The snow had stopped. Sure, the temperature in the valley was probably in the low teens, but the figure trudging in the snow looked like he would be all right. Jeremiah thought nothing of it, nothing until a few days later when he visited the general store in Livingston. The local paper ran a front page story about a woman, not a man like he had assumed, who had died in the hospital from exposure. A highway patrolman found her on the shoulder just one mile outside a small community in which she could have found warmth in a local resident's home.

Jeremiah then bought a snowmobile, a set of high-powered binoculars and a telescope. He purchased a box of self-activating hand and foot warmers and a large thermos that he would fill with hot soup or coffee. Every winter after that, like a sentinel, he kept watch on the valley below, an eye out for stranded vehicles, their drivers and passengers.

It was November 1981. Or was it '82? Regardless, a freak November storm swirled and raged and dumped four feet of snow overnight. Jeremiah couldn't see a thing through the plate glass window. An utter whiteout. But the sky was clear and blue the next morning, and with the binoculars he scanned the highway. White smoke, small puffs drifting up from a vast snowdrift. How can that be? Let's take a closer look. To the telescope.

Jeremiah adjusted the focus and zoomed in on the source of the mysterious smoke. That's not a snowdrift, but an eighteen-wheeler down there. You can make out the shape, rectangular, and maybe sixty feet long. The truck engine must have idled all night. And she's still running. Look at those white plumes trailing up from two stacks. There seems to be a pattern. Three short puffs, three long puffs, three more short puffs. S-O-S. The driver must know Morse code. Time to warm up the snowmobile.

Snowmobiling over and around glistening, white mounds and dodging exposed barbed wire fences, Jeremiah lost sight of the rig several times. But he had a clear view of the smoke signals and followed them like a sailor tracking the North Star. The storm had smothered the countryside into submission and left it with a sense of finality. It had dealt its blow, leaving snowdrifts as high as rooftops in a few places, and then marched onward.

Sledding toward the interstate, three times Jeremiah had to dig his vehicle out of snowdrifts. When he at last reached the buried highway, he found the truck cab tilted forward at forty-five degrees. Nobody could possibly be inside. The engine was still idling, but no more smoke signals. How did the driver manipulate the accelerator? The snowmobile circled the rig again and stopped near the driver's door. Jeremiah strapped on snowshoes and climbed down from the vehicle.

"Hello," he yelled, both hands cupped around his mouth. "Where are you?" His voice fell hollow on the white landscape. He circled the truck looking for signs of life. Nothing.

Jeremiah then pulled himself up on the side of the truck cab, snowshoes flat against a front tire. The rig was an old Peterbilt. Jeremiah pushed his face against the driver's window. Nobody inside. Then he lost his grip and half-jumped, half-dove onto the white pillow below. Climbing to his feet, Jeremiah looked under the truck. He felt warmth emanating from the clattering engine so he pushed his head and neck and shoulders under the cab.

White and bright outside, dim and hazy under the rig, it took a minute for Jeremiah's eyes to adjust. And there's a man, propped up against the engine block. The figure's eyes slowly opened. Look at those creases circling bloodshot eyes. A dead man coming back to life. Jeremiah stared, astonished, speechless.

"Sheesh, I thought you'd never get here," the man said. "I'd almost sell my soul for a hot cup of coffee."

It took a half hour to maneuver the rigid trucker from under the cab and onto the back of the snowmobile. Unsure if the trucker had enough strength to hang on to the snowmobile on the trip to the Bozeman Medical Center, Jeremiah wrapped a cargo strap around them both and ratcheted the buckle tight against his chest. One falls, we both fall.

Snowmobiling along the highway shoulder was a little easier than riding the backcountry. Still, it was a slow, arduous and lonely trip; the road remained closed and there was no traffic, no sign of life. The temperature hovered in the single digits, and driving just ten miles an hour was bone-chilling, despite the expensive gloves, goggles and parka Jeremiah wore. So Jeremiah kept the speed down, balancing the need to get the trucker out of the frigid air with the possibility that by driving too fast he could arrive with a frozen corpse.

It turned out the trucker was as rugged as the granite outcroppings on Old Onion Top. Stubborn, too. The next day, when the road reopened, he crawled out of bed and limped downstairs before anyone could stop him. He found his rescuer in the lobby, and insisted on going back to his rig. He was worried sick about it, stranded on the side of the road.

Jeremiah relented and in a borrowed jeep drove the man back to his eighteen-wheeler. On the way, the trucker explained how he ended up underneath the truck cab hugging the diesel engine. He was making an emergency roadside repair, he said, but the hydraulic fluid that operates the cab jack had frozen so he couldn't lower the cab and he couldn't climb up inside it either. The only choice, crawl up next to that engine and stay warm. Yanking and releasing the linkage attached to the accelerator, he sent up the S-O-S call—three short pulls, three long ones, three more short ones.

Back at the rescue site, the temperature had risen into the low thirties, warm enough to thaw the thick, heavy hydraulic fluid. The truck cab creaked and moaned but slowly dropped into position. Then the damn fool trucker, one day after nearly becoming an ice sculpture, he drives another forty miles and delivers his load of alfalfa hay to a dude ranch. The ranch owner wouldn't let him touch a bale, insisted his boys do the manual labor. The trucker laid up at the dude ranch two more days, thawing out. But his left foot was black and numb, wouldn't come back to life. He had stood all night, right foot on top of left, so the bottom foot froze longer and deeper than the top foot. Turned out to be a good strategy, said the old sawbones up in Missoula who performed the surgery. Upon the trucker's discharge from the hospital, the surgeon told the trucker: "If you had spent the night flat-footed, I would have had to cut off both feet."

Thirty-nine

"So that's why that woman called you Ahab," Jeremy said.

"What woman is that?"

"That crazy woman wearing the hard hat at the post office in Texas," Jeremy said, trying to wrap his mind around this strange turn of events. "And hold on. You visited us a couple times since that happened. I mean, sure you walked with a little limp, a hitch in your git-along, as you would say, but you *always* walked kind of funny. So, why didn't you say anything?"

"Aw, heck, I don't know. Talk is cheap."

Jeremy shook his head and rolled his eyes. He started to comment on his granddad's stoic and introverted character, but never mind.

Ubi rubbed his throbbing left leg. "I don't think I can drive," he said, standing on one foot, "until this swelling goes down. That could be hours, days."

"We got fresh fuel, hot chocolate, donuts," Jeremy said with a sense of urgency. "Only a couple hundred miles to go. We're almost to the finish line."

"It won't be the end of the world if we miss the bus. Let's get a motel room. We can make a phone call tonight and explain."

"The Attorney General will sick the highway patrol on us, or drive out himself, pick us up like escaped convicts," Jeremy said. "I can't stand to even think about that humiliation. And besides, I didn't sleep in a nasty trailer with rats, fend off prostitutes, ride all night in cars and buses, get bit in the crotch by a scorpion, just to get this close and quit."

"Wait a minute. Prostitutes?" Ubi asked. "What's that about?"

"There was only one, actually, at the Fifth Wheel Truck Stop in Oklahoma City."

"Aw, hell, Jeremy, that place has always been known for lot lizards," Ubi said with the familiar smirk that had begun to irritate Jeremy. "I could have told you that."

"But you weren't there," Jeremy snapped. "Like all those other times. Birthdays and Christmas and even before that when Mom was a kid."

"How do you know what happened before you were born?"

"Some people talk about their feelings, Grandpa."

Ubi clutched the handrail on Old Ironsides and looked down at the nub below his knee. He couldn't believe Jeremy was talking to him like that, like an adult. Ubi scrunched up his nose, stared at the stub. An old man down to his last leg. He then realized that Jeremy was still holding his boot.

"Can I have my foot back?"

Jeremy slung the prosthetic foot by the shoelace. It hit Ubi in the gut.

"Jeremy, look," Ubi stammered. "You're right on all counts, but I can't help what I am. This road life is the only thing that keeps me sane. Your grandmother accepted it and we had a good life. Now, your mom and me, we reconciled, finally, when you were about seven. But I don't know what to say except I'm here now and I want to help."

"You really want to help, Grandpa?"

"I mean what I say, Jeremy."

"Okay . . . then, teach me to drive your truck."

Forty

Patient and calm, Ubi delivered driving instructions. "Don't wrestle her, Jeremy. Shifting gears is not brute force, but technique."

Jeremy adjusted the driver's seat back a notch. Was he taller than Grandpa Truck? He pushed the clutch toward the floor and maneuvered the stick shift into second gear like he was told. This clutch pedal must be super spring-loaded. Foot's getting tired already. Jeremy's clutch foot slipped. The truck frame and cab bounced up and down, shaking and jostling the riders. Ubi nodded encouragement. Not bad for the first time.

Old Ironsides growled across the parking lot. "Let's stay off the interstate for a little while," Ubi instructed, "until you get the feel of the rig."

Listening to Ubi's firm yet gentle voice, Jeremy maneuvered the stick shift up and down and across the H pattern. Simple enough. Run the rpms up to 1,600. Lightly tap the clutch. Ease it out of gear and into neutral. Tap clutch again. Slip 'er into next gear. After he had negotiated the truck into fifth gear, Jeremy performed the tricky split shift. While maneuvering the shifter, flip the air-activated switch on the stick, go all the way back to first gear, and run through the gear sequence again. With the split shift method, the mystery of Grandpa Truck's flying elbow and surging truck rpms had been solved.

At about fifty miles and hour Old Ironsides tracked straight and heavy. Just listen to Grandpa and keep both hands on the wheel and we'll make it to Philly same time as Molly.

Jeremy wasn't thrilled taking on this role, driving an eighteen-wheeler with no license, no experience. If something happened, well, Grandpa Truck would have to do the double-talking, ticket paying, bail posting. Sheesh, don't even think about getting caught. After ten miles of frontage road driving, Jeremy eased Old Ironsides onto the freeway ramp.

171

"Running through the gears is easy," Ubi said. "Downshifting is a different animal. But with this light load, you might be able to stay in the same gear until we exit the toll road. When you approach the tollbooth, just coast in and do like I say. You got good brakes. You got a pulling truck that is very forgiving. And you got a good head on your shoulders. It'll be all right. If we get pulled over, let me do the bullshitting. This is a hardship case. And we're heading to a specialist in Philadelphia. Got no time to wait on an ambulance."

"And somebody's going to believe that?"

"How many people do you know with a fake foot?"

"None."

"So, like I said, let me do the talking."

"Okay, but how did you keep your driver's license with that artificial foot?" Jeremy asked, suddenly remembering Grandpa's subtle limp.

"I had to pass a few tests. Take an extra physical exam, but no big deal."

With Jeremy at the helm, Old Ironsides drifted up and down the hills. It wasn't easy, keeping the trailer tracking in the middle of the lane. And it wasn't pretty; more than once the truck drifted right and Ubi winced at tires grinding on the rumble strip. But after you get 'er in top gear, just accelerate a little on the downhill and keep your foot in it going up. Old Ironsides is geared low, climbs like a mountain goat. And on a steep descent, the transmission works like brakes and holds her back. Let the truck do the work.

Old Ironsides purred down the right lane. New fuel filters had done the trick. Thinking ahead, Ubi quizzed Jeremy on the location of Liberty High School.

"It's on Delaware Pike. I can get you there from the house," he answered. "But I've never come from this direction."

"Jiminy Cricket, you don't know?" Ubi asked, thinking it incredulous that Jeremy wasn't one hundred percent sure how to get to the school he had attended for three years.

"Geez, Grandpa, gimmee a break."

"Okay, okay, never mind." Ubi said.

Ubi wasn't sure why he kept his old map collection. Maybe he wasn't ready to let go of those glorious days rambling unfettered across the continent. He grimaced and crawled into the sleeper. He dug out a thick bundle of city and state maps, red rubber band stretched tight around the huge wad. Many were yellowed and faded and coffee-stained. Some were outdated, printed before the new wave of construction and urban sprawl that afflicted most of America in the 60s and 70s and 80s. A few were clean and relatively new, such as the Philadelphia map that he unfolded on his lap.

"All right. You just keep 'er between the ditches," Ubi said. "I'll find it."

Searching for Delaware Pike, Ubi thought about how Jeremy snapped at him back at the pancake house parking lot. Probably should take it easy on the lad. Been a rough trip and now he's facing an uncertain future. Maybe should have called the AG and surrendered. No, that's not right. They'll be no white flags hanging from Old Ironsides' CB antennae. Never been one to capitulate, not going to start now. And besides, out on the road, Jeremy's getting a life lesson they don't teach at Liberty High.

Jeremy somehow got the transmission stuck in neutral. When he pushed in the clutch and shoved the shifter where he thought the appropriate gear should be, the transmission screeched like a thousand fingernails clawing the same chalkboard. Ubi made a face as if his other foot was being amputated.

"Forget about the clutch," Ubi said. "We don't need it. All you gotta do is bring the rpms up to 1,500."

But Jeremy couldn't master the stiff accelerator. The engine raced high above the 1,500 mark and then plunged dramatically below it. Old Ironsides rapidly lost speed. Ubi asked Jeremy if he could hold the engine at about 1,100 rpms. Then, leaning across the truck cab, Ubi slipped the stick shift into gear. No grinding or shaking.

"It's not as easy as you make it look," Jeremy said. "I feel like I'm tearing the transmission into pieces of shrapnel."

"You're doing fine. Now put your foot in it, we got another hill up ahead."

Jeremy managed two clumsy shifts that shook the cab, but he eventually pushed Old Ironsides up to the speed limit. The rig traversed South-Central Pennsylvania without Jeremy having to shift any more gears.

"The old girl's got guts," Jeremy said, his confidence building. "I'll give her that."

"So does the driver," Ubi said, looking across the cab at his grandson.

"Maybe we should get on the CB, see if there's any Smokeys up ahead."

"No thanks," Ubi said. "I mean, you can if you want to."

"You don't chat much on the CB, Grandpa. Why not?"

"Talk is cheap."

"Why did I even ask?"

"What's that?"

"Nothing."

About twenty miles west of Philadelphia, Ubi pointed out the exit and the far right tollbooth that read WIDE LOADS. Jeremy's right foot tapped the firm air brakes and Ubi's head lurched forward.

"Brakes are a little touchy," Ubi said. "Just drop 'er into neutral, coast to a stop. Then start in second gear, ease up to the booth that way."

At the tollbooth, Ubi doled out the cash, sheesh, more than twenty-five bucks. Jeremy said he thought he could make it to the high school okay. But first a cigarette and donut break. Jeremy pushed Old Ironsides herky-jerky onto the side of the road where other motorists were also parked. What Jeremy had said down the road needed to come out, the part about Grandpa Truck not being around, but that was in the rearview mirror. Time to work together, in tandem, finish what they had started.

Ubi massaged the stump below his knee. Jeremy ran through the low gears, bucking and shaking the cab. He negotiated through the split shift without chipping or shearing off any teeth in the gears spinning below. Rookie driver at the helm, Old Ironsides carried on.

Ubi had found a route to Liberty High School in which Jeremy had to navigate only three left turns. Jeremy scratched a few gears, found the wrong hole twice and the cab shook like it had crossed a set of railroad tracks. But Jeremy was an able student. Old Ironsides plodded down Delaware Pike toward Liberty High School.

Easing the rig into the back lot behind the stadium, Ubi and Jeremy looked out on three busloads of campers milling about, toting luggage, hugging family and friends.

"Grandpa, tell me again, where's the parking brakes? You got so many switches and valves over here, I can't remember which ones to pull or push or what."

Ubi pointed out two plastic knobs, yellow and red. Jeremy pulled them with a firm grasp. A loud popping noise erupted from under the truck and trailer. Jeremy let go a deep breath. The magnitude of what he had done, what he and Grandpa Truck had done, was yet to unfold.

Forty-one

Donald and Katherine Taylor were sitting in the Jaguar at the high school stadium when the buses rolled in from Blue Lake. Looking through a spotless windshield, their eyes scanned the students as they tumbled out. But at a parking lot entrance to their left, a tractor-trailer rig that looked like a giant caterpillar weaved its way between scattered sedans and sports cars.

Back when the twins were in kindergarten, Donald had seen pictures of Old Ironsides hanging on their bedroom wall next to a bulletin board plastered with postcards from across the continent, all from Grandpa Truck of course. But the twins little shrine did not do justice to the imposing Peterbilt, up close and personal. Donald and Katherine gaped at the eighteen-wheeler. It had high cheekbones and setback eyes, broad chest and shoulders. It was rugged, masculine and clean with white wheels, polished aluminum bumper and chrome stacks.

And damned if that isn't Jeremy behind the wheel.

"What the hell is Jeremy doing driving that old truck?" Donald barked.

"I don't know, but he looks very, uh, earthy," Katherine said as she opened the car door.

"Don't they know they're lucky they weren't arrested," Donald said. "Why, I had—"

"The state police, the FBI and the Department of Transportation on lookout," Katherine interrupted. "We know."

Katherine got out of the car and disappeared into the crowd gathering around the rig. Donald slipped from behind the wheel, smoothed a few wrinkles from his suit coat and leaned against the fender. This is ridiculous. He's had Jeremy out on the road in this rig how long? Got everybody worried to death. Couldn't he call? And prosecution of Ubi Sunt is not out of the question. A man should be accountable for his actions.

176

More than a dozen band members, their friends and family, and all three bus drivers strolled up for close inspection. Jeremy remained in the driver's seat. He scanned the crowd for Molly. Ubi wrestled with the prosthetic foot, wincing and gritting his teeth, and managed to buckle it back on. They both climbed down from the rig and stood before the large grill.

The curious crowd encircled Old Ironsides. Ubi leaned on his right foot and propped himself up against the heavy-duty front bumper. His lower left leg continued to ache, but he blocked out the pain as best he could and explained that he bought Old Ironsides, brand new, in Denver—1956. It had a Caterpillar diesel engine that he enjoyed tinkering with. He had driven the truck almost two million miles. Anyone who wanted to look inside was welcome. Mind the mess, though. We've been running hard for a few days.

Jeremy chatted with friends from the band camp. What happened? Thought you were coming with us, but you slipped off at that rest area and now pull up behind the wheel of a prehistoric eighteen-wheeler. Geez, what's up with that?

Jeremy was purposefully vague with his friends, laughing and dropping a few subtle hints. Then Katherine squeezed forward and reached out for a hug. While they embraced, she whispered in his ear, "I understand you did what you felt like you had to do, but you had us worried to *death*."

"I'm sorry, grandmother," Jeremy said, "but, well . . ." Jeremy stammered and couldn't complete his thought.

"Let me see your hands," Katherine said, backing up a step. "Hmm, no broken fingers. You forget how to use a pay phone? And your grandfather, Ubi, well, suffice it to say you're lucky that you two weren't arrested."

With the crowd buzzing about the old rig, Molly stood alone, yards away from anyone. She shifted her weight from side to side. For some unknown reason, Jeremy had been driving Old Ironsides, riding up on a white horse like the hero in one of those corny westerns he used to watch as a little boy with Grandpa Truck. And now Grandpa Truck and Old Ironsides once again had center stage. Like always. She would wait for the crowd to thin out.

177

The tiny band director, Miss Ketchum, five feet tall and ninety-five pounds, was now scaling Old Ironsides like Spiderman climbing a skyscraper. She grabbed the handrail, pulled herself up, then clutched the big steering wheel and scrambled into the front seat. Wow, so high up. You can see all the way to the interstate.

Back on the ground minutes later, Miss Ketchum reached up for Ubi's hand and squeezed it. Ubi wrapped his long, gnarled fingers around her short, stubby ones. She commented on what fine, young people Jeremy and Molly are, and then asked a favor.

"When I was about five, my dad drove a rig to Florida on a regular run. I begged for a ride. He promised, someday, but he just up and quit and opened a small music shop. I never got that ride. I would love to take a spin in your truck," she said. "Just say when."

"Stick around and we can do it today," Ubi said, nodding. "After everybody leaves."

"Okay," Miss Ketchum said, her eyes full of surprise. "I have some paperwork to do at my office in the band hall. I'll be back in an hour."

The crowd drifted away. The two grandfathers still had not spoken to each other, had not acknowledged the other's existence. Ubi found Molly and Jeremy talking and standing beside a light pole. How long had it been? Five years? Maybe six, or seven? Too damn long, you old fool.

Ubi limped over to his two grandchildren. Jeremy melted away, muttered something about being thirsty. Molly remained at arm's length. The little girl who used to swing and hang on her Grandpa Truck's arms and legs like climbing a tree had grown into a young woman. Thin brown hair pulled back in a ponytail. Tall and slender like her mother, yet muscular from marching and swimming.

"I'm sorry, Molly," Ubi said. "I just found out a few days ago."

"It's okay, Grandpa," Molly said. "I'm sure you've been busy."

"If only I had known, I would've dropped everything," Ubi said, drawing a heavy breath, his chest rising and falling. He took one step closer. "I hate flying, my ears pop and explode like firecrackers, but I would've caught the first plane out of Amarillo. Surely you know that."

"I understand, Grandpa," Molly said. "But you've removed yourself so far from us that, that, we can't reach you. We can't find you when something happens."

"You're right. I should have done a better job of keeping in touch. A better job of making myself more accessible."

"A better job of being a father and grandfather."

"Those are harsh words," Ubi said, realizing Molly was the sort who told you straight up what's on her mind. Like her momma. "But I guess you're right. I guess I had that coming."

"You live life on your terms, Grandpa, and that's not fair to us," Molly said, her stern voice like a mother admonishing a small child. "It was fun and mysterious when we were kids, but not any more. Not after what happened."

"I know, I know," Ubi said. "I should've kept that pager. I never even put batteries in it. I can think of a thousand things I wish I had done."

"But you can't change the past," Molly said and crossed her arms.

An awkward silence hung heavy between the two. When Ubi felt he could stand the tension no longer, he stepped up to Molly and held out his arms. She maintained her posture. Ubi raised his hands, slowly, and rested them on her shoulders. He looked straight at her stern face. Long eyelashes, thin nose, angular chin, like her mother's. Ubi was ready to say something that was very difficult for him, something that *he* had never heard in the Texas Boys' Home, the orphanage where he grew up, something he hadn't heard until he married Molly's grandmother. He knew those words were long overdue.

"I love you, Molly."

The granddaughter's solemn face looked like it was breaking apart. Molly slid her head across Ubi's shoulder and buried it in his chest. Grandpa Truck had let them down in a thousand ways, remaining aloof, distant, out of touch. But it didn't seem like that big a deal until Mom and Dad died. That's just how things were. And, of course, what happened to Mom and Dad could no way be blamed on him. Still, that doesn't make it right, staying gone so long. Ubi wrapped his arms around Molly, closed his eyes, and pulled her close. The world disappeared.

A line of vehicles rolled out onto Delaware Pike. The stadium parking lot was about empty, save the Jaguar and Old Ironsides.

Molly slung her travel bag in the car trunk. Jeremy retrieved his backpack and the sax case from the truck sleeper. Donald continued leaning against his car. He hadn't said a word to Ubi and Ubi wasn't about to be the one to offer the peace pipe. The two adversaries glared at each other across the asphalt lot, leaned on their disparate vehicles. Their lives and how they viewed the world was reflected in the machines they owned and drove.

The Jaguar was lean and sleek and sexy. Quick and agile like a cat. It was modern, cosmopolitan, sophisticated. Imported from Europe. The Peterbilt was massive, bulky and cumbersome. Slow moving, but when it got to rolling—thunderous like a bison. It was archaic, a relic from another era. Simple in design. American made.

Both men took intense pride in their vehicles. And to each one, the other's mode of transportation was baffling. Katherine stood between the two. Obstinate men and their damned pride. She felt like smacking their heads together and telling them to grow up. She figured her role would be that of mediator, someone who could build a bridge, mend fences. Yet all that would take time. Not something to be done in a school parking lot. So let's get out of here and see if we can get started rehabilitating these two old curmudgeons. She asked Ubi to walk with her to the Jaguar. Standing within earshot of both men, she made her move.

"Anybody want to get something to eat?" Katherine said.

Silence. Then feet shuffling.

"How about dinner, later tonight," Ubi said. "I saw a motel a few exits back. I could use a shower first."

Donald ran his fingers through his silver-black hair. (He thought nobody noticed how his barber touched it up twice a month.) Dinner with the infidel didn't sound appealing to him, but he held his tongue. After all, Jeremy and Molly were safely home. And no doubt, Ubi would grow bored and drift away, like always. So he would suffer through dinner to appease everyone. Then, when it came time to say good night, he would invite the vagabond to his office tomorrow for a little come-to-Jesus meeting. Set him straight and send him back to Texas understanding he was out of place here on the East Coast.

"Are you talking about the Valley Forge Inn?" Katherine asked.

"That's the place," Ubi said. "Best I remember, food's not bad. How about eight o'clock?"

"It's a date."

The Jaguar scooted down the drive, brother-sister, husband-wife, riding quietly inside. Ubi climbed up in Old Ironsides, grabbed a pillow from the bunk, and rested his head on the steering wheel. Thirty minutes later, an electric golf cart rolled up, Miss Ketchum behind the wheel. "Swiped it from the football coach," the band director said and stepped down from the cart. She bounced on her feet. "I can't wait to ride in your truck. I've heard you call it Old Ironsides."

Miss Ketchum climbed aboard. Ubi cranked the starter and the diesel growled. He pushed against the clutch pedal, but it barely budged. Lightning bolts shot up his left leg. He clamped his eyes shut. Squeezed the black knob at the top of the stick shift.

"What's the matter?"

"I can't drive."

PART III

Sojourn

"Elbow Room!"

— *Daniel Boone*

Forty-two

Ubi was fortunate to get a room at the Valley Forge Inn. Tourist season, the brusque front desk clerk said, but we have a cancellation. And no, we don't have a truckers' discount. Besides, I saw someone drop you off in a Volkswagen. Midget lady driving.

Back in the rented room, Ubi found an ironing board in the tiny closet. Short bursts of steam smoothed the wrinkles from a pair of khakis and a green, long-sleeve collared shirt, but there was nothing that could mitigate that face, the curlicues, creases, and semi-circles that were etched into his forehead and below his eyes like back roads squiggling across a highway map.

While he showered and shaved, Ubi confronted the reality that he hadn't planned anything other than getting Jeremy home. He had hit the road on impulse. And driving out here, he thought only about the next mile. That journey was now in the rear view mirror, except that he still had the trailer to deliver, which posed a challenge now that his leg felt like a pincushion with one thousand needles constantly stabbing it. But more importantly, what about the grandkids' future? They had one summer and one more year of high school before they presumably went off to college. A college education—that's what their mother and father wanted, expected. And obviously, they would be living with Katherine and Donald.

As for tonight, Ubi expected to face the question: How long until you return to Texas? His left leg burned and ached as he sat on the bed and slipped on the prosthetic foot. Ubi sensed Molly and Jeremy would be expecting him to say or do something, make a speech or an announcement. It was his move. He had elected to drive Jeremy home in the rig and not notify his grandparents that he was okay and thus assuage their anxiety. Sheesh, put the shoe on the other foot. How would you feel?

Ubi limped down the long, carpeted corridor toward the lobby. So, where do you go now? A square peg won't fit in a round hole.

184

Ubi was sitting at the coffee counter flipping through the local newspaper when the Jaguar pulled into the parking lot. He folded back the classified ads section and stood to greet the foursome. The waitress took their orders and reported to the head cook. What a glum bunch. Never seen so many long faces.

Back at the table, small talk had fallen mostly flat. Insipid conversation about the current heat wave and Phillies losing streak. Little eye contact. Just five hurting people with different outlooks on how to move forward, but no one willing to take the first step. They couldn't talk about Jeremy bolting and hitching rides almost two thousand miles to Texas. Couldn't talk about Ubi's role in the conspiracy, the road back, the side trip with the Indiana girls. Couldn't talk about Donald's brash behavior toward Molly and the camp staff.

Ubi and Donald still hadn't shaken hands; other than a few grunts they hadn't said much of anything to each other throughout dinner. The waitress slipped the tab under the George Washington figurine that graced the center of the table. Both men reached for the check. Now standing, facing each other, they pulled on opposite ends of the thin piece of cardboard.

"I got it."

"Allow me."

"Please. I insist."

"You've done enough."

"I haven't done anything."

"Sure, you have. You helped an underage fugitive."

"Why do you think he left in the first place?"

"Unimportant."

"The hell you say."

"I don't need a Johnny-come-lately telling me how to run this family. You can mount your old horse and ride out of Dodge anytime, Tex."

Katherine jumped to her feet and said, "You two, quit your piping, for God's sake."

The two men continued pulling opposite ends of the check, hands stretched across the table, glaring. Ubi's eyes were thin slits. Donald's jaw was locked tight.

A man wearing a suit coat and tie approached the table. "Gentlemen," he said in a stern, yet soft voice. "May I be of assistance? Why don't we divide the check in half?"

Ubi let it go. He rolled up and tucked the newspaper under his right arm, grabbed his wallet from his back pocket, and dropped two twenties on the table. Jeremy and Molly and Katherine sat stupefied. The two bulls had finally locked horns. In public. And everything seemed to be happening in slow motion.

"I'm not going anywhere," Ubi said. "The next few days, I'll be looking for a place to live." He pointed the rolled-up newspaper across the table at Donald. "And I'm going to be spending some time with these kids."

Ubi took two steps toward the door, then stopped. "I'm sorry if I embarrassed any of you," he said. "Jeremy, Molly, I mean it. I'll be sticking around for a while. I'll be in touch." Ubi limped across the dining room and exited through a door connected to the motel.

Donald handed his credit card to the man in the suit. He took a long sip of water. Looking over the top of the glass, he had watched the feeble trucker exit the dining room. Shouldn't be hard to catch him. Donald excused himself, said he was headed to the restroom. He found Ubi hobbling down the long hallway, near an ice machine.

"Hey, truck driver," Donald yelled. Ubi stopped and turned around. A young woman pushing a cart stacked with clean towels veered left, between the two men, and quickly disappeared down a corridor. "This is not over. I will have you in my office. Soon."

"You're not coming between me and the kids," Ubi barked, his face burning.

"I'm not through with you," Donald said, pointing down the hallway at Ubi.

Ubi turned his back to the son of a bitch, plodded down the corridor. He felt eyes burning in his back. Things are getting out of hand. This ain't the time, or place.

Donald put his head down and hustled down the hallway with long strides. He looked up. His wife was standing near the men's room, hands on hips, scowling.

"You get lost?"

The next morning, Ubi called Patriot Van Lines. He explained the trailer was just outside Philadelphia, but he couldn't drive due to an injured foot. The dispatcher remembered Ubi. He had worked for Deaton Van Lines when Ubi drove for that company. After ten minutes sharing old war stories, they got down to business. Can't make it the last fifty miles to Trenton? No problem for an old pro like Ubi Sunt. The dispatcher arranged for a local driver to pick up the trailer at the high school stadium parking lot. The driver would also deliver a check for the mileage from Oklahoma to Philadelphia. A man like Ubi Sunt, well, you treat him with respect. He couldn't finish the job, the last fifty miles. So what? Who kicks a dog when it's down?

The young Patriot driver rolled into the stadium parking lot that afternoon driving a Volvo. Sloping hood and low to the ground, it looked like a large pickup truck. The driver's long, stringy hair spilled out from under a Cummings Diesel cap. He had just earned his Class A commercial license which allowed him to drive eighteen-wheelers. Ubi asked him to pull Old Ironsides out from under the trailer and park it in the corner of the lot where Miss Ketchum said it would be safe. And don't forget, you still owe her a ride.

Ubi shrugged, watched the kid wrestle Old Ironsides across the asphalt lot. The youngster smiled and handed Ubi the key. "They don't make 'em like that any more," he said. "I've never driven a truck with no power steering."

"It's called arm strong steering," Ubi said, flexing a bicep that bulged under the sleeve of a white T-shirt. He was hobbled, all right, after losing his left foot in Montana, but he wasn't ready for the rocking chair. Not yet, damnit.

Ubi watched the kid back the Volvo under the Patriot trailer. His foot came off the clutch too fast and the Volvo slammed and shook the trailer as the fifth wheel latched with a loud thwack. Ubi smiled. He'll learn. A minute later, the truck was rolling down Delaware Pike toward the freeway.

Ubi had a rental car delivered to the motel the following morning. A little two-door Pontiac. Head almost rubs against the ceiling. Oh well, it's got an automatic transmission. No clutch. Left foot can rest on the floorboard.

Ubi spent that afternoon going through old newspapers at the public library. A librarian went to a back room and pulled papers for the date of the accident and several more issues that immediately followed the tragedy. Ubi printed copies of several stories. The headlines screamed of heartbreak and tragedy.

Philadelphia couple badly injured in collision with 18-wheeler
Two die in hospital from injuries sustained in recent accident
Trucking company faulted in twin fatality

The next morning, Ubi rolled westbound down the turnpike in his rental car. Another dreary day; smog, fog and haze obscured the sun. It wasn't hard to find the accident site. The memorial stretched almost fifty yards. Ubi eased the automobile onto the shoulder and hit the four-way flashers. He surveyed the roadside.

Knee-high wooden crosses planted in tall grass. Some homemade. Others store-bought. Purple, red and blue artificial flower bouquets strewn along the roadside, windblown by cars and trucks zipping by. Plastic figurines, men and women wearing robes, angels with hands folded in prayer, a dove.

Ubi always figured he would be the one to die on the side of the highway, like in one of those melodramatic country songs he enjoyed. Of course, it would have to be on top of a mountain pass, rescuing a busload of children. A stupid fantasy. Yet not a bad way to go.

Ubi unlatched the seat belt. A big rig thundered past and shook the car side to side. Is this how it feels when Old Ironsides sails by? Ubi checked the mirror. All clear. He pushed open the small door and it bounced on the hinges. Climbing up and out of a low-slung car was the converse of tumbling down from the Peterbilt. How do people drive these miniature vehicles? Ubi put both feet on solid ground. With a grunt, he pulled himself to his feet. He studied each artifact. Jeanne and Martin had many fine friends.

Ubi shuffled toward a small, wooden cross and yanked it out of the soft ground. He then worked his way to a plastic wreath mounted on wire mesh, stooped, gathered it up and clutched it to his chest. Back at the car, he softly placed both items in the trunk. Working deliberately for the next hour, Ubi pulled up every cross, flower, vine and bird, and gently laid them to rest in the trunk. He was staring, transfixed, when he heard a car roll up on the shoulder behind him. He turned and saw a black and white sedan with red and blue lights mounted on the roof. The officer approached. He looked to be at least sixty-five years old. Short and barrel-chested. A police chief from a nearby small community—Laurel Springs.

"I was on my way to the station and saw you pulled over with the trunk up. Figured I'd better check on you," the chief said.

"I'm all right."

The chief looked up and down the highway shoulder. "I drive by here every day, and almost every day for the last few weeks somebody stops and leaves either a cross or some flowers." He took several steps toward the rental car and looked inside the trunk. "Why did you do that?"

"Just let them be," Ubi muttered. "Let them be."

"What are you talking about?"

"I understand friends want to recognize and honor them, but this isn't the place," Ubi said. "I'm headed to the cemetery. That's where all this stuff belongs."

Ubi put all his weight on both feet for the first time in two days.

"You all right, mister?"

Ubi nodded, yes. The chief pointed to the license plates on the rental car—New York. "You don't sound like you're from New York," he said.

"Texas."

The chief nodded. "I've been in law enforcement for almost forty years, never seen a roadside memorial like this. They must have had a large family."

Ubi interpreted that comment to be the police chief's polite way of asking if he was related to the victims. "The couple is my daughter and my son-in-law," he said.

"I'm very sorry," the chief said and bowed his head. A charter bus swished past in the right lane, the driver oblivious to the two cars and men on the shoulder. "Some folks might be upset with you picking up all this . . . uh, stuff."

"It's just not dignified," Ubi said, a long frown creeping across his face. "Mourning and memorials belong in the cemetery."

"I don't have a problem with what you're doing," the chief said. "A little rain and wind and a few weeks later everything gets scattered, a big mess."

Ubi closed the trunk lid. Next stop, Atlantic Memorial Park. At the cemetery, Ubi carried the crosses and artificial flowers and other mementos to the twin graves. A pale evening sun drifted behind a grove of maple trees and disappeared.

Forty-three

Ubi woke with a crook in his neck and a pang in his chest. Something wasn't right. He had to go back to the cemetery. For the second time in less than twenty-four hours, Ubi found himself at Atlantic Memorial Park. He dug into his khakis front pocket and extracted a handmade rosary—small wooden crucifix, medallion with the image of Mary, and fifty-nine tiny wooden beads all connected by miniscule chain links. He knelt at the foot of the graves, thanked God for the soft, green grass that was easy on his knees and began to pray. He recited from memory various prayers the way he had been taught at the Boys Ranch in Texas, back on the rugged Edwards Plateau where he had grown up after the Orphan Train dumped him at its last stop in San Antonio. The Jesuit priests who adopted him and ran the facility made praying the rosary part of the daily routine. After supper, everyone knelt together in the dining hall, rosary beads wrapped around their fingers.

Remembering those days, Ubi suddenly realized his grandchildren were now orphans, too. But unlike Ubi, who had no idea who his mother and father were, they had roots.

Reciting and counting the prayers on the beads, Ubi knelt at the graves for a half hour. Or was it longer? A maple tree's shadow had traveled across several rows of graves and was now at his feet. Ubi pushed himself upright and looked down on Jeanne and Martin's pink granite headstones. He shoved the rosary beads back in his front pocket.

"Sorry I wasn't here," Ubi said aloud, staring directly at Jeanne's headstone. "Sorry for a lot of things, Sweetums."

*   *   *   *   *

"Jeanne, your father's on the phone," the mother said, poking her head in her daughter's bedroom. "He's calling from California."

191

Jeanne placed the biology textbook face down on the bed where she was studying and made her way into the kitchen. "Hi, Daddy."

"Congratulations on the scholarship. Mom told me all about it. We are so proud of you."

"Thanks. I'm so excited. Can you believe it? I'm going to college on the East Coast." Jeanne's voice came across high-pitched and squeaky on the pay phone receiver. "That is, if I don't flunk this biology final."

"You'll do fine, Sweetums," the distant voice on the phone said. "You worry too much."

"When are you getting in? Still planning on next Thursday, right?"

"That's what I need to talk to you about."

"Don't tell me you're going to miss graduation."

"Well, something came up. It's one of our top clients. They give us more tonnage and better loads than any other company."

"Where are you going this time, Dad? Timbuktu?"

"Please don't be like that, Jeanne. I know you're upset and I understand," Ubi said, frustrated. "And I'm sorry, but I'll be home soon."

"So, where? Where this time, Dad?"

"Ontario. I have to load tomorrow, and have just four days to get there from Sacramento."

"So, you'll be in Canada when your daughter, the class salutatorian receives her high school diploma."

"I'm so sorry, sweetie. You know I'd be there if I could, but—"

"It's all right, Dad," Jeanne said. "I need to get back to studying."

Jeanne handed the phone back to her mother before Ubi could apologize again. The upset mother was short with her husband, too, and soon hung up the phone.

Then—BAM! A sound like muffled thunder coming from Jeanne's bedroom. A peek through the crack in the door. She's lying on the bed, facedown. The hardback biology book upturned on the floor, crumpled against the baseboard. And three feet above it, a hole in the sheetrock.

* * * * *

Ubi fiddled with the rosary in his pocket. He found his handkerchief and blew his nose. "Sounds like an air horn," he said, his voice drifting across the empty graveyard. Ubi's neck was bent at forty-five degrees. His head hung heavy and bobbed as he commenced his soliloquy.

"I can't change the past, Sweetums, but I promise you I'll be here for the kids. And that goes for you, too, Martin." Ubi shifted his gaze to Martin's headstone. "You were a better father, a better man by far, than I have been or could be. But I vow to you both, right here and right now, I will not forsake Molly and Jeremy. I will be here for them. I promise."

Ubi blew his nose again. From the corner of his eye, he saw a small car circle behind him and stop near a concrete bench.

Molly.

Better late than never, Molly muttered to herself, unstrapping her seat belt. She slipped from behind the steering wheel and padded up to Ubi. Red eyes and red nose. Grandpa's been crying? Never expected to see that. Molly gazed at the memorial items Ubi moved from the crash site. "You brought all this stuff from the side of the road, Grandpa?"

"I thought it would better honor Jeanne and Martin here," Ubi said.

"You have no right to do that," Molly said. "Lots of people have stopped, still do, and pray. I mean, Grandpa, what do you think you are doing?"

"People should come here, a peaceful place, to pay their respects," Ubi said.

"That's not your decision."

"Molly, I understand. But look, the highway is loud and cruel and violent and unforgiving. It's not an appropriate place for a memorial."

Molly was taken aback to hear Grandpa Truck talking like that. The highway had always been a glorious place to him. "Sounds like you're down on the road," she said.

"I'm down on a lot of things," Ubi snapped. "I'm down on that truck driver and the company that owns the rig—bad brakes, maypop tires. I'm down on this fake foot. I'm down on bad fuel and bumper-to-bumper traffic. I'm down on people who are always in a hurry." Ubi stopped when he realized he was getting worked up. He didn't want to rant, especially not here, not in front of his granddaughter. His head drooped again. His right foot pawed the grass. "But mostly, I'm down on myself."

Ubi pointed toward the bench near the maple tree. The twosome sat side-by-side. The old trucker regained his composure. "I don't want that stretch of highway to determine how they're remembered. They should be honored for being great parents and a passionate museum director and important writer. Strangers driving by don't need to know someone was killed in that particular spot. It seems cruel, like they are forever haunting the highway there."

Ubi shifted his weight to his right side. "I guess Jeremy told you I'm down to my last leg."

Molly nodded. "Yeah. Sorry, Grandpa," she said in a monotone.

"You think I'm out of line, don't you?"

Molly's eyes opened wide. Grandpa Truck had asked her opinion. That wasn't like him, or like her other grandfather. Both men had to have the first and last say on any topic.

"I see your point," Molly said. "But if you're going to be the caretaker here, you need to straighten those bluebonnets that fell over."

"Bluebonnets, that's the Texas state flower," Ubi said. He pushed up from the bench, leaning on his right foot. How did he miss that? Ubi limped back to the graves and rearranged and straightened the bouquet of plastic bluebonnets.

"One of Mama's high school friends from Texas brought them," Molly explained when Ubi returned to the bench, grunting as he sat down "She flew out for the funeral service."

Ubi locked his eyes on the bluebonnets. Other folks flew in from Texas. Why hadn't he? Of course, the answer was easy. He chose to live a distant life in the High Plains. The remote and open expanse had soothed his soul, but could not save it.

"She asked about you, Grandpa."

"Huh? Who?"

"The woman with the bluebonnets, she asked about you. Well, actually, she asked about Old Ironsides first," Molly said and forced a smile. "She said you took her for a spin in that old truck she'll always remember. Like riding an elephant."

"You remember her name?"

Molly shook her head, no.

"Could've been almost anybody back home in Paisano," Ubi said. "Sheesh, that was long ago."

Ubi and Molly sat in silence. A six-foot brick wall that surrounded the cemetery muffled the din from the highway outside. "How often do you come here, Molly?"

"Every day after school, up until summer band camp, anyway. So I've got some catching up to do," Molly said. After a heavy pause, she looked up at her grandfather. "But not as much as you."

Ubi bristled at that comment, but nevertheless forced a grin. "Guess I had that coming. One thing for sure, you've got your mother's wit and—"

"Sharp tongue?"

"No, her sense of humor and her, uh —"

"Keen intellect?"

"That's it. And you're not bad at finishing other people's sentences."

"I help when I can."

Ubi crossed his good right foot over the bad left one and leaned back. Sheesh, this girl was something else, got spunk like her mama. The two sat silently for several minutes, staring at various grave markers. While Ubi was lost in his ruminations and regrets, Molly turned and examined her grandfather's face. The skin under his eyes had sagged and looked like lakes for catching tears. But those lakes were dry. She couldn't imagine him ever crying, perhaps weeping like when she drove up, but never out and out wailing. Still, Grandpa was no longer the folk hero she remembered as a young girl. He looked tired.

Ubi cleared his throat and said, "I'm not going anywhere. Not until you and Jeremy graduate next spring."

"That's almost a year. Think you can hold out that long? I know how antsy you get in this part of the country," Molly said. "Everything's so crammed together. Fast-paced and loud."

"I'm looking forward to it," Ubi said. "I'm going house hunting soon, plan to rent a place and buy a car."

Molly wrapped her arms around her Grandfather's neck and kissed him on the cheek. "That'll be nice."

Ubi then walked Molly to her car. She opened the door and paused. "I've got a question about something you said earlier."

"Okay, shoot."

"What is a maypop tire?"

"Aw, heck. A maypop. That's a bald tire, one that may pop at any time."

"You are something else, Grandpa."

Forty-four

Ubi hunkered down at the Valley Forge Inn for several days running up a hefty long-distance telephone bill. He needed money to implement his strategy for this new life in a foreign land. That meant daily calls to his accountant in Amarillo. His life savings was tied up in certificates of deposit and U.S savings bonds. No risky Wall Street stocks for this old boy. Get rich quick. Get broke quicker. No thank you.

Ubi's accountant tried to talk him out of liquidating everything, but it was like standing in front of a blue norther and shouting at it to turn around and go back to Canada. A nice-sized check would soon be mailed to the Keystone Savings & Loan branch where Ubi had opened a modest account. It should be enough to buy a used car and make monthly rent and utility payments for many years.

It took three days to reach Stormy Stolz, the truck driver that worked for Ubi hauling grain. Ubi bought a clean, used Peterbilt and hired Stormy to drive it several years ago, back when Ubi was swamped with accounts. He had built relationships with storage bin operators, feed store owners and slaughterhouse managers. They were impressed with Ubi's punctuality and no-nonsense approach.

The search for a driver was a long one, but paid dividends because Stormy had a work ethic like Ubi. Stormy's wife, Meredith, eventually took over the accounting chores. She worked from home, which was only thirty miles from Ubi's small compound, just around the corner to folks in the far reaches of the Panhandle.

After the trio had built themselves a nice little niche hauling grain, Ubi bought himself another rig so he could put Old Ironsides up in dry dock, sandblast the barnacles, take her down to bare metal and rebuild her from stem to stern for the truck museum.

"You want to sell out?" Stormy said from his home phone, Meredith listening on the bedroom extension. "I ain't no bidness man, Ubi, you know that. I'm a truck driver."

"Your wife can handle the paperwork, Stormy. And I'll have my accountant come out and explain taxes and all that fun stuff. Hell, he kept the IRS off my back; he can do it for anybody."

"That's fine, Ubi, but I don't have a lot of savings. How much are we talking about?"

"Not much. Just a little bit a month," Ubi said.

"How long?" Stormy asked. "Forever?"

Meredith then broke in. She kept Ubi's books. She knew a profitable business when she saw one. "Let us talk, Ubi, and we'll get back to you in a few days."

After hanging up, Stormy looked at his wife. "Ubi Sunt wants to sell out and move to the East Coast? He's lost his damn mind."

The cashier's check from the Amarillo accountant rolled in. Time to get out of this tin can on four wheels. But a rust-free, sturdy pickup was a rare commodity in this urban landscape. Ubi finally found one in a farming community near the New York state line. After a three-hour bus ride, he drove off in a used, GMC half-ton with automatic transmission, air conditioning and power door locks. And no more arm strong steering. You could turn the steering wheel with one pinky. What luxury.

Ubi enjoyed moseying around in the pick'em up, as he called it, cruising backstreets and looking for a small house to rent near the high school. And back at the high school he had an oral agreement with Miss Ketchum that he could leave Old Ironsides in a corner of the stadium parking lot until he could drive it to the museum in Iowa or find a large garage.

A week later, Ubi settled into a two-bedroom bungalow on a narrow, tree-lined street on the city's west side. Ubi's first phone call from his new home was to Amarillo. The accountant said he had met with Stormy and Meredith. A smooth transition had been arranged. Ubi would finance the business himself. Two Peterbilts and the compound—ten acres, house and garage—would be repaid with a ten-year note. Everything could be handled either by mail or a newfangled technology called a fax machine in which paperwork is transmitted over telephone wires like magic.

Ubi's second call from his new home was to Molly and Jeremy, living at Katherine and Donald's townhome near downtown. Jeremy was out, but Ubi gave the address and phone number to Molly with an invitation for a visit. When the grandkids arrived a few days later, they brought a house-warming present.

"It's an answering machine," Molly explained. "So you won't miss any calls. And you can check messages from a pay phone."

Ubi hated those gadgets. Call someone and you don't get a real person but a recorded voice. And when you leave a message, Jiminy Cricket, they never call back. But this was part of being more accessible, or more responsible, as Jeanne would have said.

Molly and Jeremy connected the wires and cables and soon had Ubi contemplating what sort of greeting he would record. They flatly rejected his request for them to do the job.

"It's your home," Molly said. "It needs to be your voice."

Ubi mulled the unpleasant task over supper. He had smoked two chickens on a barbecue pit welded from an old propane tank he found in a scrap pile in a vacant lot. Ubi met the high school metal works teacher, Dennis Denison, one day when he stopped to admire Old Ironsides in the stadium parking lot. The teacher said if Ubi ever needed a favor, just ask. So the two men fired up the welding torches at the school's metal shop. It took several hours to complete the transformation from abandoned, junk steel to a Texas-style barbecue pit.

Molly and Jeremy had never seen anything like this homemade contraption. Smoke pouring from a piece of pipe welded to one end, Grandpa slipping chunks of oak he had picked up on his rounds through a door cut in the opposite end. And the chicken made them believers. Juicy, but thoroughly-cooked. Spicy and smoke-flavored without being drowned in sweet and sticky sauce.

Just before the twins left, Ubi sat before the answering machine, took a deep breath. Here goes. "Whatever you're selling, I ain't buying. I either already got it or don't need it. If you're running for office, I already voted, absent-tee, probably for your opponent. If you're a bill collector, the check's in the mail. But if you want to drink a beer or cup of coffee, wait for the beep and leave a message."

Ubi played back the recording for the grandkids. They laughed and winced and rolled their eyes. Grandpa was unconventional, all right, especially compared to their *other* grandfather.

Ubi received his first message the next day when he returned from a doctor's visit to have the prosthetic foot adjusted for a better fit.

"Hello, Mr. Sunt. My name is Yvonne Wilson and I'm calling on behalf of Taylor, Malone and Jones here in Philadelphia. Mr. Taylor would like to schedule an appointment with you as soon as possible."

Sheesh, how did he get the number so quickly? Should've had it unlisted. Ubi returned the call the next morning. Yvonne set an appointment one week away. Ubi had a week to prepare, to consider what Donald Newton Taylor III had been conjuring up in his downtown law office, up on the seventh floor.

Two days before the meeting, a delivery van dropped off a dozen boxes from Texas. Stormy and Meredith had come through, shipped him some clothes and personal effects as promised. Now where's that old suit? Got just enough time to get it to the Korean woman who runs the dry cleaners near that old tavern. One more thing. Seems like there was a barber's pole spinning red, white and blue stripes just down the street from the grocery store. Better stop and get the ears lowered.

On meeting day, Ubi drove the GMC downtown, into the belly of the beast. He scanned the streets and parking lots and side roads for another pickup. Found only one. Climbing the steps before the office building, the suit coat rubbed and scratched his neck and shoulders and forearms. How could anyone get used to wearing one of these every day?

The elevator door opened and Yvonne looked up from her desk. Only appointment at this time is the Texas truck driver. But this man is clean-shaven, fresh haircut, and that suit fits his sturdy frame well. Must be in sales. No, he's too old for that. Maybe a friend of Donald's. Still, not a bad-looking guy for seventy or so.

Ubi offered his hand across the desk and introduced himself. Yvonne stood and unruffled her dress where it had bunched up at her lap. She took Ubi's hand. My, how scratchy, rough, it is. "So, you're the gentleman from Texas? Please have a seat in here," Yvonne said, pointing to a leather chair and sofa in the adjoining waiting room.

"I'd rather stand," Ubi said.

"Very well. I'll tell Mr. Taylor you're here."

Yvonne slipped behind a wood-paneled door and left Ubi alone. Ubi scanned the walls. Framed photographs of Donald and Katherine all over Europe, standing before the Eiffel Tower, Westminster Abbey, the Colosseum. At least he enjoys traveling. Yvonne soon returned and invited Ubi into an empty office. Among several framed photographs on the credenza was a studio portrait of Molly, Jeremy, Jeanne and Martin. Ubi lowered his eyes. A knife to the heart.

Waiting for Donald, Ubi ran through the scenario he expected to face. The twins had already explained that Donald was executor of Jeanne and Martin's estate; thus he had control over their inheritance and a stranglehold on their financial future. Ubi didn't have a problem with that. Donald, no doubt, was rolling in the dough and would be a good steward of whatever assets Jeanne and Martin had left behind. But what if something happened to Donald and Katherine? He probably had that figured out, too. A trustee would be appointed legal guardian and Ubi would be expected to humbly step aside.

Ten minutes later, Donald appeared wearing a custom-tailored Italian suit; his silver-black hair had a fresh coat of paint. The men exchanged pleasantries, settled into chairs on opposing sides of Donald's large oak desk.

Waiting for Donald to commence the meeting, Ubi again mulled the myriad possible scenarios. He wasn't ready to extend an olive branch, but after all, they both wanted the best for Jeremy and Molly. Ubi sat and waited, back straight, head thrust forward, eyes wide open. Surely the two men could find some common ground.

"It's a protective order, also called a restraining order," Donald said, reaching across the desk, holding an envelope. "Any reasonable person would agree that harboring a teenage runaway like you did, crossing numerous state lines. Well, let's just say that sort of behavior is unacceptable."

Ubi opened the envelope, scanned the document.

"It means you are allowed only supervised visitation," Donald said. "No more backyard barbecues. You may attend events such as football games where they march at halftime, but you must remain in the bleachers."

"This is only good until February," Ubi said, looking up. "The twins turn eighteen then."

"A lot can happen between now and then," Donald said, leaning across the desk. "Suffice it to say, I am ready to pull the trigger. I have the documentation prepared to present to the authorities that could lead to your arrest. So, simply stay away from Molly and Jeremy. It's best for you. It's best for them."

Ubi felt himself slumping in the chair. He tried to pull himself up, but couldn't stop sliding down. Then Donald fired off more questions.

"How long a lease did you sign for the rental property?"

"Twelve months."

"Pity you wasted your money. I understand you bought a vehicle. I need to know what kind and color."

"GMC pickup truck. White."

"Figures. Another truck. Very well. It would be wise that it is not found on school grounds or at the cemetery when the children are present. Or, of course, at my home, unless I am there and we have approved an official visit."

Ubi sat in the chair, frozen, embalmed. He was petrified wood, unable to confront his adversary.

Now Donald was standing up, moving from behind his desk and holding the door open. "That'll be all. Have a good day," he said.

It seemed the elevator took forever to come clattering to a stop on the seventh floor. The door opened and Ubi stepped in beside a man in a blue uniform with a nametag, Tony, above the left pocket. Tony said he'd been working on the elevator because it often hung up for no reason, stranding people.

"And you can make it stop between floors," Tony said and pushed the button marked five. The elevator shuddered to a stop.

Ubi grabbed a handrail. "See that. You could sit here as long as you want. And an intern on the fourth floor and her boyfriend have been doing it regularly," Tony said with a wink.

"Why don't you just fix it?"

"We got an estimate, but the building owner wants to save a buck. He ordered me to repair it. I'm waiting on parts."

"Who's the tightwad building owner?" Ubi asked.

"You just visited him on the seventh floor."

Out in the parking lot, Ubi cranked the pickup and reflected on what just happened. Blindsided. Sucker punched. The two warriors had been sparring when the sly attorney slipped one in under the rib cage. And the worst part, you went down without a peep. What next?

Forty-five

Where the hell is Old Ironsides? Ubi circled the parking lot twice—still no Peterbilt. After meeting with Donald, Ubi felt a sudden, inexplicable urge to see his truck. But it was gone. Ubi walked at a fast limp down the hall to the band director's office and pushed back the door so hard it bounced against the wooden stop.

"My truck's gone," Ubi bellowed. "Do you know where it is?"

"Uh, no. Are you sure it's not there?" Miss Ketchum said, looking up from her desk.

"Sure, I'm sure." Ubi thrust his head forward. "It's pretty hard to miss a Peterbilt."

Miss Ketchum stood up and walked around her desk. Her eyes came up to Ubi's chest. "I park out front during summer break," she said, "so I haven't been in the back lot for several days. When was the last time you saw it?"

"Yesterday morning. I drive by almost every day to check on it."

"Let me call the school district police," Miss Ketchum said and picked up the telephone receiver that hung on the wall by the door. "There must be some mistake."

Fifteen minutes later, a woman in a police uniform arrived and explained they had orders from a school board member to tow the truck. It was illegally parked. She gave Ubi the phone number and address for the storage yard where Old Ironsides had been unceremoniously deposited.

"Why would a school board member care about that truck sitting in the back lot, not bothering anybody?" Miss Ketchum mused. "We've got several acres of open asphalt. Besides, everyone except diehard teachers like me is on summer break. It's not like there's a football game tonight and we need the parking spaces."

"I'm just following orders," the officer said and hung her thumbs inside a wide belt. "Maybe somebody made a mistake. Maybe they thought it was an abandoned vehicle."

Ubi cringed at the insult. Innocent as it was, it still hurt. Old Ironsides abandoned? Not on your life.

While the women continued speculating about who instigated the event, Ubi slowly came out of a stupor. It was only a hunch, but he asked Miss Ketchum, "Do you know the names of all the school board members?"

"No, but I can look them up." Miss Ketchum opened a desk drawer and found a recent newsletter that featured all seven members. "Here you go."

Ubi scanned the black-and-white page and immediately recognized a photo. Third from left was Donald Newton Taylor III. Ubi grabbed a pencil off the desk and circled the Attorney General's mug shot. "There's the culprit."

"That's Molly and Jeremy's other grandfather. Why would he have your truck towed?"

"Remember summer band camp?" Ubi asked. "Jeremy no-showed."

Miss Ketchum nodded. "And he was with you in Old Ironsides. Guess that didn't set too well with Mr. Taylor."

"Obviously not," Ubi said. His eyebrows formed a V that met just above the bridge of his nose. "Wait till I get my hands on him." Ubi caught Miss Ketchum frowning, looking a little scared. "Guess I better be headed to the storage yard," he said. "Guess I better look for another place to keep Old Ironsides."

Ubi found Bailey Towing, Paint & Body an hour after leaving the high school. It wasn't far from Sid's Truck Stop in East Philadelphia. Maybe he could leave Old Ironsides there. When things settled down in the fall, he'd drive the truck to the museum in Iowa.

Ubi parked the pickup out front and entered through the steel front door, checkbook in back pocket, ready to pay a king's ransom. One hundred twenty bucks? Jiminy Cricket, what a rip off. Ubi groaned but wrote the check and handed it to the man behind the counter. Ubi noticed the man was wearing his hair with a long mane down the back, but close-cropped on both sides.

"What kind of haircut is that?" Ubi asked in a grouchy and blunt tone.

"It's called a mullet. Where the hell you been, mister? Under a rock?"

"Texas."

"Like I said," the man snapped and led Ubi out the back door and through a garage littered with dead batteries and blown-out tires. What a mess. You can tell a lot about an operation by how they keep their shop. Wouldn't trust these guys to install a set of wiper blades. Let's just find Old Ironsides and get the hell outta here, get over to Sid's. It'll be nice to see a friendly face. Should've visited him before now, especially since we're practically neighbors.

Ubi approached Old Ironsides from the rear bumper. Walking around the passenger side, he saw black symbols and markings spray-painted across the door and side of the sleeper, some sort of cryptic alphabet. Circling the truck, Ubi found that the front had also been desecrated with paint that had dripped and oozed down the grill and bumper. And the driver's door was defiled with more aerosol paint.

"What the hell is this?"

"What do you mean," the man said.

"This graffiti on my truck."

"It wasn't like that?"

"Hell no, it wasn't." Ubi set his jaw and stared at the man. He didn't know why, but that haircut bothered him.

The man pointed at a faded sign hanging on the sagging fence. "Don't they teach you to read in Texas?" he asked. "Not responsible for damage to vehicles."

Ubi found it hard to believe that people would sneak into a crowded and filthy lot just to spray paint somebody's truck. "When did you tow it?" he asked.

"Damn if I know," the man said. "It was sitting out front when I arrived this morning at seven."

"So it sat out front all last night?" Ubi asked. "On the street? In this neighborhood?"

"Well, yeah, guess so. Larry handles the graveyard shift and I don't think he has a gate key."

Too angry to speak, Ubi climbed in the truck. He pushed in the clutch, mashed the starter switch and the diesel engine let out an angry roar. Ubi finessed the stick shift into a low gear and with a steady left foot released the clutch. Damn, the sawed-off old leg was burning like Satan was holding a torch to it. Ubi grimaced and ushered Old Ironsides between a van with four flats and a beverage truck with the hood pointing up at forty-five degrees, jumper cables dangling over the front grill. Ubi eased the truck through the gate and onto the street. He set the brakes, looked down to see old mullet head had followed him and was closing the gate. This was not gong to be easy.

"You got a commercial license?" Ubi asked from his perch in the driver's seat.

"Of course I do," the man snapped. "I'm a tow truck operator."

"I need a favor. Can you drive my rig to the truck stop?"

"I can't go anywhere, mister. I'm on call. This is our busy time of day. Could be an accident on the interstate any time."

Ubi eased down the side of the truck, careful not to put any weight on the left foot. "I spent six months restoring this truck and your driver left it out in the street overnight where he knows it's going to be vandalized," Ubi said, his tone softer. "Just look around, every fence and building in sight has been marked up. Least you can do is help me out, son. I can't push in the clutch, damn foot's acting up." Ubi balanced himself on his right foot. He bent over, grunted, reached down and unlatched the prosthetic foot. He held it up in front of the man's face.

The tow truck driver arced his shoulders. "Damn, mister, I ain't never seen nothing like that. You're down to one good leg."

"So, are you going to help me out or not?"

The last thing Sid Quatro expected to see on a hot summer afternoon was Old Ironsides rolling into his truck stop, defaced with graffiti, and driven by some stranger with a mane like what you would see on a saddle horse.

Ubi had followed in the GMC and parked out front. He explained the circumstances of his return to Philadelphia. Sid knew part of the story because he had helped launch Jeremy's odyssey weeks ago.

"I would have called to warn you," Sid explained, "but the kid was dead set on being the Pony Express. And I don't even have your number."

Sid quickly rolled up the overhead door to an empty tire bay and the man backed Old Ironsides inside. While the two old friends caught up on the recent turn of events, the tow truck driver was chain smoking in the parking lot, anxious to get back to the wrecking yard before his boss found out he had abandoned his post. Out of courtesy to the man, Ubi cut the conversation short and drove him back in the GMC. The man looked relieved when they pulled up in front of the sad fence and dilapidated sheet metal building. The boss's Lincoln wasn't parked out front, so he was in the clear.

Forty-six

Living in a pulsating metropolis took a toll on Ubi's nerves. He had never been around so many people for so long. The nonstop sirens, blasting car horns and thumping automobile stereos rubbed him raw. And the way those auto alarms beeped all night, sheesh, the thieves and vandals must be working overtime. The urban racket propelled Ubi into the lush green and wooded hills west of Philadelphia where he wandered down tree-lined back roads looking for nothing in particular.

Ubi often left the house before the sun's first rays peeked between the skyscrapers and downtown office buildings. And he always stopped at the cemetery on the way home. Sitting on his favorite concrete bench near a young maple tree, he reflected on the price he was now paying for his remote lifestyle. Why didn't he rent that Philadelphia apartment Jeanne had picked out ten years back? Because he'd probably be lying here too, that's why. And that wouldn't have prevented the accident. Wouldn't have put new tires and fresh brakes on the tractor-trailer rig that rammed their car out on the turnpike. So why keep beating yourself up? Who the hell knew their lives would be snuffed out like a candle? Who the hell knows anything, anyway? It's all guesswork. Speculation. Maybe talking to God is like talking to that recorder hooked up to the telephone. Leave a message. Ain't nobody home.

Ubi sometimes lingered on the bench until one of the cemetery workers tapped him on the shoulder. "Sorry, sir, but we gots to close the gate now. Time to go home."

Ubi often returned to his rented home well after sunset. At one point in late June, he hadn't seen the neighborhood, or the city, in full sunlight for six consecutive days.

Ubi sometimes lingered at Sid's truck stop. Sid had furnished him with a can of solvent that made your eyes burn and nose hairs twitch. Little by little, Ubi scoured away the jumbled figures, numbers, geometric shapes, inverted letters. But the work was performed by a listless hand, a man whose passion for his task had waned. This wasn't the same diligent worker who had restored that '56 cabover Peterbilt back in the Texas Panhandle.

July Fourth marked the summer's midpoint. And Philadelphia, cradle of liberty, celebrated with fireworks and parades and music like Ubi had never seen. What revelry. After the holiday, Ubi spent most of his days cruising the Pennsylvania countryside, driving and thinking and not thinking, and stopping for a burger and a Ballantine beer at a favorite tavern. Back home in the evening, the first thing he did was check the answering machine. There were occasional messages from the grandkids, and they had met him twice for lunch, but Ubi figured Jeremy and Molly were too busy. That and the likelihood that Donald had them cowed.

One Saturday morning, a few days before Labor Day, Ubi retrieved the paper from the front porch as usual. Something was stirring in the vacant lot across the street. Something in those weeds. Grasshoppers? Naw, this ain't Texas. Still, something's fluttering about. Then an orange-and-black butterfly flew up, circled several times and landed among low-hanging limbs in the front yard elm.

"You rascal," Ubi said, looking up. "You git. You hear me? Fly away before it gets too cold." Ubi turned and hobbled up the sidewalk to the front porch. He opened the front door and looked back. "Go on now. This is your time to be free. Fly, fly away." Ubi waved at the butterfly with the back of his hand. The butterfly circled several times and disappeared down the street.

Ubi stepped inside the house and flipped the light switch. What the? Who's that lying facedown under a blanket on the couch? Didn't see that a minute ago. Sheesh, walked right past. The figure rolled onto its side and the cover fell to the floor revealing long, thin legs draped over one armrest and a head full of shaggy brown hair pushed up against the other. Sonofagun, can't be but one person.

"Jeremy? When did you get here?"

Jeremy sat up, yawned, stretched his arms overhead. "How can a man get a cup of hot chocolate around here?"

Ubi returned to the kitchen, and a minute later was handing Jeremy a white porcelain cup, hot to the touch. Steam meandered toward the ceiling. Hot chocolate for his old road mate. Ubi wished they were back on the road together.

Stirring and sipping, the grandson explained that he had arrived about two a.m.—used the key Ubi had given him and Molly.

"He's intolerable," Jeremy said. "Insufferable. That trip out West to see you, he hung that over my head like a noose. But I was doing my best to live with it. Molly and I agreed to lie low, especially after we learned about the restraining order. That's why we didn't call or drop by much. After school starts, we figured we would get together more often, see you on the way home, weekends, you know." Jeremy sipped the hot chocolate. He blinked several times and continued. "Things happen fast in the fall, with marching band and classes and stuff, so it would be hard for him to keep such a close watch on us. We were hoping to just ride things out."

"So what the hell happened?" Ubi asked. "You two get into it?"

Jeremy took another drink. His eyes were coming alive, red-rimmed and on fire. "I'm in his study last night looking for a yellow marker to highlight passages in a book I'm reading, *Of Human Bondage*, for fall credit in English. So I accidentally bump over the wastebasket and some papers spill on the floor. I'm picking them up and suddenly I'm holding an envelope with my name on it. It's slit wide open."

"What's inside the envelope?"

"Nothing, it's empty."

"Damn," Ubi said, shaking his head. "He's reading your mail."

"No shit, Grandpa. And guess what address is in the top left corner?"

Ubi fiddled with his coffee cup, turned it around in his hands, gripped the small handle. "I give up. Where's the letter from?"

"South Bend, Indiana."

That night, Ubi tossed in bed, sleepless and restless. Somebody needs to show that man how the cow at the cabbage.

Forty-seven

Oh my stars, you should have seen Donald's face when he returned from lunch today—beet red, flushed like he had been called before the state bar and had his license suspended. I've worked for Donald twenty years and have never seen him so out of sorts. Hold my calls, was all he said before slamming his office door behind him.

Apparently he was stuck in the elevator between the third and fourth floors for ten minutes. People waiting to go up or down heard all this yelling and screaming coming from the elevator shaft. They said it was an awful argument, mostly one-sided. A booming voice with a southern or rural twang was the loudest and most profane. And that person used some colorful language, odd sayings like, "You're plowing a little too close to the cotton," and, "Last time you jumped on me with all four feet, but this time it's gonna be a different tune." But my favorite was, "Get down off your high horse." The thought of somebody confronting Donald in such a manner, in a stalled elevator, well I'm certain no one has dared such a bold move before. And like I said, I've known the man twenty years.

Right after Donald closed himself up in his office, I rushed to the window. A man who looked to be in his late seventies was headed across the parking lot toward a white pickup truck. Favoring his left leg, he walked with a limp.

Forty-eight

Caught between two warring grandfathers is no place to be, Katherine explained sitting on Ubi's couch. And about the night Jeremy slept over here. Donald would have been knocking on your door, waving all sorts of legal paperwork in your face, had I not talked him out of it. Through four decades of marriage, Katherine had always been the one with the cool head, the one who could placate her husband, the one who would convince him to just let some things ride. So Jeremy's one night on Grandpa Truck's couch was no cause for alarm, she explained to her husband—he probably had girl trouble. That's normal for boys his age.

Anxious to hear what the dear old vagabond had to say, Katherine accepted Ubi's invitation for an afternoon visit. Far as she was concerned, the grandkids *should* be free to visit when they wanted, provided they showed good judgment. But she knew her husband was not a man easily crossed. She would like to help, yet she'd seen what happens to people who went up against Donald Newton Taylor III. It wasn't pretty.

"What about dinner Sunday?" Ubi asked "You, Molly and Jeremy."

Katherine's long, thin lips curved into a smile. You crafty old devil, Ubi Sunt. As long as the twins are with me, Donald can hardly object to a visit. Maybe it *was* time to call Donald's bluff. When he realized what an ass he was being, that carrying a grudge was hurtful to the family, maybe he'd back off. And if he wouldn't lighten up, she had an ace in the hole.

Katherine hadn't said anything about that little incident with the receptionist, Yvonne, down in Boca Raton twelve years ago. In the sailboat, of all places. But Katherine knew. And he knew that she knew, although they had never discussed it. So, she felt it best for Jeremy and Molly to see their crusty, eccentric Grandpa Truck more often. And if Donald wanted to cross her on this, well, her hole card was a wild card; she could embarrass and humiliate him, not to

213

mention put a dent in his wallet. Oh no, she wasn't looking for a divorce. She still loved him, albeit the relationship was a strained and often difficult one. But for once, she had the upper hand. For once, she would have control. For once, she held the cards. And it tasted . . . oh, so sweet. Okay, we'll be guests for dinner. Just say when.

The morning of the visit, Ubi woke early, slow smoking a beef brisket on the barbecue pit. After tending the fire all day and sipping several Lucky Lagers, it was no surprise that Grandpa Truck's eyes were a little bloodshot.

Standing in the backyard chatting with Jeremy, Ubi closed the damper on the smoker's chimney to snuff out the coals and embers. A cigarette would be nice, but better not. Once you start again, it's hell to stop.

Then a mischievous, arcing smile lit up Jeremy's face. "I got a hold of South Bend," he said, eyes sparkling, radiating.

Ubi leaned close to Jeremy. "What's up?"

"Terri and Kelli are coming to the East Coast this spring, resuming their quest to visit all the state capitals, starting down south." Jeremy counted off the capital cities on his fingers. "Atlanta, Columbia, Raleigh, Richmond, Dover — "

"Harrisburg," Ubi said.

"Ten-four, Grandpa. And Harrisburg is just up the road, maybe an hour or so drive."

Ubi's jaw dropped in surprise. Crevices ran coast-to-coast across his forehead. Those Indiana gals were special. And to see Jeremy strike up a romance on the road with cute Kelli—freckles and all—well, it made *him* feel young again. When was the last time that happened?

"So, here's the plan," Jeremy said. "Before they visit Harrisburg, they're coming to Philadelphia for a few days."

"Y'all better stop by for a visit," Ubi said. "By the way, did you ever find out what happened to the missing letter?"

"Nope. I snooped and dug through that study every chance I got for days," Jeremy said. "He had to know somebody was digging around in there. And actually, one time, I heard him blame it on Grandmother."

"What did Katherine say?"

"She blew him smooth off, said he was paranoid."

"Did you ever confront him?"

"No, I didn't. Last summer out on the road, I learned to choose your battles."

"Do you think he knows that you are onto him? You know, about reading your mail."

"Probably not. And I had Kelli write another letter, a Dear John letter, calling the whole thing off."

"Clever."

"So far as the Attorney General knows—"

"You call him the Attorney General?"

"I thought I told you that back in Texas," Jeremy said. "Molly came up with that name a long time ago. And it especially fits after all that crap with the restraining order blew up. Anyway, far as he knows, the Indiana girls are history."

"Okay," Ubi said. The last vestiges of smoke trickled from the chimney. "But did Kelli tell you what she wrote in that first letter?"

"Yep, she said it was perfectly innocent."

Ubi inhaled, breathed in the smoke. It smelled like Texas.

Forty-nine

Hazy and humid August surrendered to clear and cool September. The pleasant afternoons spurred Ubi into refurbishing Old Ironsides, but it was painstaking and slow. The solvent and electric sander he used to erase and rub out the markings left the truck spotted. Matching the paint would be next to impossible. To do it right, he would again have to take it down to bare metal. Another complete paint job so soon after the last one? Ubi wasn't excited about that.

Ubi spent Friday nights sitting in the bleachers at Liberty High School football games. He learned where the band families sat and joined them. They didn't care much about the game, but during halftime everyone stood and applauded every song. Their enthusiasm struck a chord with Ubi. He cheered and rubbed shoulders with the folks packed tightly together, all smiling and bobbing up and down to the rhythm and beat. Week after week, the band's halftime show eclipsed the football team's performance.

The band parents quickly accepted Molly and Jeremy's eccentric grandfather into the fold. "I just adore that old man's country accent," a band mom said.

One family invited Ubi to dinner. His reply was, "I ain't so busy."

"What does that mean? Ain't so busy."

After a few more questions, the confusion was cleared up. Ubi was saying something to the effect, "I'm not so busy that I can't take time to accept your invitation."

"We still laugh about that one," a band mom later recalled. "Anybody want a cup of coffee from the concession stand? Ain't so busy."

On a somber note, some families offered condolences, heartbroken about what happened last spring. But for others, broaching the subject was too painful and they reverted to small talk.

While Ubi mixed with the band families, Donald and Katherine sat high above the field in a glass shell that was reserved for sportswriters and school district big wigs. If Donald ran across Ubi, before or after the game, he didn't acknowledge it. But Katherine would always nod or wave or come up and say hi. She had grown fond of old Grandpa Truck, his Texas drawl and his unpretentious demeanor. Refreshing. And being friendly to Ubi was good for the twins. It looked like Ubi was here to stay, at least until spring graduation. Donald needs to get over it. Animosity poisons families.

Ubi often hung around after the game. He watched the band members load their instruments into a semi-trailer pulled by a faded, mustard-yellow rental truck. Ubi examined it up close, poking his head under the back of the cab. Volvo with a 430 Detroit diesel. Thirteen-speed transmission. But look at the oil puddle under it. Listen to it idle. Missing badly. Might need new injectors. Ubi made friends with the driver and they would talk shop during the fourth quarter when the Screaming Eagles football squad wasn't screaming anymore. At one point in the season their record was one win and five losses.

The annual rivalry game with the Ashbury Heights Falcons arrived on a bitterly cold Friday night in November. Falcons versus Eagles, two proud birds of prey. Ubi was bundling up in layers when the phone rang. It was the band director, Miss Ketchum. She was hysterical and couldn't complete a sentence.

"That yellow piece of shit."

"Huh?"

"That puke yellow truck we rented. It's a hunk of junk."

"Sheesh, I coulda told you that."

"It broke down in the parking lot outside the band hall, loaded with all of our equipment. This is a road game at Ashbury Heights, thirty miles away. We've got two hours until kickoff."

Ubi then knew why Miss Ketchum had called. "We can use Old Ironsides," he said. "You never did get that ride."

"If we could do that," Miss Ketchum said, her voice rising with fresh hope, "I'll have them rename the school in your honor."

"No need to do that," Ubi said, his mind racing. "Just relax, I'll run down to Sid's Truck Stop and get the truck. Then meet you at the school."

"Fantastic, and make it quick as you can," Miss Ketchum said. "This is our biggest night of the year. The football team may be pathetic, but we so love showing up the Ashbury Heights Band."

Ubi pushed the pickup across town to Sid's faster than he'd driven any vehicle since racing that Maverick through the Ozarks last summer. But it was still a thirty-minute drive; he had time to worry about his left leg. A specialist had adjusted the prosthetic foot and he had gone to physical therapy a few times. It fit and felt much better. But could he operate that stiff old clutch? Both possibilities loomed large until the GMC pickup veered into the truck stop lot and Ubi realized Sid's was closed. Oh, shit. Forgot Sid had mentioned he was going to cut back on hours. Business was slow. Ubi had Sid's home phone number in an address book at the rent house. That did no good. Gonna have to break in. Good thing Sid is old school and doesn't have an electronic security system with those motion detectors. Good thing he doesn't have that Doberman anymore, too. Ubi snooped around the perimeter of the three-bay garage, pulling doorknobs. No luck. Then he tried all three rollup, overhead bay doors. The first two wouldn't budge, but the third one had a little play in it. Ubi found a two-by-four near the dumpster and used it to pry up the door a couple feet. Squirming and kicking on his back like an upturned insect, he managed to get his head through, but his belly hung up. Sheesh, the old khakis have been fitting tight, come to think of it. Need to find somebody thin, somebody skinny as a rail like Jeremy. And need to find 'em quick.

Ubi stood on the curb. Looked both ways. Not much traffic on a blustery November night in this part of town. What's that noise? A booming car stereo. A four-door sedan. Those chrome wheels must cost a bundle. And she's riding just inches above the asphalt. Must have removed all the shock absorbers. Hoodlums? Thugs? Gang members? So what.

Ubi stepped into the street and held his hands above his head. The driver turned down the godawful pounding coming from the car speakers and craned his neck out the window. "Who said stick 'em up?" he said with a snicker, looking at his four passengers to see if they were laughing.

Ubi ignored the joke. "Hey, you want to make twenty quick bucks? One of you kids has to slide under that garage door and unlatch it so I can get my truck out."

"You want us to break into that truck stop for twenty dollars?"

"Okay, thirty. That's my rig locked inside and I need it right away."

The driver leaned over the back seat and said to a wiry youngster, "Stick, we got a job for you."

Stick pulled his sweatshirt hood over his head and climbed out of the car. Ubi watched him look left and right and then drop to his knees before the garage door. Slithering and wiggling, he slowly disappeared inside the shop. Ubi shouted through the crack in the door how to open the overhead latch. A minute later, Ubi climbed in Old Ironsides and pushed hard on the clutch with his left foot. A little pain, but he could handle it. Ubi then jammed a thumb against the starter knob. The sleepy diesel stretched and yawned, shaking and vibrating the truck cab. The young men riding in the low-slung car had all climbed out to watch. A broken down old man in a broken down old truck.

Ubi flipped on the amber clearance markers but left the headlights off. The Peterbilt silhouette eased out of the garage—a hibernating bear climbing out of a mountainside cave. Ubi pulled the truck forward into the lot and set the brakes. He rolled down the overhead door, locked it and exited the side door, locking it behind him. He then approached Stick, cash in hand. He refused the money.

"We're cool, Gramps," Stick said, holding up two elongated hands. "Dat's a wild old truck you got there."

"I'm not stealing it, if that's what you're thinking," Ubi said. "This is my friend's truck stop and I'm keeping it here to repaint after some thugs sprayed graffiti all over it. I have to help out some friends and haul a trailer for them tonight."

All five teenagers were now standing near the curb. "Youz guys hear dat? He's gotta do a friend a favor," the driver and apparent leader said with a smirk. "But he's da one paying somebody to break inta the shop. Sounds like some shit I woulda made up." The others laughed and pushed their hands deep inside their sagging jeans pockets.

"All right, all right," Ubi said. "I gotta roll. You boys stay out of trouble and don't break into any more buildings unless I say so."

Ubi and Old Ironsides rumbled down the dark street. Taillights disappeared around a corner. The gang leader asked Stick why he had refused Ubi's money.

"What's the matta witch you? Thirty bucks woulda bought enough gas to cruise all night."

"Did you see the paint job on that truck?" Stick said. "All spotted like a fucking Jersey cow?"

"Yeah. So what."

"I tagged it one night last summer when it was sitting on the street at that junk yard."

"I outta slap the shit out of you," the leader said. "Wasting good paint like that."

Twenty minutes later at the high school, Old Ironsides rolled down the driveway toward the band hall. The headlight beams blinded Miss Ketchum. She immediately started waving and hopping like she was performing jumping jacks. The rental truck driver had already unhooked the asthmatic Freightliner, coughing, choking and spitting, and parked it out of the way. Ubi backed under the trailer, which was painted with gold letters and an eagle, wings fully expanded. Working quickly despite his limp, Ubi connected the air hoses and electrical line.

Tiny Miss Ketchum climbed up the side of the cab like a human fly. Sitting in the shotgun seat, she opened a plastic pill bottle full of white tablets.

"I can usually make it until the second quarter," she said, throwing her head back and swallowing two tablets dry. "But this has already been a long night and we're not even at the stadium."

Old Ironsides rolled into the stadium parking lot just as the football team kicked off. The band members swamped the truck, wouldn't give Ubi room to maneuver. In the cab, Ubi tugged the cable hanging from the ceiling, long and low like a foghorn. The crowd parted. Up in the skybox, Katherine and Donald heard the discharge. They stood and peered over the end zone bleachers—a clear view of the scene below.

"What's going on?" Donald asked. "Some kind of commotion down there."

"Oh, my. It looks like Old Ironsides," Katherine answered.

Donald grabbed a sportswriter's binoculars. "Let me see." Looking down on the parking lot, he recognized the forty-five-foot trailer Old Ironsides was pulling. "What happened to that yellow diesel we leased?"

"Probably broke down," Katherine answered. "Miss Ketchum said it was a piece of you know what."

Donald and Katherine traded the binoculars several times. Worker ants were climbing into the trailer and distributing drums, horns, flags, pennants and other props. In no time, the ants had stripped the trailer clean and were adjusting chin and shoulder straps. About ten minutes later, the Liberty High School Band, wearing gold uniforms with green trim, strutted down the stadium entrance blasting out their fight song—*Fly Like an Eagle*. And a student wearing an eagle costume with a white crown and yellow beak raced down the sidelines, wings unfolded. Up the stadium steps the band marched, playing and stamping into the reserved section near the fifty-yard line. Parents and students jumped to their feet, energized, clapping their hands and stomping the aluminum bleachers in time with the song.

But out on the field, the Falcons scored a lightning-fast touchdown on a run down the sideline by a star player who has a track scholarship waiting. The teams traded punts until just before halftime when the Screaming Eagles quarterback surprised everyone with a sneak up the middle for thirty yards. With seconds on the clock, a long field goal attempt caught a tail wind and drifted through the uprights. Half time score: Ashbury Heights 7. Liberty 3.

Earlier on the drive to the stadium, Miss Ketchum insisted Ubi watch the halftime show from the sidelines as the band's guest of honor. Ubi managed to stand for the entire performance and marveled at the simultaneous marching, drumming and instrumentation. He followed Jeremy bobbing back and forth and breathing life into the same saxophone he had carried across the country and back last summer. If that instrument could talk. Wait a minute, Jeremy's making that sax talk right now. And there goes high-stepping Molly and her flute, nimble fingers working the keys.

Under the windy and cold conditions, the game stagnated until late in the fourth quarter when the Screaming Eagles came down from their nest. The offensive line pushed back the defenders, opening creases that the fullback exploited with short bursts of power. The coach continued calling his sturdy fullback's number. Like Old Ironsides pulling a steep grade in low gear, the fullback churned out the yardage, dragging tacklers with him. With two minutes left in the game, the Screaming Eagles crossed mid-field. The coach signaled time out. The players dropped to one knee, gulped sports drinks, and took long, deep breaths. Then the coach climbed onto a bench, raised his right hand, signaled Miss Ketchum up in the stands that he wanted *that* song.

The drummers and horn section broke into a wall of sound. The pep squad, cheerleaders, students and most of the parents stomped the aluminum bleachers. The Eagles side of the stadium was louder than anything Ubi could ever remember hearing. He looked up into the stands behind him. Either he was dizzy from the pain in his left leg or the bleachers were swaying. Then the student body raised their hands high above their heads, fingers curled up like claws. And would you listen to 'em chanting, waving their hands like a bird flying.

"I want to fly like an eagle, to the sea."

With the visitor's side of the stadium yelling the team on, the Screaming Eagles rushed onto the field and huddled up. Play after play, the hefty fullback bit hard on his mouthpiece, took the quarterback's handoff and plunged into the line. The defense knew what was coming but was helpless to stop it. The fullback rolled up the yards, four, five, six at a time. The opposing coach then called timeout and changed his defense, stacking the line to bottle up the Eagles running back. Two plays later, the quarterback faked a handoff and scampered around the right side into the end zone.

The Screaming Eagles side of the stadium erupted. Hands held high. Clenched fists held high. An index finger held high like the team was number one even though it had a losing record. Jumping up and down hugs. Hugs with strangers. High-fives and more hugs. Liberty had prevailed.

Back in the parking lot, the band members loaded their instruments into the trailer while Miss Ketchum checked things off on a clipboard. Satisfied that all was accounted for and in order, she directed Jeremy and another band member to close and lock the trailer doors. Jeremy and Molly spotted Grandpa Truck huddled out of the wind, cradling a Styrofoam cup of coffee under the bleachers. They introduced a few friends and shared childhood memories of rides in Old Ironsides. The band members then climbed into a yellow school bus. The vehicle bounced over several speed bumps and onto the street. As the taillights disappeared, Miss Ketchum tucked her clipboard under her arm and approached Ubi.

"I know the band didn't block anybody or tackle anybody, but we energized that crowd and the team. We made a difference," she said, wrapping an arm around Ubi's waist.

"When the football team needed the band, the band came through," Ubi said.

"It's been a long year, winning only one game before tonight. But this was magical. Thank you for saving the day." Miss Ketchum stood on her toes and pecked Ubi on his cheek. "Do you mind if I ride home with my boyfriend? We haven't spent much time together lately. Just leave the trailer where you picked it up and we'll unload it tomorrow."

Ubi bid Miss Ketchum good night and climbed into Old Ironsides. He had driven to the stadium fueled by pure adrenaline. But the left leg was back to its old painful ways. Could he make the return trip? Reaching up to the console, Ubi pushed in the parking brake valves. He had parked on a slope and the rig inched forward. Without using the clutch, he slipped the stick shift into gear and the truck rolled free. He could drive like that, slipping gears and timing stop lights, and make it back to the stadium okay. It was late evening and the traffic would be light. Ubi goosed the accelerator and headed toward the exit. A silver Jaguar suddenly cut him off, made Ubi lock up the brakes. The Jaguar zipped into the street and disappeared.

"Why did you have to do that?" Katherine scolded. "You purposely went out of your way to interfere."

"Oops, sorry about that," Donald said, the corner of his mouth upturned in a sneer. "Didn't see it."

"Didn't see an eighteen-wheeler? Donald, you are so jealous you're green around gills."

Fifty

Metal works and auto mechanics teacher, Dennis Denison, relished his Saturday mornings at Liberty High School. That's when he could tinker with his latest lesson idea like how to extract a broken spark plug from an engine block. The morning after the big game against Ashbury Heights, he rolled up in his yellow Volkswagen Thing, an unfinished project he bought dirt-cheap last year, and stopped before Old Ironsides. What a shame. Look at the paint. Desecrated by delinquents. Hmmm, looks like somebody has begun removing the graffiti. See the spots sanded and buffed down to bare metal?

Dennis climbed out of the VW, zipped his lined windbreaker up to the neck, and pulled his collar up. He walked to the back of the rig. Now the truck's shaking. What the heck? And somebody's crawling out of the sleeper. It's the old-timer with the funny name like something they would teach in Latin class. The man who took an old propane tank and turned it into a Texas smoker.

Ubi climbed down from the rig, favoring his left leg. He recognized the friendly shop teacher, a kindred spirit who liked to mess and fiddle with stuff, making something out of nothing.

"How 'bout a cup of coffee?" Dennis said. "I'll fire up a pot in the lounge."

Ubi followed the teacher inside and explained he had camped out in the rig, too tired to drive home. Dennis went to work pouring water, scooping coffee grounds, flipping a switch. A few minutes later, he poured two cups of steaming salvation. The two men pulled up hard plastic chairs before a round table. Ubi's left leg felt more swollen and more painful than he could remember.

"If you don't mind me saying, you don't look too good."

Ubi dismissed the comment and forced a grin. He reached in his shirt pocket and pulled out a small packet of BC Powder. Ubi tore open the little envelope and shook the white contents into his coffee. Stirring the concoction vigorously, Ubi examined the insulated

225

coffee mug with red, cursive letters stenciled on it—*Virtue, Liberty and Independence.*

"That sounds like something we'd say in Texas," Ubi said, taking a sip, then another.

"It's our state motto," Dennis said.

"No kidding. Well, I lived by that motto myself. But last night I witnessed something different, something I had been missing out on."

"What's that?"

"Teamwork. Those kids and parents and coaches, they all pull together."

"That was a great night," Dennis said. A couple of quiet sips passed. Dennis leaned across the table. "Last night, Miss Ketchum mentioned some thugs spray-painted your truck. This morning I saw it for the first time. Damn shame."

"It happened after it was towed. A wrecker driver left it sitting out overnight in front of a wrecking yard."

"It looks like you could use some help restoring it," Dennis said. "I mean, it was looking good when you arrived last summer. What a shame to see it like that, all, all . . . well you know."

Ubi mulled the offer, sipping the coffee. Help repainting Old Ironsides? Sheesh, why would he want that?

"I've always worked alone."

"But you just said that last night you saw firsthand the value of teamwork," Dennis continued. "If you don't mind me saying, you could use some assistance. I saw you wincing when you climbed down from the truck just now. I don't see how you can put weight on that left leg at all, much less work on this rig."

"I'm not going to lie to you," Ubi said. "Sometimes it hurts like hell. I've had it looked at. And it was feeling better until last night. So, yes, I know I'm going to have to do something about it."

"I can check with our school nurse, see if she can refer somebody," Dennis said. "Meanwhile, I have sanding machines and students who need a class project for their senior portfolio."

Ubi stood and grimaced, his leg burning again. His cup was half empty, but he wanted a warm-up anyway.

"Don't take this wrong, Mr. Sunt, but —"

"Call me Ubi."

"Okay. Ubi, you need to learn to accept some help. Help with your truck and help with that bad leg."

Ubi topped off his mug. "You make a decent cup off coffee, schoolteacher." He held up the glass pot and looked at Dennis, a way of asking without words if he needed a refill. Dennis waved him off. Ubi sat down again. The lounge was empty except for the two men. The shop teacher fiddled with his watch, waiting for a reply. Ubi sat silently. With the long years on the road now in the rear view mirror, he reflected on Old Ironsides' future.

He hadn't done a good job of keeping in touch with the Iowa Truck Museum. After the trip with Jeremy last summer, he called the director and explained that for personal reasons he had to postpone delivery. But that was his last communication. And now all these setbacks—the aching stump at the bottom of his left leg, a vandalized truck, a feud with Donald—had delayed those plans indefinitely. Still, Old Ironsides belongs on display at that museum. For posterity. To let folks experience a little piece of transportation history. So this project would be unlike the restoration work back home. This would be teamwork, all right. But what about these kids? Who would keep an eye on 'em so they didn't screw up?

"I would have to supervise," Ubi said.

"Of course, of course," Dennis answered, waving his hand excited that the long silence had ended and Ubi was interested in his idea. "But you have to be available during class time."

Ubi chuckled. "Ain't so busy."

The following week, Ubi showed four seniors how to unbolt Old Ironsides' twin stacks so the truck would fit inside the high school shop bay. Initially, the young men and the old trucker had little in common. But Old Ironsides spanned generations, lifestyles, cultures; it was a bridge between the past and present, a highway that connected the Southwest to the Northeast. Although their attention to detail was somewhat lacking, the kids' enthusiasm was uplifting. And they weren't bad company, once you figured out what language they were speaking.

The students' slang and urban culture was both peculiar and intriguing. *Youz guys* was like saying y'all. *Dint* wasn't always a depression in the sheet metal; sometimes it was the contraction

227

didn't. *Dat* was that. *Dis* was this. An *idear* was a promising thought. And *get outta town* was like saying you must be joking.

And of course, Ubi's exclamations such as *sheesh* and *Jiminy Cricket* and *holy smokes* and *for crying out loud, keep your cotton-picking hands to yourself this ain't no place for horseplay* amused the students. They gradually incorporated the phrases into their lexicon.

"Sheesh, whoever used the cotton picking sander last dint do a good job rolling up the extension cord. What a mess. Dis looks like a rat's nest, for crying out loud."

The students had the most fun with the manner in which Ubi used "fixing to."

"Get it through your heads, fixin' don't always mean repairing something," Ubi explained one day when confusion reigned over his comment that he was "fixin' to take a leak." The students assumed he was about to replace a hose that had been dripping. But Ubi meant that he was going to the men's room.

"It's like you're about to, or getting ready, to do something," Ubi explained. "Like, hand me that wrench. I'm fixing to unbolt the mirror bracket."

Invigorated by the restoration work, Ubi contacted the Iowa Truck Museum. After the twins graduated in May, he would deliver Old Ironsides to her rightful place of high honor.

"Of course, we're still interested," the director said. "Call when it's ready and we'll make room to display it at the main entrance. Summertime is a good time."

Fifty-one

Despite her husband's objections, Katherine set a place for Ubi at the Thanksgiving dinner table. Jeremy's summer adventure with Grandpa Truck was six months ago. Get over it, dear. And Ubi, sorry that Donald had your truck towed and it was spray-painted, but it's time to move on. I hear from the grandkids that the restoration work at the high school metal shop is coming along nicely. Please keep it cordial, gentlemen. No sports or politics.

"So, Ubi, I guess you saw the Eagles beat the Cowboys 31-7 on Monday Night Football."

"I said no sports," Katherine fumed.

"What about the election? An Arkansas Democrat trounced *two* Texans," Donald said. "How do you feel about that?"

"Dear, must you?"

Although the two men acted civilly toward each other at the dinner table, Katherine felt she needed the same carving knife she used on the turkey to cut the tension in the room. My goodness, they should be able to put up with each other for a couple afternoons during the holidays. And who knows what next year brings? Molly and Jeremy have both applied to various universities, all far from home. No surprise there.

Ubi spent most of Christmas break alone. He revisited the dog-eared pages of poetry volumes he carried with him on the road. Some of the collections were gifts from his wife, Sherry. Others he had picked up over the years. Reading on the road, up in the bunk at night, he sometimes fell asleep with his favorite voices: Dickinson, Frost, and Walt Whitman, who had a local connection. Roads and schools, a shopping center and a major bridge over the Delaware River were named in Whitman's honor.

Ubi considered picking up the pen again, like he did when he was waiting weekends for a load. Messing with words was fun. Like shifting gears and driving Old Ironsides, it took finesse and patience and confidence. But hold on. Who are you kidding? Driving an eighteen-wheeler is like writing poetry? Well, maybe. The cadence running through ten, thirteen gears, rising and falling rpms, then a steady hum and . . . sheesh, why does a person torture himself like that?

Ubi looked forward to school resuming. He would catch up with those characters, students he had befriended, and finish repainting Old Ironsides. Back in early December, he ordered the same shade of red paint from the dealer in Texas that he had used before. But there was a problem. Mr. Dennison couldn't get permission to paint in his shop anything larger than a lawnmower. Regulations, he said—school, city, state, federal—required a ventilated painting booth. So Ubi visited the owner of the wrecking yard and body shop where his truck had been sullied. It took a little arm-twisting, but things worked out.

"It happened right here, right in front of *your* gate where *your* driver left it," Ubi said, standing in the man's office, pointing out the window to the curb where Old Ironsides had been hogtied, dragged and abandoned. "Besides, it's a senior class project for some students at Liberty High. Those kids been busting ass for weeks. Now all that's left to do is paint it. They've worked hard, sowed the seeds. So help 'em reap the harvest." The owner relented, allowed Ubi and his boys access to his painting booth.

Throughout January and February, a wintry mix of ice, sleet and snow shrouded the East Coast in a blanket of misery. Everyone complained, at school, at work, at home, about the daily grind of shoveling sidewalks and driveways and scraping and defrosting windshields. The city snowplow drivers worked overtime pushing the frozen mess into Peterbilt-sized piles of slush where large tractors loaded buckets and buckets into dump trucks that hauled away the wet and heavy mess. Just when workers had wedged a toehold in city streets and people could get around again, another storm would pounce and immobilize the metropolis and surrounding counties. Then the whole process started anew.

The snow and frozen roads curtailed Ubi's countryside meanderings as well. But he found fulfillment by bundling up and limping a half-mile to the public library where he spent numerous days prowling the poetry section. Then there were the long nights.

Watching television left him empty. Bored and restless, he sometimes scrawled verses on the back of envelopes, utility bills, scratch pads. He left the paper scraps with numerous scratch outs scattered about the house. During their infrequent visits, Jeremy and Molly came across the scraps of paper with short verses scribbled on them. It reminded them of the postcard poetry he often mailed when they were in grade school. One day, for no apparent reason, the twins gave him a bound leather notebook. Ubi then compiled his poetry in the journal. Not a bad antidote for wintertime, big city claustrophobia.

Big dreams, long road.
Big wheels, heavy load.
Keep 'em turning.
Long days, short years.
Slow down, face fears.
Keep on learning.

Winter gradually loosened its glacial grip on Eastern Pennsylvania. The budding dogwoods and cherry trees, honeysuckle and marigolds marked the inevitable change of seasons. But fickle spring was a tease. A morning cruise through the countryside could quickly become an afternoon dash back to the city. Slippery roads. Wipers slapping at wet snow outside. Defroster blowing warm air inside.

On one such trip, a small town policeman pulled over Ubi's pickup for going a few miles over the speed limit. Ubi handed over his driver's license.

"Texas? Geez, mister, you're a long way from home. And you're expired. I mean your license is expired. Of course, if *you* had expired we wouldn't be having this conversation."

Ubi was taken aback. Officer has a sense of humor, a little morbid, maybe, but refreshing in its own way. So many tense folks back East. The policeman wrote Ubi a warning.

The next day, Ubi visited the state department of motor vehicles branch near his house. The young officer standing behind the counter wouldn't renew his license. To keep a commercial license, a driver has to pass a physical exam every two years.

"I need to take a physical?" Ubi said, frowning. "Sheesh, I plum forgot."

The next morning, Ubi visited a clinic that performs routine physical exams for drivers who hold a commercial license. A petite, young nurse with a tantalizing smile and braided hair, stethoscope dangling from her neck, examined his Texas driver's license. This old-timer must've taken a wrong turn in Forth Worth.

Ubi's eyesight was keen, almost 20-20. Pulse okay. Blood pressure borderline high. All that coffee, he explained. Ubi then had to take off his shoes to be measured and weighed. He hoisted himself on the exam bench. Stiff, white paper crumpled under his weight. Off came the right shoe. Now the left. Ubi unbuckled the two small latches at the ankle, and pulled.

"Let me help," the nurse said, gently tugging at the black boot until it wiggled free. "Oh, you're wearing a prosthetic foot," she said, unfazed, holding the boot. "When did this happen?"

"About ten years back," Ubi answered.

"You must've been in an accident."

"It was bit off."

"Are you kidding me?" The nurse said, feigning surprise by dropping her lower jaw. "Alligator?"

"Nope."

"Shark attack?"

Ubi shook his head. "Negatory."

"What?"

"Ditch Dragon."

"Ditch Dragon?" the nurse repeated. "I think you're pulling my leg."

"You been pulling mine."

The nurse flashed a warm smile. "You are something else, Mr. Tex," she said and tossed a friendly, backhanded slap at Ubi's left arm, her stethoscope shaking all around.

"I got a special waiver to drive," Ubi said. "Look on the back of my old license."

"I'm sorry to be the one to break the news," she said, "but if you want a Pennsylvania commercial license, sir, you're going to have to take a road test."

"A driving test?" Ubi said, squinting. "I've been driving eighteen-wheelers since before you were born. I've driven across forty-eight states, eight Canadian provinces, more'n three million miles. And I have to take a driving test?"

"With this strapped to your calf you do," the nurse said, turning Ubi's prosthetic foot over in her hands. "As far as the state of Pennsylvania is concerned, it doesn't matter if you drove to the moon and back six times."

"I gotta think about this," Ubi said, wiggling on the exam bench.

"It's none of my business," the nurse asked, "but why do you want to drive a truck?"

"Why do you want to be a doctor?" Ubi snapped. The lighthearted conversation had turned sullen.

"Sorry if I touched a nerve, sir."

Ubi slipped on his right work boot and slid down from the exam bench. "My foot, please," he said. Ubi strapped the contraption on his left leg and yanked open the door. The knob banged the wall, leaving a hole in the sheet rock. He ambled down the corridor. The nurse followed at a distance.

Outside in the parking lot, Ubi slammed the pickup's automatic transmission into reverse and backed out of his parking space. A blaring horn warned how close he had come to getting hit. Ubi pulled back in the parking spot and killed the engine. He sat there for ten minutes, maybe more. Mind racing. Passing a driving test was impossible; he couldn't work the clutch. No commercial license. No identity. No badge of honor. A nobody. And this meant someone else would have to drive the Peterbilt to the Iowa Truck Museum. But he wanted to be the one to ride Old Ironsides on the last roundup, the final drive up the trail to the green meadow the old mare so richly deserved. Have to figure all that out later, but right now—something more urgent.

Ubi hobbled back into the clinic, past the receptionist, "Sir, you can't go in there," and found the young physician examining an X-ray. The nurse blinked and stared at the Texan who had just stormed out of the clinic. Didn't even pay his bill. "May I help you, sir?"

"I'm sorry about how I acted," Ubi said. "Yes, I'm old and crotchety, and this damn stump where my left foot used ta be is acting up, and for the first time in sixty years I have no driver's license. Still, that's no excuse." Ubi held out his right hand. "Please accept my apology."

"Apology accepted." The nurse took Ubi's hand, squinted at this strange man from a faraway place, and squeezed it tightly. "So what's up with this Ditch Dragon anyway?"

"Aw heck, that's a scary story I used to tell the grandkids. Ditch Dragons live on the side of the road and come out at night to get truck drivers. Like this." Ubi raised both arms over his head and curled his fingers downward to look like claws.

"Sounds like you got a lot of stories."

Ubi nodded. Then a sad smile crept across his face. A minute later, standing at the front desk with an open checkbook, he asked the receptionist to add an extra charge for the damaged wall.

Fifty-two

The twins turned eighteen on Valentine's Day. Actually, Molly was born a few minutes before midnight on February thirteenth. Jeremy arrived shortly after. But they always celebrated their birthday on the fourteenth. Ubi had invited them over for dinner, a crockpot of beef and vegetable stew that had simmered all day. And carrot cake that he baked himself. Been practicing all week. Ubi gave them each a framed black-and-white photograph of his wedding day, back in Paisano, Texas. The picture was among the personal effects he had shipped from home. Here in the Philadelphia area, he had found a local business that restored and copied old photographs. Their grandmother, Sherry, beamed and radiated warmth, smiling with a champagne flute in her hand. And look how handsome Grandpa Truck was in that tuxedo. Young and tall and smiling.

Ubi was anxious to hear what Molly and Jeremy had to say about the restraining order, which he thought was now null and void. They were eighteen, adults. They should be able to do what they pleased and go where they wanted. But the subject never came up. Instead, the talk was all about spring graduation, summer vacation and then college in the fall.

Jeremy said he had recently called South Bend, talked with Kelli. The two sisters had opened a small business selling all things Studebaker: hoses, horns, brake shoes, decals, manuals. They could track down almost anything, and would then mail the parts to Studebaker owners across the United States, Canada, Europe, even Australia. Kelli was in charge of advertising. She had placed ads in newsletters published by Studebaker clubs across the world. Business was humming along like the Golden Hawk on an open road, Kelli said. So they were postponing their quest to visit state capitols until summer. They had just hired an old timer who worked at the Studebaker factory and knew their grandfather. He should be able to run things for a few weeks in June. They planned to swing through Pennsylvania first, then head down south. So, be ready to roll, Jeremy.

"That's what I'm doing after graduation," Jeremy said. "Hitting the highway, staying gone as long as I can. I've saved money from my tutoring job, and I can live cheap if I have to."

"What about college?" Ubi said. "I know your parents invested and saved for it. They expected both of you to enroll somewhere."

"I've been accepted at several schools," Jeremy said and crossed his arms. "I got it narrowed down between Missouri, Colorado or Washington."

"Far, farther and farthest away," Molly interjected. "That's how Grandma Katherine describes it."

"The Ozarks are nice," Ubi said and winked. "If you choose Missouri, you'd be near the Current River."

"Oh, I know," Jeremy said, "Believe me. I know."

"And how about you, Miss Molly?"

"I'm off to band tryouts at the University of North Carolina."

"Huh?"

"That's Grandma Katherine's alma mater. We visited when I was a junior and I fell in love with the school, the campus, everything."

"Katherine does have that Southern charm about her," Ubi said. "I need to thank her for putting up with all the . . . well you know, all the stuff between me and Donald."

Serving squares of carrot cake to the twins, Ubi realized Molly and Jeremy's plans did not include old Grandpa Truck. Looking ahead to graduation day, they were both itching to move on. For Ubi, it would be the first time he could remember when other folks were doing the leaving and he was doing the staying behind. It didn't feel good. Was this how Sherry felt all those years they were married? And what about Jeanne? Many times when she was a little girl she would wave good-bye, holding mama's hand, tears rolling down her cheeks. Standing on the other side of the road makes a mountain of difference.

Ubi walked to the curb with the grandkids and watched the Pontiac that Donald bought for them disappear around the corner. Again, he felt a twinge of self-pity, or was it envy. After all the conversation about the future, about plans after graduation, neither one asked Grandpa Truck what he planned to do.

But even if they had asked, Ubi held no answer.

Easter Sunday found Ubi back at the Taylors for dinner. Ham and fresh green beans and potatoes au gratin served on white china. The stalemate, the truce between the two grandfathers held up. But Ubi felt the clock ticking. Graduation was all the talk. And he was happy for the twins. Martin and Jeanne had laid a strong foundation for these kids, one that held up after their sad and untimely departure, one that held up despite the troubles between him and Donald. And that thought made him ponder whether he had done more harm than good. He barged into their lives during a time of crisis. Still, somebody needed to counter Donald and his autocratic rule. Katherine tried. She rebuffed him at times, but he could steamroll her just like everybody else who stood in his way. Maybe that confrontation in the elevator was wrong. Then again, maybe it did some good. Would he do it all again? Would he sell out and leave rural Texas for this metropolitan way of life? Ten-four, he would.

The following Monday, Ubi's boys bolted the exhaust stacks back onto the truck. The paint job was complete and Old Ironsides stood polished and gleaming. Ubi popped two aspirin, then took the Peterbilt for a little spin, four young men riding in the shotgun seat and sleeper. Ubi drove them to their favorite hoagie shop where they dragged the owner out to see the classic diesel rig.

"The beauty and the beast," one student said, pointing to Ubi sitting in the driver's seat.

"Who's the beauty?" the cafe owner asked, "and who's the beast?"

Back at the high school, Ubi parked in front of the brick marquee at the main entrance. Dennis the shop teacher snapped photographs as the boys posed in front of the rig, beaming and clowning around, climbing, hanging onto the bumper and side rails.

"Hey, Mistuh Soont, stand here in front of da grill for a pitcher wid us."

Ubi stood in the middle, two teenagers on the left, two on the right, while Dennis took pictures. "I'm gonna' miss you monkeyshines."

"Send us a postcard from the museum in Iowa. Wouldya, Mr. Soont?"

"Okay, but I didn't know you guys could read."

"I didn't say you had to write anything on it. Just send a pitcher."

Although it was a short drive, Ubi's prosthetic foot didn't hold up well. The pain felt like the time a bull hauler in Omaha accidentally poked him in the thigh with an electric cattle prod. Proud and vainglorious and conscious of his image as the tough old Texan, Ubi managed to conceal his agony for the short trip. But how was he going to get Old Ironsides to the Iowa Truck Museum? No way could he drive eleven hundred miles with his leg quivering and shaking like this. He had some prescription pain pills back at the house, in the medicine chest, but he wasn't going to load up on them. And he didn't know or trust anyone to drive Old Ironsides. Jeremy might be able to handle the rig since there would be no trailer behind it, but they were pushing their luck when they made that grand entrance in the high school parking lot last summer. Besides, Jeremy had his own road adventures waiting and they didn't include him or his truck.

That afternoon, Ubi drove down to Sid's. Time to check on his old friend.

"How's Jeremy?" Sid asked, pouring two cups of coffee. "He put any meat on those bones?"

"If he did, I can't tell," Ubi said, positioning himself on a swivel stool. "He's actually grown a few inches, so if anything, it makes him look even skinnier."

"I could tell he's a good kid just by the way he handled himself. Can't put my finger on it, but I could tell." Sid circled around the counter and took the swivel stool next to Ubi. "What's on your mind?"

"Jiminy Cricket, Sid, can't a fella just stop to say howdy to an old friend?"

"Sure."

"Well, then, howdy. How's the missus?"

"Bout the same."

"How's bizness?"

"Bout the same."

"Good. Guess I'll be going then," Ubi said and rose from the stool like he was leaving.

Sid cracked a smile, a rare occurrence these days, clinging to a business that barely covered the utilities, taxes and doctor bills. "If I hold out another year, I got the place paid off. Hope to sell it then, but the price of real estate in this part of town is dropping like the Phillies in September."

After a few moments silence, Ubi said, "I'm looking for another truck."

"Hell, you can't drive the one you got, Ubi, with that bum leg."

"I'm looking for a truck that can pull a fair-sized trailer," Ubi said. "Something that can handle Old Ironsides."

"What the hell are you up to now?"

"I'm still taking the truck to Iowa like I planned, to the museum. But like you said, I can't even drive it around the block." Ubi stared into the black coffee. "So, I'm fixing to haul it on a flatbed trailer. Gonna need about a twenty-four-footer and a bigger pickup truck to haul it with."

Sid shuffled over to a metal rack that was stuffed with truckers' tabloids and copies of *Equipment Digest*. Back at the coffee counter, he handed Ubi the paper.

Ubi flipped through the pages. "Look at these prices."

"Aw hell, Ubi, everybody knows you still got the first penny you made. I heard you squeaking when you walked in."

"Maybe that's why I ain't destitute in my old age," Ubi said. "You and me both seen more'n our share of hot shots driving new rigs with all the chrome trimming. Then a few months later you see the truck at the dealership—repossessed."

Sid grinned. Ubi Sunt was about as flashy as that cast iron skillet in the kitchen. And like that blackened piece of cookware, he was durable, reliable, consistent—but when he got hot, boy, he got hot.

Owning a truck stop had kept Sid plugged into the local used vehicle market. Several dealers bought tires and diesel fuel from him on occasion. He offered to call around and see what he could find.

It took three weeks combing the want ads, then test-driving and haggling, but a New Jersey truck and trailer dealer managed to

239

separate Ubi from some of the thousands of dollars he had saved over the years. Ubi traded in the GMC and returned from Jersey behind the wheel of a one-ton Dodge pickup with a Cummins diesel, automatic transmission and dual wheels on the drive axle. The Dodge pulled a twenty-four-foot flatbed trailer equipped with three axles, electric brakes and oversized tires and wheels that could handle the heavy Peterbilt.

Ubi decided to take his new rig on a test run. With the four high school shop students watching, he eased Old Ironsides up the heavy-duty steel ramps onto the trailer. The trailer creaked and groaned and shuddered. The Dodge's front end raised up and pawed at the sky. One of the boys waved him forward, and Ubi evenly positioned the truck's weight over the trailer axles. The team then threaded several heavy chains through various points on old Ironsides' steel frame and attached iron hooks to the trailer side rails. Pumping up and down on industrial steel binders, they ratcheted down Old Ironsides for the ride.

Ubi's face suddenly took on a melancholy appearance, mouth turned downward, eyes lowered. Old Ironsides looks like she's on a gurney.

The big Dodge came with four doors and a full-size back seat. The gang climbed in for a spin. Damn thing handles all right. But it looks a little eerie, peering in the rearview and seeing that Peterbilt staring back at you.

Graduation day arrived like it was shot out of a cannon. One day it was weeks away, then it was tomorrow. Ubi had dry-cleaned the same suit he wore to visit Donald at his office last summer. Fresh hair cut. A dozen roses for Miss Molly. Cards for both kids, fat with twenty-dollar bills. Too much money? Oh well. You know what they say, ain't never seen a hearse pulling a U-Haul.

Molly walked across the stage first. *Boy, she favors her mother.* Ubi reached in his coat pocket for a tissue. Then Jeremy. Holding his diploma in one hand, he tossed his mortarboard into the air. Holy smokes! He got a haircut. You can see his neck and ears and forehead. Bet he lost twenty pounds.

That afternoon, five folks who had a tumultuous dinner at the Valley Forge Inn a year ago returned to the battlefield site for a celebration dinner. The same waitress seated them with a cautious smile. Katherine, ever the peacemaker, smiled at the waitress and whispered in her ear as they all pulled up chairs. "Not to worry, dear," she said. "The boys are on their best behavior."

Two days later, Molly and Katherine left for North Carolina. The girls said they would be gone three weeks. Katherine had big plans showing her granddaughter around the state. "Mountains and pine forests and beaches, you will absolutely love it, Molly."

And Ubi's archenemy had called to ask about a little trip of his own. Donald was an avid golfer. He and a business friend were taking a golfing vacation to Mississippi. Ubi sat with his road atlas on the kitchen table and chatted on the phone for thirty minutes.

"What route do you suggest?" Donald asked. "Anything worth seeing on the way? Good food? Bad food? Anything else?"

"Don't get stuck in any elevators," Ubi said, taking a chance on how Donald would react.

"You know, people still talk about that, uh, *conversation* we had," Donald said.

Ubi detected a hint of a smile with that comment. He wished Donald happy trails and hung up the phone in a daze. He just had a civil, half-hour conversation with his antagonist. Ubi walked outside, looked up for the Big Dipper like he used to back in Texas. What had just happened? The road had brought Donald and Ubi together, that's what happened. The road was the common denominator, the missing link. The road did something nobody else could, not even Katherine the noble arbitrator. The road was the great healer.

Later that week on a warm sunny morning, Ubi sat on the back porch, newspaper in his lap. Something was stirring in those weeds by the fence. Ubi ambled toward the plants and looked down. Aw heck, look at the monarchs, fluttering about with orange and black wings. Diving and darting. Seeking sunshine.

A familiar sound out in the street then shook Ubi from his trance. Twin mufflers on a Studebaker Golden Hawk. Ubi limped through the gate and into the front yard. A convertible with Indiana plates was sitting in the driveway. Terri, Kelli and Jeremy all scrambled out. None of them used the car doors. Tents and sleeping bags and backpacks were piled high in the back seat. What an adventure they would be having. And wait a minute. Is that a puppy in Kelli's arms?

"It's a Miniature Pinscher," Kelli explained, "or Min Pin for short. Isn't she cute?"

Ubi reached under the tiny dog's black and brownish-colored snout, scratched it. The dog's pointed ears stood straight up. Its mouth turned upward in what looked like a smirk.

"Kinda cute," Ubi said, still scratching the animal's neck. "What's her name?"

The girls and Jeremy grinned at each other, but said nothing.

"Well, what's her name?" Ubi asked again.

"Tex."

"Aw heck, a little runt like that. Should have named her Rhode Island."

The Indiana girls insisted on seeing Old Ironsides. Oh, that's right, Ubi recalled, they had only seen that rental car, the Maverick, and had never laid eyes on the Peterbilt. The foursome rode the Hawk over to the high school. They marveled at the shimmering and gleaming paint that Ubi's boys had polished to a point where you could shave in the reflection. Jeremy spun stories about riding in Old Ironsides as a little boy and shared more tales about the remainder of the trip last summer.

"Driving Old Ironsides is like sitting on top of a volcano," Jeremy said. "All that energy pulsing under your feet."

"It's riding a white tornado," Ubi chipped in.

"Like the running of the bulls in Pamplona, but you are hanging on to the back of the beast itself." Jeremy smiled with a long distance look in his eyes. "But sometimes, it's so smooth you could swear you were riding a magic carpet."

Terri and Kelli winked at each other and rolled their eyes. Let the boys have their fun.

Back at the house drinking ice tea, a long and awkward silence lingered between Jeremy and his Grandpa Truck. Recognizing the uncomfortable situation, Terri and Kelli both hugged Ubi and pecked him on the cheek, said they would wait in the car.

Ubi said to Jeremy in a low voice, "I won't be here when you get back."

Jeremy looked at the floor. "I know. You told me the lease is up this month and you didn't renew it."

"By the way, I had an interesting chat with Donald. He thinks him and a buddy can drive straight through to Mississippi, then play eighteen holes of golf."

"What'd you say?"

"I told him he's nuts, take your time and enjoy the ride. He said he'd think about it, but I expect he'll rush headlong down the road anyway. Most folks do." Ubi sipped his tea. Ice cubes clanked against the glass. "You ever pick a school?"

Jeremy pushed his lips together in a flat smile and shook his head no.

"You better make up your mind."

"I know, Grandpa. I've narrowed it down to a couple choices. Just need a little time to clear my head."

"A road trip should do that," Ubi said. "Now that Donald and I are on speaking terms, I'll be checking with him and Katherine to find out where I'll be traveling to this fall when I visit you at college."

"College. Sounds kind of funny," Jeremy said. "I thought I might want to take a semester off, traveling, exploring."

"You got a whole summer to do that," Ubi said. "You want to end up like me?"

Jeremy looked away, then back at Ubi. "A man could do worse."

The kitchen now felt small and stuffy. Ubi dumped the ice cubs in the sink. He looked at his grandson. "Last summer, we had the best and worst trip of my life. I wanted to talk to you about what happened to Jeanne and Martin but could never find the words. And I had two thousand miles to do it." Ubi swallowed a lump the size of those ice cubes melting in the sink. "I know it's too late now, but I want you to know that it wasn't because I don't care, it's just—"

"Grandpa," Jeremy said, feeling the need to interrupt, to show mercy on the man he still didn't completely understand, but respected. "You showed character in what you did this last year. Talk is cheap."

A hush fell on the kitchen. Ubi folded a kitchen towel, two, three times, then hung it on the oven door. "Jeremy, about what happened

243

on the road on your way to find me. You know, those visions of Jeanne and Martin."

"You mean, do I still see them?" Jeremy looked at Ubi square in the face. "Yes, I do, but it's not like before when I was trying to bring them back. Now, well it's hard to explain, but it's more like looking at a photograph. It's okay now. It's comfortable. Almost like when it happens, I'm—"

"But you were haunted, Jeremy," Ubi said. "At least that's my impression."

"I was, but our road trip changed that, I think. I hadn't truly accepted what happened until I ran away."

"Hmm," Ubi muttered and nodded. "I wished I could have said something. Done something."

Jeremy looked up at the ceiling, then at Ubi. The kitchen clocked ticked, relentless. The refrigerator hummed softly. Jeremy finally broke the silence. "Guess I better not keep the girls waiting." Jeremy's wiry arms suddenly wrapped around the old trucker's neck. For a skinny kid, that boy's got a solid grip. "Love you, Grandpa," Jeremy whispered and pulled Ubi's head tight against his own.

Ubi breathed heavy, his chest rising and falling, and sighed. Time to buck up and utter those three words more terrifying than driving down Donner Pass with no brakes. Ubi pushed Jeremy back a little and rested both hands on his shoulders. Their foreheads touched lightly. "Thanks for coming to Texas. Thanks for coming to get me, Jeremy," Ubi said with a soft voice. A second later, he relaxed his grip and leaned back for one last close-up. "You be careful. And take care of them gals, too."

"Ten-four, Grandpa. Big ten-four."

Ubi dropped his hands to his side. Jeremy smiled a crooked smile. Both men headed toward the kitchen door but bumped each other at the jamb. Nervous laughter. Ubi held back and made sure Jeremy went first over the threshold into bright sunshine.

Ubi watched his grandson's lanky frame stroll down the sidewalk toward the convertible. He saw Jeremy's left hand touch his face like he was wiping dust from an eyelid. But this ain't Oklahoma. There ain't no dust here.

"Hey, Jeremy," he shouted. "Hold up. I forgot something."

Jeremy turned and looked at old Grandpa Truck. Sheesh, what a story his life had been. All that traveling. All that trucking. And now, he's hobbling around on one good leg, too proud to use a walker like we all suggested. Wonder what he wants?

Ubi pushed hard on his left foot and walked without limping, without wincing. He stopped a few feet away and beamed like he had just topped a Montana mountain pass with a vista that stretched to the Pacific Ocean. "Love you, too, Jeremy," he said without hesitation, without his voice cracking, without a single teardrop. There would be time for that later. "Love you, too."

Jeremy reached out and took Ubi's hand with a strong grasp. They pumped hands until Ubi slowly released his grip. "And stay away from the Ditch Dragon," Ubi said as Terri cranked up the Studebaker's powerful V-8.

Jeremy hopped in the back seat. Terri stomped the gas pedal. The rear tires spun just a little, then gripped the road. The car leapt forward. Terri turned toward the back seat and asked Jeremy something. Although the rumbling exhaust drowned out her voice, Ubi thought he could read Terri's lips: "What's the Ditch Dragon?"

Ubi stood on the sidewalk and watched the Golden Hawk raise its wings and fly down the narrow street out of sight. This time, the traveler was the one being left behind. How does it feel now, road master? How does it feel to watch everyone else drive away while you're shackled to the same bed again tonight?

That evening, Ubi worked on his latest poem.

young
old
timid
 bold,
lure of the open road,
reaches out
takes hold
of us all

Fifty-three

Inertia—Sir Isaac Newton's first law of motion—a thing at rest will remain at rest until acted on by an outside force.

Three days after the others had hit the highway, Ubi remained cemented to the couch. The outside forces were gone. Ubi's wife beckoning him home—gone to cancer long ago. Daughter and wonderful son-in-law leaving messages with his dispatchers, urging him to visit—gone in a flash on the road last year. Grandchildren—gone and grown, exploring the world on their own. Nervous dispatchers who needed a hot load covered—gone to the young breed of truckers with satellite communications and lightning-fast trucks.

One morning after a summer thunderstorm drenched the city, washing the stifling air clean, Ubi pried himself from the sofa. He roamed the neighborhood, visiting businesses where he was on a first-name basis with the owners and workers. Adios, y'all, I'm fixing to hit the road for Iowa. At noon, he wandered home and a found a U-Haul truck parked out front, rear door open.

Uh-oh, somebody's moving in. Haven't even finished packing yet.

Two young men using an appliance dolly rolled a big-screen TV down the steel ramp and up the sidewalk. Ubi watched them wedge it in the front door. Stuck. Can't get in. Can't get out.

"You boys should take the door of its hinges," Ubi said, watching from the sidewalk. "Get a hammer and screwdriver, pop those steel pins out and the whole door comes off. That way you gain an inch clearance."

The young men had to borrow Ubi's tools, but a few minutes later they had the TV inside, plugged in and tuned to a soccer game. Then they helped Ubi stack several boxes of his personal items into the back seat of the Dodge truck. They could keep the couch and bedroom set he bought at a garage sale. And the smoker, let me show you how to start a fire and adjust the damper so you don't burn the meat, or the house down.

The men soon emptied the U-Haul and drove away on a beer run. Ubi pulled the door behind him and heard the lock click with a tone of finality. The big Dodge plodded through the neighborhood; Ubi's left arm dangled out the window. An open cardboard box stuffed with maps rested on the seat beside him.

An hour later, Ubi pulled into Sid's where he had left Old Ironsides locked up safe in an empty bay. Good old Sid—another painful good-bye.

Sid helped Ubi hook up to the flatbed trailer parked out back. Ubi then inched Old Ironsides onto the trailer. Chains tightened, fuel tanks topped off, ready to roll, the two men shared one last cup of coffee.

"Where are you going to live, Ubi? You sold everything in Texas. You didn't renew the lease on the house here."

"That's what the grandkids and everybody else have been asking me." Ubi stared out the plate glass window. "Figure I'll hang out at the truck museum for a while, then drift out to the Panhandle, check on Stormy and Meredith, the couple that bought me out last fall."

"Then what?" Sid kept pressing.

"Go back to the Boys Ranch where I grew up, maybe look around, offer myself for a little volunteer work, fixing up things. And of course visit the cemetery where Sherry is."

"You're still not answering my question," Sid said. "After your farewell tour, then what?"

Ubi stood and circled behind the coffee counter. He poured a refill and looked up at Sid. A blank stare.

Sid stared back and said, "You don't know."

Ubi took a sip of coffee. "I'll figure it out on the road."

"Why don't you help me with this truck stop? We could milk a few good years out of it." Sid was talking fast, thinking fast. Way too fast for Ubi.

"Thanks for the offer old friend," Ubi said. "I'll keep it in mind."

Fifty-four

Because he planned to traverse five states with an expired Texas driver's license, Ubi determined it best to travel the back roads and keep a low profile. What kind of fast-talking would he have to come up with if he was stopped? And cruising these state routes would be a chance to preview some countryside. For years, Ubi often hustled along the heaving and crowded interstates and bypassed pleasures like what Josephina was writing about in her travelogue.

As for the rig itself, Ubi was confident in its ability to handle the steep grades and S-curves crossing the Alleghenies and the Ohio and Mississippi rivers. The truck had excellent brakes and deep tire tread all the way around. The first night out, in Gettysburg, Ubi parked in a vacant lot beside a grocery store that was closed for the evening. A decent-looking coffee shop waited across the street. Ubi pulled himself onto the flatbed trailer and into Old Ironsides. How many nights had he spent in this bunk?

The next morning, Ubi and the Dodge and Old Ironsides circumvented Pittsburgh, swinging south and then northward in a wide arc. Mist and showers made the road slick, but the rig handled well, no hydroplaning, firm traction on all five axles. Late afternoon, Ubi approached the Ohio River at an old toll bridge near the small community of East Liverpool. Narrow and steep, the crescent-shaped iron bridge arced above the river like a rusty rainbow. Ubi felt the truck downshift at the bottom of the bridge. The diesel growled and got serious about the task. Ubi leaned forward and patted the dashboard. "Show me what you got."

Down on the riverbank, an elderly couple on an afternoon stroll stopped to take a break. They huddled under an umbrella. The husband gazed at the bridge. He saw only Old Ironsides, now at the apex, with no driver. The Dodge and flatbed were obscured by guardrails and fog. The man arched his back and stood straight. He

248

pointed a shaky index finger at an antique Peterbilt crossing this relic of a bridge.

"That looks like a ghost truck."

Before the man's wife could turn her head and adjust her spectacles, Old Ironsides had disappeared into a low-hanging cloud on the bridge's downhill side.

"Where?"

"Up on the bridge," the man replied. "Uh-oh, it's already gone."

"Honey, sometimes you scare me."

Continuing westward, Ubi meandered across Ohio and Indiana along two lane roads and state highways. He sometimes wandered into towns that did not appear on maps. Weaving and wending down forgotten roads lined with never-ending rows of corn and wheat, bunking out in empty parking lots in small towns, the measured pace suited the old truck driver's demeanor. Nerves unraveling from a year living in a major metropolis began to heal.

Five days after leaving Philadelphia, Ubi still hadn't made much ground. He continued the languid pace in western Illinois, slipping along a curvaceous two-lane highway that played peek-a-boo with the mother of all American rivers—the Mississippi, great bisector of the continent, artery of nine states, conduit of exploration for Marquette, Joliet and La Salle.

Now, where and how to cross.

Ubi lingered at a rest area and gazed across the river. The sun burned a fiery crimson shade of red and disappeared behind the Iowa hills. Swirling purple and pink clouds looked down on the big river. Ubi climbed out of the Dodge for a better view. Leaning on the front bumper, he swiveled his head back east. Look at this—a three-hundred-sixty degree sunset. Sundown out west, but the eastern sky's glowing as well—shades of red, magenta, violet. Beats watching television on a crummy couch with four walls closing in.

When the curtain opened on the first act of tonight's celestial showcase, the Big Dipper entered stage right. Ubi strained his neck watching a dot-to-dot puzzle in the sky grow brighter. He then remembered that pint of handcrafted, Kentucky bourbon whiskey he picked up in Mt. Vernon yesterday. He reached into the truck, grabbed the whiskey, a road atlas and a flashlight. Propped up against the Dodge's hood, he flipped through the pages, still unsure where and how to cross the Mississippi. Crossed it one hundred times before. Why so hesitant?

Ubi continued staring, eyes fixed on the river. He opened the small bottle with the tan label and inhaled. That'll blow the road dust out of your nostrils. A careful sip. Throat burning. Neck twitching. Would be nice to share it with someone, but when a fella's ready for strong drink, then what's wrong with a little nip alone?

Ubi took another slash and swished the bourbon like mouthwash. Now back to this body of water that has defined our country's midsection and produced so many folk heroes. This is the true mark between East and West. Sure, you got the Rocky Mountains and the Great Divide, but the Mississippi is where the green and wet and populous East yields to the semi-arid, brown and sparse West. This is where the annual rainfall begins to drop and agriculture slowly gravitates from farming to ranching. This is where your blood pressure drops and you raise a toast to the folks who pushed westward more'n one hundred years ago in them little old prairie schooners. Sheesh, those are the kind of ancestors to be proud of.

Ubi raised the bottle high above his head and tilted his neck back. The whiskey bubbled and gurgled inside the tinted brown bottle. Ubi's mouth and tongue tingled. He swallowed. The whiskey floated down his throat, warm and soothing. Ubi set the bottle on the truck hood and found the thread, that thought about crossing the Mississippi, point of no return.

Might not see Jeremy and Molly again, and those kids in metal shop, and the spunky band director, Miss Ketchum, and Sid and his old truck stop—what a port in a hurricane that was. And of course, Katherine and Donald, glad that feud finally simmered and died, don't need to carry around such animosity, way too heavy a load no matter what rig you drive

Fifty-five

The next day, Ubi pushed the Dodge with that odd-shifting automatic transmission one hundred fifty miles northward, paralleling the river, still on the Illinois side. The road caressed the riverbank, hugged it tightly and let go to angle toward high ground and sure footing. And Ubi embraced the road like never before, bent fingers wrapped around a steering wheel that directed the Dodge's path. Throughout the day, he pulled over at numerous wide spots and scenic turnouts to drink in the view—magnificent cottonwoods clinging to sandy bluffs—and let pass the line of impatient cars, motorcycles, and motor homes that were tailing him.

At one such turnout, Ubi noticed fine print on his Illinois state map that depicted a ferry crossing. It was only twenty or so miles north, just below where the Cedar River joins the Mississippi. Could the ferry handle his rig? Should he trust the ferryman with Old Ironsides' safe passage? Won't hurt to take a look.

Ubi dropped down into the river valley, flat and quiet with scattered mobile homes and equipment sheds and infinite rows of corn. Thriving from a wet spring, stalks were shoulder high and jungle thick. Ubi took what looked like the road to the ferry, drove a mile, but faced a large, wooden barricade. Beyond that roadblock, the river rolled past, carrying tree trunks and massive stumps with roots dangling. Must have had some heavy rainfall upstream. And damn, there goes a refrigerator. Who woulda guessed that a refrigerator could float? Turning around, the Dodge drive tires slung mud and the trailer got sideways before Ubi could correct the steering. That was close. Better drive to the nearest town, Slippery Elm, and ask for directions. Sheesh, hate to do that. Asking for directions is like surrendering. Oh well, it's back through the corn forest and up the sandy valley into Slippery Elm. Crossing the Mississippi River with Old Ironsides on a ferry would be worth it.

The two women working at the gas station were a mother-daughter team. They knew all about the ferry. The heavyset mother pointed to it on a county map pinned to the wall. The petite daughter said the ferry was running, all right, and it was the last one still operating on the Mississippi, as far as she knew.

"Can it handle that rig?" Ubi pointed out a window at Old Ironsides riding tall and proud on the flatbed.

"It carries eighteen-wheel grain trucks all the time," the mother said, dumping used coffee grounds and a paper filter into the trash.

The two women explained the best route down to the ferry. The mother had just refilled the coffee basket with a new filter and fresh coffee grounds. A moment later, black gold trickled into the pot. Smell that fresh java. Ubi helped himself to a jumbo cup.

"You sell diesel?" Ubi asked.

"Sure we do. Got a pump out back," the daughter answered. "If you don't mind me asking, why are you so fired up to ride that little old ferry?"

"Well," Ubi said, sipping coffee, pondering the question. "I'd like to cross the big muddy some other way than on a highway. Rolling over these interstate bridges you hardly slow down at all. I want to feel the spray in my face, feel the river pitching and heaving and rolling under my feet, and see up close the giant cottonwoods."

While Ubi was speaking, the mother had stopped wiping down the front counter and laid her damp rag on the glass. The daughter just stood and stared. Lots of strangers roll through here, but this man was carved out of some type of hardwood they had never seen.

"And this is the last time that Peterbilt will cross the Mississippi."

"What do you mean?"

"I bought that truck in 1956, brand new. Drove her the equivalent of twenty-five trips around the equator," Ubi said. "So Old Ironsides here is going to be enshrined for posterity at the Iowa Truck Museum, just west of Cedar Falls."

"Maybe we'll come visit," said the mother. "That's only a four-hour drive."

"You should. By the way, the river's running like there was serious flooding upstream."

"Oh, yeah," the daughter said. "They had lots of rain a few days ago up in Minnesota, Wisconsin and even parts of Iowa."

"Can the ferry handle the river rising like that?"

"Only one way to find out," said the daughter. "You want to float the river with the ghosts of Mark Twain, and I appreciate that, but on the other hand, it sounds like you have some precious cargo riding up on that flatbed."

"If it gets too dangerous, those boys will shut down," the mother interjected. "They know what they're doing."

Chatting with the women about corn prices, land prices, diesel prices and tourists, Ubi sipped the coffee until the bottom of the cup was looking back at him. Hit the spot don't do that java justice, bull's eye is more like it. Then Ubi eased the Dodge up to the fuel bay and topped off both tanks. With the hose pulsating and the dollars and gallons scrolling by on the pump, Ubi looked at Old Ironsides and sighed. "Wish it was you taking a drink instead."

The ferry landing was right where the store gals said it would be. Ubi pulled his red Peterbilt cap down tight to block the heavy mist that was hanging low. He dropped the transmission in park, stomped the emergency brake pedal and climbed out of the rig. Ubi found a few pieces of driftwood and kicked them under trailer tires. The truck was sitting on a slight incline and he wasn't taking any chances.

Looking across the river, Ubi spotted the ferry. A flatbed with guardrails on the sides and swinging steel gates on the front and back so you can load and unload from either end. Got a two-story pilothouse with four sides glass and a shanty for the deckhand. Looks like a two-man operation.

Ubi peered through the heavy haze and across the river. He followed a tractor-trailer rig easing down a concrete ramp and then across a steel plate onto the ferry. A couple minutes later, the boat churned forward. The swift current slapped the guardrails and sprayed the deck like a rainstorm. The surge continued nonstop for six minutes until the ferry bumped the dock. The deck hand exited the shanty and wrapped chains around cement posts jutting out of the concrete boat dock. He swung open the iron gate. The grain truck clanked across a steel plate and climbed the concrete ramp on the Illinois side.

Ubi approached the wiry deck hand. His jeans were grease-covered, as if he was constantly wiping his hands on them. He pulled on the bill of a forest-green cap from Bo's Bait and Tackle—

New Orleans. A salty, white stain arced across the base of the hat just below the outline of a catfish with long whiskers.

"Call me Junior," the deckhand said, lips peeled back, exposing swollen red gums and charcoal-colored teeth.

Ubi reached for Junior's extended hand. "Ubi Sunt, and I'm glad to be headed back across the right side of the river."

"Well, hold on, mister," Junior said. "That all depends on which side you're from."

Ubi acknowledged that sentiment with a smile and a nod. "That's true," he said. "Got so excited about finally heading west, forgot folks don't all look at the world the same way. Like most things, it depends on which side of the road you're driving on."

Junior named his price for the ferry crossing, five bucks, and said, "You're de last run of the day. Been rougher dan a roller coaster in an earthquake since dey opened the gates upstream. Spray and waves been pounding the deck all mawning. River's come up three feet in de last two hours." Junior pointed to a steel pole planted in mud, painted with yellow lines that marked 1962 and 1976 historic flood stages. "Been raining for a week in Minnesota and Wisconsin. So now we're getting de runoff."

Ubi climbed up the riverbank to the Dodge. Following Junior's hand signals, he eased the truck and trailer across the steel deck plate—clang, clang, clang—and onto the boat. He put the truck transmission in park and depressed the emergency brake.

Using a wet boot, Junior nudged the chock blocks under the front and rear pickup wheels. "Dat's a nice old Peterbilt you got there. What year?"

"Nineteen fifty-six."

"Oughta be in a museum."

"Will be in a few days. If you can get me across this river."

"I'll get you dere, no problem," Junior said, examining the swift and chalky–brown current. "But it might not be pretty. Ain't nothing like an ornery river."

Ubi watched the man watching the river. "I thought government engineers had it all figgered out," Ubi said. "Dams and locks. Flood control."

Junior let out a dismissive snicker. "Hmmmph." He grabbed the cold and wet steel rail, leaned forward and shoved his face into the wind and spray. "I worked this river from N'awlins to La Cross, Wisconsin. Cain't nobody tame the Mississippi. Dey tried it all, like you said, dams, locks, levees. She still breaks their shackles. Some things are meant to be wild and free."

Junior turned around, wrapped an arm around the guardrail. He straightened his cap. Caught his breath. Ubi squinted into the drizzle. He was trying to make sense of it all, this raging river man with a Cajun accent. "How long you been doing this?"

"Tirty-tree years."

"Thirty-three years?" Ubi repeated, not sure he understood the man.

"Dat's right. Tirty-tree."

"What about the pilot?"

"Aw, he just a rookie."

"So, how long?"

"Tirty-one years."

"Then, let's do it."

Junior unwrapped the chains that held fast the boat and slung them on the deck. They landed with a cracking steel-on-steel thud. He nodded to the glass tower above. The pilot engaged the boat transmission. The ferry pushed off into the chalky, turbulent water. A wave smashed the side of the boat and rocked it like a bathtub toy. Then another crashed over the guardrail and onto the deck. Ubi gripped the side of his trailer with both hands. Taking baby steps, he made his way for the dry Dodge cab.

Another wave washed over the ferry and snapped Ubi's head back, ripping his cap from his head and blurring his vision. He wrapped a forearm around the chain that held Old Ironsides fast to the trailer. Out of the corner of his eye, he saw Junior lying flat on his back, arms and legs flapping like a minnow. Another wave crashed over the deck and swept Junior against the guardrail.

Ubi then heard a loud groan and a pop and felt the chain loosen. He had inadvertently grabbed the steel binder that held taut the chain. The boat rocked again and Old Ironsides slipped a couple feet toward the back of the trailer.

The pilot had no idea the drama unfolding on the deck below—one man down and an unchained vehicle on board—because a boat dock that had broken free upstream was bearing down on the ferry.

The captain steered hard to the left. Another massive wave pushed the boat downstream. Ubi wrapped both arms around the chains, still on his feet, aware that he if he lost his grip and hit the deck he could be pinned against the guardrail like Junior. The ferry heaved and pitched side-to-side as it floated down the foamy river. The pilot recognized a deep bank on the Illinois side, a cliff that had been carved from a sandy hill by years of pounding river water. That meant the river eddied on the opposite side and the depth would be shallower, a point bar where he could possibly evade the current and ground the boat. The pilot radioed his intentions to the river authority and pointed the boat toward the point bar on the Iowa side.

Ubi felt the boat pitch and lean toward the downstream side. His drenched shirt and khakis hung heavy and clung to his body. His arms, hands, fingers were cramping and slipping down the wet chain. Another furious wave broke over the Dodge and Old Ironsides. The Peterbilt's rear axles crash-landed on the boat deck with a sickening bang. Old Ironsides was now resting on its haunches, back axles on the boat deck and front axle still on the flatbed trailer. The Peterbilt was rearing up like an angry stallion pawing at the gray sky. Another set of waves like that and she'll come tumbling off that flatbed, bust through the gate and drop into the river.

The pilot in the glass control tower looked down, helpless to do anything but ram the boat into the sandbar. When the ferry hit the bank, the chain that had secured Old Ironsides to the trailer broke free. Taking small and careful steps, Ubi dragged the chain toward Old Ironsides' front bumper. He ducked under the truck and wrapped the chain around the front axle. He affixed the large hook at the chain's end to a link, and with twitching and throbbing muscles, pulled it as tight as his heaving arms could manage.

Another wave splashed the ferry, but the chain held the rig in place. Old Ironsides washing overboard? Not on your life. Not after all these years together. This truck ain't going nowhere but to her shrine in Iowa.

Ubi then looked across the deck and saw Junior sitting upright, no hat, shirt ripped and torn, but holding his thumb up in the air, a victory sign, grinning with those big, infected-looking gums and black teeth. Just as Ubi smiled back, the largest wave yet blasted over the boat and ripped his hands free. He somersaulted in the swirling water and crashed against the guardrail. Junior grabbed the same guardrail and was on his knees, ready to work his way toward Ubi, but the boat rocked and threw him on his back.

When Junior looked up, the man was gone.

Junior pulled himself to his feet, yelling and pointing at what looked like a man floating on his belly. The pilot jammed the throttle handle downward, pushing the diesel engine to full capacity. Over there, look, that's him.

A mile down the river, Junior leaned over the guardrail and pointed out the figure he thought was Ubi Sunt, floating and protected from the swift river by a natural jetty. The pilot maneuvered toward the river bank.

But upon close examination, it was apparent they had been chasing a tree trunk, water-logged yet bobbing in the river. Years ago, that tree trunk was thick and solid, probably an oak.

Nothing but driftwood now.

Epilogue

"Uncle Jeremy, are we there yet?"

A four-wheel-drive van stuffed door-to-door with cousins and tents and sleeping bags rolled down the interstate, shoulder-high rows of corn waving at them from both sides of the road.

"I think you missed the exit, honey," said the woman riding in the front seat.

Jeremy turned the wheel to the left, hit the gas and pushed the vehicle through the soggy median. A shortcut. The vehicle pulled into a parking lot, mud cakes flapping from four tires.

"Uncle Jeremy, this place looks like a big old barn."

Inside the steel, two-story building, several youngsters approached a vehicle unlike any they had ever seen. Tires bigger than the top of your head. Two smoke stacks higher than the chimney at home. Front end looks like a tank or locomotive. Jeremy boosted the kids up the steps into the passenger seat and sleeper berth. He then pulled himself into the driver's seat.

"You drove this truck, Uncle Jeremy?"

"That's right. I sure did."

"What was it like?"

"Were you scared?"

"Did you ever crash?"

Jeremy wrapped his left hand around the steering wheel. He caressed the black knob attached to the stick shift with his right.

"How come you were driving this truck, Uncle Jeremy?"

"Yeah, how come *you* got to drive it?"

"It's a long story that happened way before any of you guys were born."

"We want to know."

"Yeah, tell us."

"Well, it all started at Sid's Truck Stop. It's closed now, but . . . "

ABOUT THE AUTHOR

FRED AFFLERBACH'S first published works appeared in truckers' tabloids and newspapers in the 1970s and 80s when he traversed the contiguous 48 states and Western Canada as an independent truck driver. At age 50, he retired from the road and earned journalism and English degrees at Texas State University. Writing for Central Texas newspapers, Fred has earned numerous Texas Associated Press awards. His debut novel, *Roll On*, was published in 2012 by Academy Chicago.

www.fredafflerbach.com